EXPLICIT

Lancaster #3

AVA HARRISON

Line Edit: Lawrence Editing, www.lawrenceediting.com, Gray Ink
Content: Jennifer Roberts-Hall, Becca Mysoor
Proofreader: Write Girl Editing Services, Marla Selkow Esposito
Formatting: Champagne Book Design

Dedicated to those who need help finding beauty in the broken pieces of themselves.

Please join us as we break ground on the

newest Lancaster venture.

You are cordially invited to

Antibes, France.

Saturday, June 4

Official groundbreaking ceremony to start

at 7 p.m. followed by a celebratory dinner.

CHAPTER ONE

Pierce

PRETENTIOUS FUCKING BASTARD.

I'm not surprised. He's always been a pompous ass. Goddamn Spencer Lancaster. Heir to the Lancaster family fortune, head honcho at the biggest hotel chain in America, and, most importantly, my brother. My oldest brother.

The one who has it all and has no problem reminding you. He's always loved to flaunt his wealth, and today is no different. If anything, today is even worse. With a promise to build an elite property fit for royalty on a plot of land in Antibes, France, he already has everyone whispering amongst themselves about how great he is. If that isn't enough, he's down on one knee in front of his closest friends and family, handing over his balls to a recovering addict.

And they say *I'm* the fuck-up.

Who doesn't like to have a good time? What the fuck else is there to do? I like booze, drugs, and women, but at least it doesn't own me. Unlike Olivia, my older brother Spencer's fiancée, I can hold my own. At least unlike her, I never ended up in rehab. I can stop whenever I want. Sound like a cliché? Too bad, because it's the truth.

I'm not my brothers, and I'm not expected to contribute to the family name. No one has ever asked me to work for the

1

family business, to run a chain of hotels, hell, they haven't even asked me to work at one, so if they don't want me around, why should my decision to spend time and money on my vices matter to anyone? Yet, by the nasty phone messages I've been getting from Spencer and, even more surprisingly, my other brother Grant, my "reckless lifestyle" is all that matters to them.

The irony of this situation isn't lost on me.

Spencer's constantly breathing down my neck about how I'm soiling the Lancaster name, which is completely ridiculous. *Hypocrisy much*? Here he is, promising his life away to someone who was snorting lines not even a year ago, and I'm going to be the one to bring down the name. *How is she any different from me*?

Fuck them.

I pull my flask out of my pocket and take a swig, not caring who sees. The liquid burns my throat, scorching the persistent bitter feelings that threaten to float to the surface. My entire life I've been the black sheep of the family, always overshadowed by my brothers' success. They don't even give me a chance. For years, they ignored me, all too busy with their own drama, so I kept myself busy with other distractions. Getting fucked is an easy way to forget just how irrelevant you are to the world.

"Clap your hands, Pierce."

A soft voice cuts through my inner rant, and I turn my head, looking down at Olivia's best friend, Lindsey. Her eyes are narrowed, their color so deep with thought they appear black as the night, dark and ominous. I lift my gaze back up to scan her face and am met with lips downturned in a scowl. Apparently, she's not happy to be here either. That, or she doesn't like me very much. *No, I'm always a good time.*

Brown locks fan her shoulder, resting on her translucent skin. Something twists in my gut as I watch her. Lindsey sitting in a wheelchair, helpless, sucks. A devastating accident left her pretty badly banged up and has kept her away from our typical hangouts. She used to be the life of the party, and I have to admit I miss seeing her around.

"Want some?" I point the flask in her direction.

She shakes her head.

"It wouldn't kill you to act happy for your brother," she scolds quietly. Each word comes out only a little above a whisper, but no matter the octave, her intent is present. She's totally thinking, *Suck it up, Pierce.*

I roll my eyes but do as she suggests, bringing my hands up to slowly clap. I'm not fooling anyone, especially not her, but I still put forth my best acting effort. Yeah, I'm a dick. So what? My false bravado doesn't seem to faze anyone. No one cares. They're all too excited to notice me.

Hoots and hollers are called from all around. I take it all in, watching the cheers from the sidelines. Everybody's happy for the couple. Spencer and Olivia are about to plan a wedding, one that's sure to be the soiree of the year, and apparently, this is the kickoff. My stomach twists. A strange feeling of jealousy washes over me, and it's unwelcome.

"Oh, come on, Lindsey. Don't you want to get drunk and make bad decisions?" I wiggle my eyebrows suggestively.

"Eww." Lindsey scrunches her nose in disgust. I shrug, knowing she's full of shit. Before her accident, she wanted me bad. She's alluded many times when there were copious amounts of drinks being had, just how much. It never happened, unfortunately. Not because I'm not attracted to her, but because some other girl beat her to the punch. Tonight I could use the camaraderie, and a good blow job wouldn't hurt either.

From across the expansive gray gravel where we're all standing, I watch them smile happily at each other.

I wish I could flee, but no, not until the golden couple makes a speech. Anything other than listening to my brother speak sounds like a more enjoyable way to spend my evening. Just as I'm contemplating an escape plan, I notice Spencer and Olivia making their way through the crowd, thanking everyone for traveling to Antibes to witness their engagement. I take another swig, chasing the buzz that will get me through the night.

"Let's get out of here," Lindsey suggests, worry evident in her eyes. "They won't miss us."

I recognize what she's doing. She's saving me from the awkward reunion with my brother. He knows I'm here. Obviously, being the good soldier, obeying the commands of my superiors, I came. Still sucks to be here, especially with the relationship between us so strained. Truth is I've been avoiding him for the last year, but he's been too focused on meeting Olivia, falling in love to care and apparently reconciling with Grant to notice. When I was still in high school, Grant, my middle brother had a huge falling out with the family, but seeing as he's in Antibes, celebrating with everyone, that bridge must have been mended.

I lift my flask once more to my mouth, and Lindsey shakes her head and motions to leave. She obviously realizes my alcohol consumption won't go without an argument, seeing as she's best friends with his soon-to-be wife. It's such bullshit though, as flutes of champagne are currently being passed around. What the hell does it matter if I brought my own? When I still haven't agreed to go, she speaks.

"We'll say I needed to pee and you helped wheel me out of the gravel," she declares on an loud exhale of breath, sounding frustrated at the thought.

"You're going to take the heat for my disappearing act?" I'm surprised. Dumbfounded really. Why would she do that?

"I want out of here. It's hot as hell." She fans herself. Bending at the hip, I bow to her before taking the handles of the chair. Who am I to look a gift horse in the mouth?

"Let's go, Miss Daisy." I laugh while wheeling her around like her own personal chauffeur.

CHAPTER TWO

Lindsey

I FEEL LIKE A COMPLETE IDIOT.

Truth is, having to be in a wheelchair in France, isn't ideal. I'd much rather be using my cane. But unfortunately, instead of using it, it's lying on my lap because the ground is too uneven at this location for me to do anything more than stand.

It's been a year since the accident that changed my life. Before the accident, I was the life of the party. Always jet-setting around the world, looking to have a good time. But everything changed on the drive back to New York City. My car crashed. Olivia and my driver were lucky. I wasn't, hell I'm still not lucky.

Now it hurts to walk even a few steps, let alone dance on top of a bar.

You'd think it would be better by now, but I've recently undergone corrective surgery to have the screws removed from my leg, so technically, although a shit ton of time has passed; I'm still in recovery. The surgeon said I'll be able to stop using my cane in a few weeks, but I'm not happy about having to use it at all. I've spent the last year trying to mend myself back to whole. Doctor after doctor, followed by physical therapy and still, I'm not okay.

So, here I am, being pushed by Pierce Lancaster. Nothing could be more humiliating than this.

But I saw his face. I can see it written all over every single feature. The way his green eyes darkened when Spencer spoke, and the twitch in his jaw. Even the way he brought the flask to his perfectly formed mouth.

I hadn't seen Pierce since London last year. Since I'd all but thrown myself at his feet. He didn't want me then. My cheeks warm with embarrassment. He certainly won't want me now. *So who cares if he has to push you around like a little old lady to escape his family? It's not like you have a chance anyway.*

But even knowing that doesn't calm the heat spreading across my body. No matter what I tell myself, Pierce Lancaster still does things to me. My treacherous body still wants him.

He's so damn beautiful.

Head in the game, Lindsey.

That's not going to happen so stop longing for him. You're nothing to him, never have been, never will be. If he didn't want you when you were perfect, why would he want you when you're broken?

The ground beneath my chair dips and my cane bounces in my lap, hitting my upper thigh with a thump.

"Sorry about that," Pierce says.

"It's fine," I reply, pulling my mind back to reality.

"Did I hurt you?"

"I said I'm fine," I snap. I don't want his pity. I just want to be normal, for crying out loud. I want to be the girl I used to be, even if just for a night. But no, here I am, in France, in a wheelchair.

I'm not sure what I was thinking. A part of me was so excited to get the invitation to come to Antibes. I didn't know Spencer was planning this elaborate engagement. I, like everyone else, thought they were throwing a giant party to break ground on the newest hotel in the Lancaster Holdings portfolio.

The excitement I'd had was short-lived, though. It's not that I'm not happy for Olivia. I am. It's just her life keeps moving forward and mine is stuck. Kind of like Pierce right now trying to get me over the bump in the ground.

"I can stand," I say when he tries to push the wheel through the hole in the gravel.

"Are you sure?" His voice is hesitant.

"God, Pierce. *Yes.*" I lace my fingers on the handle and push my body weight up.

I don't bother with the cane. I stand. Internally, I grimace, but I don't let my face show any signs of pain. I grit my teeth and bear the feeling radiating down the front of my left leg. *Shards of glass.* It feels like shards of glass pulling the muscle from the bone. The surgeon said I should be recovering, and in truth I am, but it's too slow for me.

Sometimes I think of myself as two people. Lindsey *before* when I had the world accessible to me, and Lindsey *now*, not so much. I was lucky to live that day, but that doesn't make this healing process any less tiring. I just had what will hopefully be my last corrective surgery, and my doctor assured me if I work hard I should be able to run again, but it feels like it will never happen.

I think that's the hardest part. As much as I loved to go out and dance, I loved to run more, and no one even knows. It was a hobby I took up years ago when shit got bad with my parents. Olivia had been off at college, so I'd packed up my shit and moved to Europe. I'd had no one. Sure, I had people to party with, people to do drugs with, but every now and then I needed to calm down, collect myself.

One of those times I tried calling my dad. He answered, and I expected him to ask me where I was, how I was, what I was doing. Instead, he asked, "How much?" I was furious. Angry. Sad.

Heartbroken. I hadn't spoken to him in three weeks.

"One hundred."

He knew what that meant. He hung up then, and as I walked to the gym, I heard the familiar ping of my phone. A deposit had been made: one hundred thousand dollars.

I didn't make it to the gym that day. Instead, I ran from where I was standing in front of the building, down the street, up a few blocks and right into Hyde Park. I kept running, and for the first time, I felt free. The scenery, the newly blooming trees, the way the sunlight illuminated across the early morning grass in the distance, it transported me to a different place.

A different time.

The endorphins I released rivaled what I got from doing coke, rivaled what I got from booze, and from there on out I was never sober. I never had to think about my problems. During the day I ran, and at night I got high. I was running from my problems in all directions.

Now I've lost all of that.

And I have nothing.

The sound of Pierce grunting removes me from my tormented thoughts. He lifts the wheelchair off the ground, his arms flexing beneath his button-down. Only Pierce could wear a baby-pink shirt, white linen pants, and sneakers and look devastatingly handsome. His hair is disheveled. Too long on top, but just long enough to pull it in the throes of passion. He always looks like he's just had sex.

I stare at him, saliva pooling in my mouth. All thoughts of my family drama behind me as I stare at this beautiful specimen. I hate that he does this to me. I hate that no matter how much time has passed, I still want him as much as I did *before*, and I hate that he'll never want me.

His gaze catches mine and his lips spread.

Shit, he caught me.

"Like what you see?" he jests. His typical cocky grin grows on his face.

"Hardly." I grimace and dramatically roll my eyes.

He raises his eyebrow. "Your chariot awaits." He motions to my wheelchair now safely away from the large divot in the ground. "Do you need help?"

"I'm good."

He eyes me warily, small lines etching away at his face with concern, but I shrug him off and take a step. I don't have my cane and the ground is horribly uneven, so this is a bad idea. But having him help me any more than he already has is the worst idea.

My left leg lifts, hits the ground, and then it happens, a pebble. Or a rock. It might even be a boulder from the way I feel myself falling forward. I brace for impact. For pain.

But I never feel it.

Instead, I feel his arms around me, cocooning me in his strong embrace. He has me. I'm safe. *I'm mortified.*

"Shit. I got you, here." He moves me in his arms as if he's my crutch and I hate it. I hate how weak I am. I hate this feeling. I want to crawl into a ball and hide. Drown my feelings.

As I sit, I glance over my shoulder. "Give me that flask."

The need to get drunk and forget my humiliation flood through me. I haven't felt this way in a long time.

That's because you're always alone.

"A girl after my own heart." He laughs as he hands it to me.

The liquid courses down the back of my throat, burning a path in its wake. When I'm done taking my sip, I return it to Pierce.

"That's all you're having?"

"Someone has to be responsible and make sure we don't

miss dinner."

"That's lame."

"Oh, shut it. Wheel me out of here."

Pierce laughs and sets us in motion. When we make it to the parking lot where the fleet of cars Spencer has rented as transportation for his guests is, I fear we won't be able to leave and will have to wait here until everyone is ready.

"No fear. I'll get a driver to take us back." Pierce walks toward one of the cars and the driver is already opening the door for us. Within five minutes we're back at the hotel.

After freshening up, I walk out of the bathroom and find Pierce staring at me. "Want me to get the chair?"

"My cane is enough. I can stand. I can walk. If it weren't for the damn location of this ceremony, I wouldn't need this chair."

"I know. To be honest, I wish you'd let me push you." He laughs. "It gives me a great excuse to not have to walk around and be social."

"Tell you what. If you don't tell, I'll pretend I can't."

"You're on." He winks.

CHAPTER THREE

Pierce

THE ESCAPE FROM THE EVENING WAS SHORT-LIVED.

Now we're at the overly fancy restaurant at the hotel Spencer rented, and my teeth are grinding together as my father delivers a toast to his favorite son. He doesn't have to say it. It's obvious. Spencer is the only one who hasn't disappointed him. Grant turned his back on the family years ago and only recently made amends, but his transgressions aren't as bad as mine.

Why the fuck am I here?

To celebrate your perfect brother.

"Hey. Stop sulking. It's not attractive," Lindsey berates, and I turn to match her stare. Cocking my head to the side, I flash her the largest, overly fake smile I can muster. It's so broad my cheeks actually hurt.

"I'm not sulking. I'm brooding," I deadpan, and she purses her lips.

"Same thing, ass," she mutters under her breath, and I can't help but laugh. As pissed as she is, it appears she's still the witty Lindsey I remember from last year. Of all people, I can appreciate that.

"Pierce," my brother's cold voice calls from behind.

I turn slowly, throwing my cocky grin his way. "Spencer.

Congratulations." My voice lacks warmth. In fact, the sarcasm oozing from me is clearly not going unnoticed. Spencer's scowl could cool the desert.

"Where were you after the proposal? Slink off to get wasted?"

His words cut through me like a sharp blade, his condescending comments making me feel like a stupid child getting caught doing something I shouldn't be doing. It's demeaning, especially since I'm not even close to wasted. My speech is clear and I'm standing upright, which is more than I want to be doing at this second.

"That was my fault, Spencer," Lindsey says demurely, and a feeling of relief floods me. I don't need her to help me, but I appreciate it. It's not often someone has my back, and Lindsey stepping up makes me feel good. "I had to pee and needed his help getting the wheelchair out of the gravel."

"How you feeling, Linds?" Spencer turns away from me without another word. His concern for Lindsey is apparent as he steps toward her and furrows his brow.

"I'm fine." She waves him off. "I only needed the wheelchair because it's hard for me to walk on uneven ground right now."

"Of course. I'm sorry we didn't think to make accommodations."

"I *can* walk, Spencer," she grits out, and Spencer's back goes ramrod straight.

I turn toward her, my eyes going wide at her harsh tone. The condition of her legs is definitely a sore spot for her. She doesn't like to be coddled or treated differently, but that's always been Lindsey. She's strong. Stronger than me. I remember before her accident she was always a tough girl. She was bossy and a force to be reckoned with, demanding attention from all those around her. She was in your face and always got her way no matter what, with only one exception ... me. The thing is I always respected

13

her for taking what she wanted, for being so strong. But seeing her now, as I look more closely, I notice her strength doesn't meet her eyes. They appear hollow and tired. Dark circles I haven't seen before are present under a light dusting of makeup. A thought pops into my head. Is it only for appearance's sake? Is this an act? Because acting is something I can understand better than anyone else.

"I'm glad Pierce could be of help to you."

Spencer's words pull me out of my thoughts and I look up to meet his glare. The corners of his eyes crinkle as he narrows his gaze. He's appraising me to see if there's any sign that I'm wasted, I'm sure. *There isn't,* I want to hiss back, but instead, I go for the tried and true sarcasm I'm best known for.

"You wound me, brother. I am a gentleman. Of course I'd help."

"One never knows with you, *Pierce.*"

The way he says my name stings. *His rebuttal stings.*

It's nothing new, but though I'd never admit it to anyone, it doesn't hurt any less with time. Pride. It's a trait all three Lancaster brothers share. It's our downfall, but most certainly mine.

With that, Spencer dismisses me and speaks to Lindsey for a few minutes before walking off without a single word more in my direction.

Asshole.

After thirty minutes I can't fake smile anymore. I let out a large, audible sigh and face the direction of the bar.

"I'm heading back to my room," Lindsey says. "I'm tired."

Bingo. This will give me the perfect excuse to bail on my brother's party. "I'll walk you back."

"I can do it myself," Lindsey snaps, causing heads to turn in our direction. Her cheeks redden with embarrassment. "I-I just

14

meant . . . I can manage." She looks down at the floor, biting her lip, it's as if she's trying to rein in her emotions over the situation.

"No doubt about that. I was only looking for a reason to escape myself," I respond to lighten the mood.

Her scowl softens, and she has the grace to appear apologetic. "Okay," she says as her lips turn up into a small smile. "I have a bottle of Jack back in my room." She shrugs. "You can help me polish it off." She gnaws on her lower lip awaiting my response.

I grin. Pierce Lancaster never turns down a chance to get fucked-up. After all, I am, in my family's eyes, a hot fucking mess. And I'm not about to lose my reputation now.

Back at her room, we decide to take shot for shot, both needing to liven up the party.

We sit across from each other as the bottle of Jack Daniel's sits neatly between us. Holding two glasses in the air, I turn to her.

"What are we drinking to?" I ask as she pours the amber liquid into the glass.

"To life?" She raises her left brow.

"That's lame," I respond. Who the fuck cheers to life? To most people, I'd been given a great one, but my family constantly reminded me that I'm wasting mine away.

"Hey . . . I almost died." She hands me a glass. "Life is important when it's about to be stripped away from you."

Damn she's right. I was wasting my life and she was given a second chance. "To life . . ." I say with a smile. Our glasses clink and then I down the dark liquid. It's warm and rough, but it does the job. "Next." I pour more into my cup and then hers.

"To family?" Her lip tips up into a wicked grin and I nod. She knows how much I *love* mine.

"To family." This one goes down smoothly, the previous shot paving the way. "To your parents sucking?"

Her mouth drops open on that one, but she recovers quickly and pushes her glass to me to refill.

"To being an only child and never being enough," she offers up when our drinks are empty.

"To being the youngest and not being enough. To not being worth their time." I shrug.

"I'll drink to that," she agrees.

Once we've polished off Lindsey's bottle of Jack, we move on to tequila, and her words begin to slur.

"Why, Lindsey Walker, I never knew you to be such a lightweight."

She scoffs. "I'm no lightweight. I just didn't eat that mush."

"Mush?"

"Shut up." She giggles.

The sound penetrates me in a way I didn't think possible. Girls and giggling typically annoy the hell out of me. I'm not into cute girls who like to cuddle afterward. Fucking and leaving are what I do best. But there has always been something about Lindsey. We've always been a lot alike. We party hard and fuck harder—*at least that's what I've heard.*

That thought bothers me. I don't know why but imagining her and another guy boils my blood. She's too good for that type of life. She deserves someone who cares for her. Someone who has their life together and isn't always looking for the next party. *Like you,* the voice in my head mocks. I'm everything that's wrong for her. I'm everything that's wrong for any girl looking for a relationship, yet I can't help but want a taste.

There's something different about Lindsey from the last time I saw her. She used to be like all the other girls who partied with me, only out to get drunk and high. But tonight, when she saw I was struggling, she put her own embarrassment aside and allowed herself to be the scapegoat for why we had to leave.

Something in that moment lit a flame in me. Anyone who'd do that for me was worth getting to know.

So now, here we are, both drunk, and I want her. Maybe that makes me a bastard, but I can't help it. Lindsey is unexplored territory and I want to conquer her.

She leans into me, slapping a hand to my shoulder. "Another shot," she goads.

I grab her hand, holding it to my chest. Our eyes meet, and the air shifts.

"No more shots, Lindsey," I assert through my drunken haze. The room is beginning to tilt out of focus. If I have another shot, I'll be useless to her and myself.

"No?" she croaks.

I pull her into me and she squeaks at the sudden movement. "I want to kiss you."

She answers my unspoken question by crushing her mouth to mine.

Thank fuck.

The touch of our mouths sends me into a heady trance, one that won't be lifted until I'm inside her. We're all hands pulling at each other's clothes, and I throw my jacket—and then my shirt—haphazardly across the room.

The tiny semblance of control we had is lost. It's explosive and I need more.

Her shoes hit the wall with a thud before I yank her around and her back slams against my chest. She flicks off the switch to the lights and plunges the room into darkness. I can barely see my fingers flicking open the buttons running down Lindsey's spine. *I can't get this dress off fast enough.*

"Fuck it," I growl, tearing at the dress and sending buttons flying.

Lindsey gasps.

"Lift your arms," I command.

She obeys.

My fingers skim up the outside of her leg, and she stiffens. I pause and wait for her to object, to stop this insanity, but when she doesn't, I don't need to be asked twice. I grab at the hem of her floor-length cotton dress and pull it up her body and over her head until she's in nothing but her bra and thong. She sits down on the couch in front of me, her arms moving around to cradle her knees to her chest. She's covering herself as if she's embarrassed, which is ridiculous.

She's phenomenal.

In the dim light of the room, I can't see enough, though. I want to turn the lights back on and feast on her beauty. I reach past her to the lamp on the side table.

"Don't," she whispers. "Don't ruin it."

I don't know what she's talking about, but I honor her request and reach around her back to unclasp her bra and let it fall to the couch. Even with only a pale light illuminating the room, I can see how exquisite she is.

"You're as perfect as I thought you'd be." The words slip out from my mouth before I can stop them, but they're the truth, no lies. Even though I've never said it before, I've always wanted Lindsey. She's always been beautiful to me.

In the past, she reminded me of a perfectly constructed painting. From far away you admire her, but you never really come close enough to see the levels of depth to the art. Now, up close, seeing her at the dinner, seeing her come to my rescue, she's even lovelier. It's like seeing each brush stroke of a masterpiece for the first time. The way they combine to make her who she is, makes her more different, more real.

More exquisite.

"I'm hardly perfect." Her voice trembles and the insecurity in her voice makes my blood boil.

"You are," I hiss.

Saliva pools in my mouth at the sight of her nipples exposed, begging to be licked. I can't think about anything but having her beneath me, so I do just that, discarding her thong and stripping her completely naked. I gaze intently at each valley and dip across her skin, and in my head, I paint each surface of her body. It feels like my universe begins and ends with her. I want to discover everything about her. I want to chase away all the insecurities inside her.

And I will.

I bend over and take her nipple in my mouth, licking first, then letting it pop out and replacing it with the other one, biting and sucking until she's lifting her hips, rubbing against me and getting the friction where she needs it, but I toy with her. I don't give her what she wants. I keep her panting. Watching her fall apart is an aphrodisiac to me. It makes me feel powerful. Strong. Wanted.

I keep her begging.

With one breast still in my mouth, I trail my hand down and then allow my fingers to part her. *Fuck.* She's so wet. Desperate for me. I love this. I love the control I wield. How, with just one look, one touch, I can have her begging at my feet.

Unstoppable.

Feeling her desperation, I remove myself from my boxers and stroke my length.

Up.

Down.

Root to tip.

A bead of moisture collects. I'm not even in her yet and I'm ready to burst. Not able to take it anymore, I pull away from her body, remove my hand from between her thighs, and reach for the condom I've got in my pants. Once sheathed, I pull her legs apart and let my eyes feast on her glistening skin like the hungry beast I am.

Looking up, I meet her stare. Lindsey ensnares me with her gaze, and all logical thoughts drift from my mind. Her desire for me is intoxicating.

I need to taste her.

And that's just what I do. Without preamble, my tongue swipes. She quivers. I lick. She squirms. I bury my head between her thighs. She screams out my name.

She's fucking fantastic.

I lift off, push her back into the couch, and lift her leg around my hip. Slowly, I drag myself up and down her skin, teasing her. She moves underneath me, trying to force me in, but I don't. I continue circling but not entering. Her nails scratch my skin, biting into my flesh, and I let out a throaty chuckle before I thrust.

A primal gasp escapes her mouth as I slam in. Bottomed out, I pause for a beat, allowing her to accommodate me before I slowly drag myself back out to the tip. Her inhale of breath at the sensation fuels me. I crash my mouth down on hers at the same time. This is what heaven must feel like. This is what it must taste like to come close to ethereal bliss.

I hungrily push my tongue into her mouth. Wanting to savor her, own her, possess her. My strokes match each slam of my body. She meets my advances, eagerly giving as well as taking. All control leaves me and I push into her even harder. One pump, two, and then I'm losing myself into an oblivion so intense, I think I'm high.

Once I return to reality, I roll off her and onto the floor, breathing heavily. The events of what just occurred run through my mind. We didn't even make it to the bed. I fucked her on a couch, missionary, and it was easily the best sex I've ever had. *What the fuck*? I'm grappling with the foreign emotions running through me, confused and feeling like a douche, when I look up to find Lindsey dressing.

"What are you doing?" I ask.

"I'm tired. Going to head to bed. You should probably head back to your room."

I can't help but feel a prick of annoyance. She's kicking *me* out? This is a first. A first I don't like at all. Here I thought she saw more. When she offered to be my excuse, I thought she understood what it was like to have a family who never approves or just plain doesn't give a damn. When we got drunk and traded family gripes, I thought she saw more of who I am. But I guess I was wrong and once again I've been thrown out. Just like the trash. My whole life I've been dispensable to my family. Never good enough and always swept to the side. Now the one person who I thought got me is doing the same? Not happening. I won't be made to look like an idiot.

I stand, grabbing my clothes and throwing them on. While pulling my shirt over my head, Lindsey speaks.

"If you want to stay, you can." Lindsey sounds unsure, hopeful. She's giving me whiplash by the second. I don't know if she's going to fuck me again or kick me out any minute, and if I'm honest, I'm not up for another bout of rejection. Because that's just what she'll do if I let her. Like my family, she'll rip me apart. She'll add a new wound, a new scar to my mental collection.

I take a deep breath and spill words I don't want to say but must for my own stubborn pride. Words I can't take back. "Nah. I'm going to head out. I helped you back, but I have shit to do."

She stiffens, her face paling. "You helped me back? What? Like I couldn't do it myself?"

Her words are ice.

"You were struggling today. I just did what any gentleman would do."

"Gentleman? You've got to be fucking kidding me," she huffs. "So, what? Was this some sort of pity screw? Because I don't need your pity, Pierce. You're more fucked-up than I'll ever be."

Her words sting, but she's right. Every word my brothers said play back in my ears. Every look of disappointment I can see behind my lids as I close them. Every memory of being alone, everything comes back to me. Lindsey leaves no room for confusion at the way she looks at me with disgust.

I'm nothing to her.

Straightening my back, I lift my internal walls up. I shrug, callous and arrogant.

"Get the fuck out," she screams, pushing at my shoulders.

"I'm out," I say, hands coming up lazily in surrender.

I walk out, Lindsey's curses and insults hitting my back as I close the door on her. My shoulders slump as I round the corner, out of her sight. I hate myself for the things I said. They were hurtful, and Lindsey didn't deserve them.

I'm a coward.

I'd rather push her away than risk the chance that she'd not want me. Honestly, hurting her this one time won't compare to what would happen to me if I let this girl in. She'll get over it. I sure as fuck know she'll get over it faster than it would take me to come back from whatever she could dish out.

Decision made, I don't turn back. I ignore the niggling thought going through my brain . . .

That I just ruined any shot of a repeat with the one girl who's ever made me want more.

CHAPTER FOUR

Pierce

Three months later

WHY I THOUGHT STOPPING AT A CLUB AND MEETING for a drink instead of hitting the road to head out east to the Hamptons was a good idea is beyond me. I could be at my family's summerhouse already. But instead of being on the road driving, I'm only just leaving the club now, which means there's no way I'll be going anywhere tonight.

I'm walking toward the valet of Swerve, the new nightclub housed at The L Hotel to grab my car. I shouldn't have come, but I couldn't say no. When Trey told me he was getting a table at the new club in my brother Grant's hotel, the opportunity to taunt my brother was too intense. I'm never going to be taken seriously by them, so I've decided to flaunt my indifference in their faces and yet that still didn't have the desired response. He didn't even show up. So once again, I did something to demand their attention and it fell on deaf ears.

This week alone, I've gone out five days, and it's only Friday, so that says a lot. God, I'm tired. I'm tired of this damn city. Tired of trying. Just plain tired.

A haze of booze and girls will do that.

A peaceful weekend is no longer in my future, though, an

escape to East Hampton long since forgotten with a bump of coke and a willing girl swaying her hips. One minute I was having one drink, the next I was getting an impromptu lap dance from my ex, and then before I could say, "let's go" we were gone. Now I'm taking the keys from the valet, who so kindly for the right price has parked my Range Rover in front of the hotel, and stepping into the car, entourage in tow to keep the party going.

I pull out onto the street.

"Where to?"

"Your place," Trey shouts from the back seat.

"Ain't going to happen." No one goes to my place. That's my one rule and Trey knows it.

"Fine, mine then." He laughs, obviously not surprised that even as fucked as I am, I'm holding true to my word. I'm not even sure why he tried. We always party at his place.

We aren't even two blocks from the corner when Josie places her hand on my crotch. "Fuck, Josie. You can't do that while I'm driving."

My ex strokes me through my jeans, making it difficult to concentrate. My dick is rock-hard beneath her touch, begging to come out and play. But right now I need to concentrate on driving or I'm fucked. She's a major distraction. Why did I think going home with my ex was a good idea?

I grit my teeth and try to move her away by shoving her hand off me, but she's having none of it. I feel her work at my zipper.

Josie and I dated in high school, though I use the word "dated" lightly. We fucked. We fucked a lot. She's a whole lot of crazy and drama, so eventually, I cut ties. But I was horny as fuck and high off my ass when I bumped into her tonight, and she's now in my car, practically sucking my dick in the front seat. She might be crazy, but she gives good head, and sometimes, like now, that's all that matters.

Hoots sound from the backseat. Trey, Linc, and one of Josie's friends are back there smoking a joint and having a heyday.

"Want a hit, Lancaster?"

Trey offers a blunt over the seat. I take it and pull a long drag. If I can't get my rocks off, I might as well feel good.

"I want the good stuff," Josie whines.

She drives me crazy. I thought I could forget that fact, but no matter how good I feel, the high-pitched bitching does nothing but annoy me.

"We'll be doing lines in less than ten, Josie girl," Linc promises.

Josie dances around in the seat, hitting my arm.

"Hey, watch it. I'm driving here," I growl.

"Lighten up, Lancaster, and have some fun," Josie snips, turning up the radio to a decibel that's bringing on a headache. I'm about to yell at her to turn it down when flashing blue lights attract my attention from behind.

"Shit," I yell. "Fuck. Get rid of that joint, Linc."

Everyone in the car scrambles to get in their seats and hide the shit. It doesn't even matter. There's no way around this. My stomach shifts uneasily as I pull over and then release my hands from the steering wheel. They shake uncontrollably.

I'm fucked.

High off my ass and fucked.

Twenty-four hours in central booking, and then the tombs, I'm finally sitting in court awaiting the judge's sentencing. I've never sat overnight. Typically, my father or Spencer comes to bail me out. Not this time, and it's giving me a strange feeling. With all my priors, the judge should throw the book at me, but I'm

Pierce Lancaster. I'll receive a slap on the hand because, let's face it, my father will make sure of it.

"Mr. Lancaster, did you hear what I said?" Judge Maddox calls from the stand.

I turn my head toward her.

"I'm sorry, Your Honor. What did you say?"

"Mr. Lancaster, you've become somewhat of a constant in this courtroom. Have you gotten so comfortable that you don't feel inclined to answer the one person who holds your fate in their hand?"

"I'm sorry, Your Honor. I was looking for someone."

"Perhaps that person isn't coming, Mr. Lancaster. Has it occurred to you that your shenanigans might have been the final straw?"

I don't say anything. *She's right.*

"It's my decision that you shall be required to log ten hours community service per week for the next three months. We'll consider your night as time served."

My shoulders droop. I'm thankful to be getting off so easily, especially without my father's presence.

"Mr. Lancaster, this is your last chance. The next time I find you in my courtroom, you will serve time. Plan on a minimum of ninety days upstate if you're back here within the next twelve months. Are we clear?"

I nod.

"Use your words, Mr. Lancaster."

"Yes, Your Honor. Crystal clear."

I'm released and ready to call for a ride when I round the corner and bump straight into Spencer. "A little late, bro. No worries. I didn't need you."

His brow rises. "You think she decided to go easy on you for no reason? What? Because you're Pierce Lancaster?" he mocks and it feels like I'm being punched in the gut. "Get this straight: nobody cares. You got a pass only because I made the call. But this is the last time."

Spencer is seething. I haven't seen him this angry with me in a very long time. Not that it hasn't been building. With all our dad's health issues, it's been Spencer more and more. He's tired. I can see it in his eyes.

"I'm sorry," I offer for the first time ever. "Does Dad know?"

"No, and he won't. He can't take that stress right now."

I hang my head in shame. Despite everything, I don't begrudge Spencer. He's worked his ass off his entire life. Things weren't just handed to him. The hotels were supposed to be Grant's, but he turned his back on the family for some time.

"I'm serious, Pierce. Get your shit together. I don't care what you do but do something. Because if you don't, you'll end up here again, and let me tell you there won't be another bailout. You better get your ass to community service every week, no excuses. The first time you miss, I'll drag your ass to jail myself."

With that, he turns his back and walks away from me.

CHAPTER FIVE

Lindsey

"Listen, Christopher. You can't do that," I say sternly, maintaining eye contact with the young man in front of me. He might be taller, but that doesn't stop me from being firm with him. I've learned in the last few months of working at the Polaris Boys Club that showing strength is as important as kindness with these teens. They might look like men but, in fact, they aren't, and they need to learn boundaries or they could potentially walk all over us. "We don't use our fists here."

"He threw the punch first," he responds, his chocolate brown eyes never leaving mine.

"I don't care. You should've walked away and gotten one of the counselors. You can be kicked out for that crap." My words must get to him because Christopher starts to nibble on his upper lip. He's not a bad kid. He's just had a tough life.

Polaris has been my home away from home for the past three months. I started volunteering here after I returned from France. It's my way of giving back. For a long time, I took my life for granted and treated people badly. But after the car accident that left me pretty banged up, everything was different. When your life flashes before your eyes, you decide to make changes. Truth is, my life needed a good cleansing. I didn't realize it at first, but after the accident, I knew it was time. After a drunken night in Antibes, I realized the time was now.

I didn't want to settle back into old habits. After Pierce's rejection, I found myself itching to numb the pain again. I was headed back down a bad path with partying and drinking. The need to do drugs was all-encompassing. So I took a long, hard look at my life. I'm lucky to be alive after the accident I was in, and I don't take that for granted, so as soon as the plane touched down back in the States, I set off to find meaning in my life.

I needed something to occupy my time, and since I have more money than I could spend in a lifetime, I decided to volunteer to help make others' lives better. My best friend Olivia's sister is dating the guy who runs Polaris. Olivia hooked me up, and I've never been happier with my decision. These boys need a wake-up call, and I've found that my limp is pretty good motivation.

I watch Christopher inspect his fingernails. It's obvious he's uncomfortable and feeling bad. "Come here." He walks until he's beside me, and I place my hand on his shoulder. My lips spread into a tight smile. "You're better than this."

And he is.

Most of these boys are trying to stay away from gangs and drugs. If not for Polaris, they'd most likely get sucked into a criminal lifestyle. Christopher's father is a gang member and drug dealer, and Christopher's mom is a single woman, working her ass off for a little more than minimum wage. She depends on Polaris to keep Christopher in line after school. If he gets kicked out, he'll most likely get pulled into his father's world and end up in jail. *Or dead.*

"Next time, get a counselor."

He nods.

"You have an hour left. Basketball or art."

His brow rises and his chin tips up. "Definitely basketball," he says, smiling wide.

"Then hit the court, Jordan."

Without another word, he's jogging toward the gym. It's always hard to be stern with the boys, but I know I have to do it sometimes. Tough love situation. Kindness and a little discipline go a long way. I learned that early on.

When I first started here, the concept was foreign to me. I'd never had either in my life, so they were hard to demonstrate to the boys. I gave in to their every demand, their every indulgence, and quickly everything became clear—if there are no boundaries, you get taken advantage of.

My childhood flashes before my own eyes as I consider these kids. I got everything I ever wanted, everything but the one thing I needed. Someone to care. So that's what I give these kids. I treat them the way I've always wanted to be treated. There are rules and rewards, but also love. Each and every boy at Polaris has a place in my heart. I stare off into the distance, remembering every kid I've worked with during my short time here.

"Hey, Lindsey. Everything okay?" Carson calls from behind me.

I sigh before turning to face him. I'm not ready to rehash the last few minutes with Christopher, especially since it's over.

"Yeah. Just a little issue with Christopher and Cass, but it's been handled," I inform him.

"Great. Thanks for taking care of things." He smiles. "I'm headed out but call if you need anything."

"I've got it under control. See you tomorrow."

He starts to walk away before turning back in my direction. "Tomorrow, we've got a new volunteer coming. He's court ordered, so I'm not sure how much we can depend on him but thought I'd give you the heads-up. I'll need you to do the introductions."

"Great. I should have some time tonight to put a packet together and get things set up."

"You're awesome, Linds. Polaris is lucky to have your help."

I beam at his praise, my chest puffing up with pride. I'm not used to compliments. Most of my life I've been ignored and left to fend for myself, but hearing him say that, knowing that Carson appreciates me, makes every rough day worth it. I respect him so much, and his opinion means everything to me.

Carson Blake hasn't had the easiest go of things over the past couple of years. He used to teach at Cranbrook Prep until a scandal with a student, Olivia's sister, Lynn, ended that run. He's still with Lynn, and Polaris is his life, but it hasn't been without trials and tribulations. He got his start working with the grade school boys. Then he recognized that the older kids need the intervention as much as the younger boys, so he made it his mission to start this chapter.

With my past, Polaris just made sense. Most times, I'm able to recognize the warning signs for potential drug use, and Carson is good at picking up on criminal activity, so together we're able to circumvent the issue and steer the boys back on the right path. It's the most rewarding thing I've ever done. After two months, Carson insisted on paying me. It's not much, but it's more than I need. Carson doesn't know, but I've been donating money to the center through a charity I founded. I understand how important this center is, and I know this was my calling. I'd love to see the equivalent opened for girls in the same situation.

———————◆◆———————

The rest of the night flies. I'm in my office charting out tomorrow's activity groups when my phone beeps with an incoming text.

Olivia: You around tonight? I'm in town!

I nearly fall out of my seat with excitement. Olivia is *never* in town. She's always globetrotting for work or with Spencer. Olivia and I have spoken several times the past few months, but I haven't seen her since the engagement party in Antibes, and the idea of seeing her has my mouth spreading into a huge smile. Spending time with one of my closest friends is definitely needed right now. Friendships don't come easy for me, and most of the people I used to hang with stopped calling me after the accident. Olivia stuck by my side, even when I was a complete bitch during recovery, which was often. Truth, I've always been a bitch, so the fact Olivia still talks to me bodes well for her character. If anyone treated me the way I treated her, I'd give them their walking cards.

Me: YES!

Me: You mean to tell me Spencer is allowing you to breathe?

Olivia: Ha! Like he has a choice. I want to see you.

Me: I'll be home within the hour. Dessert? Wine for me!

I stare at my phone and wait for her to answer. Full-fledged excitement courses through me. With all that's happened, we have so much to talk about, and a piece of cake and some girl time sounds great. Olivia doesn't drink alcohol, so now instead of drinking, we sample the best desserts the city has to offer. But no matter how yummy the cake that I'll pick up for tonight will be, I'll still need a glass of wine. I'll need liquid courage. I never told her about Pierce and me. There was no point. She wasn't here. But now everything is different and having someone to talk to about it is welcome—*needed*.

Olivia: A piece or two. I can't stay late. No sugar coma for me, I have to fly out to accompany one of my girls on a shoot tomorrow.

Me: K. See you at my place in one hour.

Olivia: K.

———————— ◆ ◆ ————————

"You did what?" Olivia bellows while simultaneously choking on a piece of the chocolate cake I bought.

I groan, already regretting my admission. *Why did I think wine was a good idea?* Wine equals loose lips.

"Why didn't you tell me before now?" Olivia pouts and not being able to answer right away, I dart my eyes around my living room. The city just outside my floor-to-ceiling windows grabs my attention. The lights flickering in the horizon from the neighboring buildings lock me into a trance.

Why didn't I tell her?

Embarrassment.

Pride.

"It wasn't one of my finer moments," I finally answer while I chew on my lip, remembering Antibes. "In fact, I'd just as soon forget it." I grimace.

"You've wanted Pierce forever. It was only a matter of time," she states. "So was it everything you dreamed it would be?" She giggles, and the sound makes my heart warm. This is what I've missed; the laid-back feeling of friendships.

"Wait, don't answer that," she says, pulling me out of my thoughts. She scrunches her nose in obvious disgust of me hooking up with him, and I can't help but laugh with her. Pierce is the youngest brother of her fiancé, so he'll be her brother-in-law soon. I'm sure she doesn't want the mental image.

"He's an asshole, and I couldn't care less if he fell off the face of the Earth," I vow.

"Yikes. What did he do to deserve the Lindsey wrath?"

"Does Pierce Lancaster have to do anything in particular to be a prick?" I purse my lips, and Olivia taps a finger to her mouth in thought.

"Nope. Good point."

We both laugh.

"Spencer is about to kill him. He got himself arrested for possession, DUI, and open container. Spence had to make a call and get him off, but this is the last time. He promised me."

None of this surprises me. I ran in the same circle as Pierce Lancaster for a long time. I know how he rolls. The fact he's still alive is a miracle based on his lifestyle choices. I should know since I'm barely alive in spite of making the same choice myself once upon a time.

"With everything going on with Spencer, the last thing he has time to do is babysit Pierce." She sighs. "Some people are incapable of change."

"I'm sorry Spencer still has to deal with that shit, but I'm glad I'm no longer in that scene. It has to get old, right?"

"One would think."

We spend the rest of the evening eating and talking about Olivia's new business pursuits. I tell her about the center and how life-changing it's been for me. Hearing her speak about helping young models inspires me. I want to do more. Now to figure out what more is. If Olivia can turn her life around and make such an impact, so can I. Olivia has lit a spark under me, and she doesn't even know it.

After a few more drinks, I'm getting tired, and I have a long day tomorrow with the new volunteer coming. I hug her good-bye and head to bed, happy with my life just the way it is.

CHAPTER SIX

Lindsey

GET TO THE CENTER EARLY TODAY, WANTING TO MAKE SURE all the stations are mapped out and volunteers are accounted for. We're one volunteer short, which means the newbie and I will have to tag team.

I look over the list of volunteers and frown. Tonya, Courtney, Jaden, and Travis are scheduled to work today—none of which do a great job with the basketball station. As much as I hate the idea, any type of exercise and the chance to get on my leg is good for me. The more I use it, the faster I'll be back to normal.

I glance at the clock. Ten minutes before our staff will begin to arrive and I have everything ready to go. I check the computer once more for information from the courts about our newest volunteer. All I've been told is that his participation here is court mandated. He must not have priors because they never send us volunteers with a criminal background. Still, I like to be sure of who I'm dealing with. I should have asked Carson.

"Hey, Linds," Courtney shouts from the hallway.

"I'm back here," I call.

Courtney comes around the corner, hair pulled into a high ponytail, blond tendrils falling around her face. She's a pretty girl, but she's a bit of a ditz. "Where am I at today?"

"I'm gonna put you at the art station," I answer.

"Awesome."

Courtney is our resident artist. If it were her choice, she'd be there every day. Unfortunately for her, there are others who fight for it as it takes the least amount of effort.

"There's a new guy hanging around the entrance." Courtney wiggles her brows. "He's cute, too."

I roll my eyes. Courtney thinks any guy with two legs is attractive. Poor girl grew up in the sticks of Kentucky, and you'd think she's never seen a man before.

I grin. "Court mandated. He's sure to be a winner."

Her smile drops. "I'm always attracted to the bad boys."

I can't help but chuckle. "Thanks for letting me know." I close the screen on my computer and stand. "I'll go greet him and start the tour."

Stretching, I let a groan escape. My muscles are tight and I bounce on my feet, hoping to loosen up a bit. Coming around the corner, I stop in my tracks.

And just like that, my day goes to hell in a handbasket.

This is bad. Really fucking bad.

Pierce Lancaster.

"What are you doing here?" I snap. My voice is harsh, much harsher than I intend. But why is he here? Why is he in my place?

Pierce's wide eyes stare back at me. "I'm here for community service," he drawls out, causing me to cock my head to the side and assess him. He notices my perusal and reads it the wrong way completely, because his eyes twinkle back mischievously as the side of his lips tips up.

"You can't be serious." I roll my eyes.

"As a heart attack," he says, smiling that signature grin of his. This time, a small dimple I never noticed before forms on his right cheek. The desire to wipe the smirk off his face is all-encompassing. I want to smack it off.

God!

He infuriates me.

Why does he have to be so goddamn handsome? It makes no difference how dashing he is when he grins like that. I still hate him. With every ounce of my body, I loathe this man. Of all the fucking places and all the volunteer positions in this city, he would end up here.

Karma hates me.

CHAPTER SEVEN

Lindsey

"DARE I ASK WHAT ACTUALLY HAPPENED THAT forced you to do community service? I doubt it's unpaid parking tickets," I hiss knowing full well he got in trouble for drugs just not knowing anything more about the story as Olivia didn't give any other details, just vague references.

His brow rises, which makes me contemplate all the ways he could have landed himself in this position. Pierce is synonymous with partying, so I wouldn't put it past him to have made a complete ass of himself or to have gotten caught in a really compromising situation with drugs. Both are unacceptable when working with young minds. These boys are already susceptible to those behaviors.

I throw my hands up in the air as he begins to talk. "Never mind. I don't even want to know." I stalk off down the hall with him following close on my heels as I bark off explanations of each room's purpose. After the fifth room, I feel him grab my shoulder and stop me.

"Linds, come on. I know we didn't exactly leave on the best terms, but you can't tell me you're not happy to see me." He smirks, which only irritates me further.

"Actually, Pierce, I'm not happy to see you. You're an ass,

and quite frankly, you aren't competent to work with these kids."

He frowns.

"If you do a good job, we'll get along just fine. When your time is up, we'll never have to see each other again, and I like that even better."

"Come on. It's no fun to hold grudges. You of all people should know how fast life can be over," he responds matter-of-factly.

I stop in my tracks. How dare he bring up my accident like he knows anything about it? His words hit a sore spot, and he knows it.

"You make it easy to hold grudges," I spit out.

"Lindsey, I'm sorry. I don't. I . . ." he trails off. "I meant to say we've had fun in the past. Wouldn't it be easier to go back to those times?"

"I much prefer hating you to any other emotion, Pierce. Like I said, you make it effortless."

I turn from him and head down the hall. He doesn't say another word while I continue to give him a tour of the building. "The basketball station needs both of us today. You may want to change out of those clothes." He looks down at his jeans and Henley tee. "Please tell me you brought shorts."

"Yeah, I have a bag in the car. I can run out and get it." He turns to leave.

"You drove here?" I blink a few times, not understanding why anyone would choose to drive in the city.

"I had someplace to be before here. It was just easier."

"Sure." He starts to go. "Pierce." I stop him again, still having more to say.

He turns back and looks at me expectantly.

"No matter our past, this job is very important to me. These kids are very important to me." I can't stress the words enough. "They need good role models, and they need to know there's a way to live that doesn't include the streets and all that comes with it. Alcohol, drugs, all of that could ruin their lives. They are highly susceptible to it based on their situations. Whatever got you in here, I don't want those boys to know anything about it."

"Lindsey, I—"

I stop his words with a raise of my hand. "You will act like a model citizen. Do we understand each other?"

He nods.

I pray he heeds my words. If he doesn't, I don't know what I'll do.

⎯⎯⎯⎯ ◆ ◆ ⎯⎯⎯⎯

"Okay, boys, this here is Pierce, and he'll be volunteering at the center for a few hours in the coming weeks. Today you get to school him in basketball."

The boys bob their heads up and down and say their hellos.

"This should be fun," I mutter under my breath. "Christopher, Xavier, and Terry, you guys take on Pierce, Rocky, and Jackson. I'll keep score."

Pierce narrows his eyes. "How do you get out of playing?"

"I'm in charge here, so you'll stop asking questions and just play." My boys chuckle at my words and I smirk. "All right, boys. Get playing."

For a solid half hour, the boys run up and down the court, shooting free throws and making three-pointers like it's no big deal. These kids are so talented. A couple have even talked about joining the basketball team at their local school, which makes me so happy. They should. They are good, and it will help keep them off the streets.

Pierce wipes sweat from his brow, leaning over as if out of shape. But as he does it, the large cutouts in the side of his shirt show his ripped abs. The man is cut from stone and my cheeks heat from staring.

Look away, Lindsey.

I berate myself for being so damn weak. The last thing I need to do is appreciate anything about Pierce Lancaster. The last time I did, it led to me dealing with a bruised ego for months and almost falling back to my old ways. The urge to lose myself in a bottle or even worse, coke, was strong. I barely pushed through the last craving. Who knows what I'd do if I ever get that weak again.

They begin to play an actual game, and I watch the corded muscles of his arms flex as he raises his hands above his head to block Xavier's attempt at a shot. I never would have imagined Pierce to be athletic, but he is. I always saw him more as a party boy than athlete. Burning the candle at both ends and not taking care of himself. But it's obvious from this little exhibition that I was wrong. He's actually really good, and the boys are loving having him play.

It irritates me.

I don't want my boys to like my enemy, and my enemy he is. He took what he wanted and left me in pieces. The words he spoke shredded my heart and left me feeling vulnerable at a time when I was already at my lowest, and I have no doubt that his words were intentional.

No matter how much of a Greek god Pierce Lancaster is, I won't be pulled back in. He can do his time here and I will play nice, but I won't let him back into my heart. He had his shot and he lost it. The most he can hope for is to earn back a little of my respect. If he treats these boys the way they deserve to be treated, I can deal with his presence here. Then, when it's time for him to go, we can part amicably. But I'll never forget his harsh words. And he doesn't deserve total forgiveness.

He of all people should know how deeply words cut.

CHAPTER EIGHT

Lindsey

"WHAT WERE YOU THINKING?" I DEMAND, BARGING into Carson's office.

He looks up from the stack of papers in his hands, a line forming on his forehead. He lifts one eyebrow at me as he gives me a puzzled look. "Am I supposed to know what you're referring to?"

"Pierce Lancaster?" I throw my hands up in the air in frustration. "Do you have any idea why he has to do community service?"

He lowers the papers to his desk, folding his hands in front of him, and stares at me. "I am aware. But I'm curious as to how you came about this information?"

"Public knowledge, Carson. Anyone can learn anything if they do some digging." The truth is, Olivia told me and I'm sure Carson knows that since his girlfriend is Olivia's sister. He's well aware of how the gossip mill works in the Miller family. "These boys and this center are my reason for living. You founded this center to teach these kids right from wrong and to make sure they don't go down that path. So, we're putting a convicted drug user and alcoholic in front of them?"

"Lindsey, we have all made mistakes," Carson says as he gives me a pointed look, and I realize how hypocritical I sound.

"Fine." I raise my hands in defeat. "But you have to admit, it's not okay that he's always in the newspaper. If these boys look him up, he's not a good role model."

"Again, I understand your concerns, but it's also a part of this program to demonstrate that mistakes are part of life, but no one is unredeemable. We want them to know that no matter where their past has taken them, their future doesn't have to be the same. Look at me. Look at you. If they looked us up, they'd see some pretty bad things too. If we changed, so can he." He sighs. "Pierce has an opportunity to show the boys that their pasts don't define them. It's a growing experience for all of them. Pierce isn't a bad guy. He just made some bad decisions."

Bad decisions? Bad decisions! Making me feel like shit is more than that! I want to scream. Instead, I inhale a sharp breath and ponder a response that might get through to him. "That could be said for a lot of former criminals, but we don't allow them through those doors," I say matter-of-factly as I place my hand on my hip.

"I know Pierce, and I know his character. I know what I'm doing, and I hope you trust me enough to not question my judgment. If he makes one wrong move, he's gone. Until then, I want you to give him a chance."

"Fat chance," I murmur under my breath.

"Lindsey, I need you to trust me. You know about my past. You know how I feel about these boys. Some of them have been with me for years. Don't you think I have their best interest at heart? I would never put the boys in harm's way or sacrifice our program if I wasn't one hundred percent sure."

"I trust you. I just"—I blow out an audible sigh—"hope he doesn't disappoint you, because the Pierce I know can't be trusted."

Carson doesn't respond. What more is there to say, anyway? I said my piece, he said his, but in the end, this is his club and I'm an employee, no matter how much my heart is invested in the children.

Having lost the fight, I turn on my heel and exit the room. As soon as I'm out, I see Pierce standing there with a frown on his face. He obviously heard everything I said, though I'm too angry to care. Serves him right for being here.

"You're that desperate to get rid of me that you need to try to hurt me?" he asks.

"You don't have a heart, Pierce. I couldn't hurt you if I tried." I turn to walk away, but he grabs me by the elbow, spinning me around so we're nose-to-nose.

"But I clearly hurt you. You cared that much about me?" His eyes bore into mine, and I attempt to avert my gaze.

"You're so full of yourself. I could never care for you."

Lies. At one time I would have done anything to have Pierce Lancaster, but now I see him for what he is—bad news. He'd drag me back into the habits I'm running from, but I won't allow that to ever happen.

"You're lying. I can see it in your eyes," he says, sounding hurt at my words. "I cared about you, too."

"You don't need to bullshit me, Pierce. I'm not your family."

He laughs, but by the way the emotion doesn't touch his eyes, it's obvious he's not laughing because he finds it funny. "That's the thing, Lindsey. You think you know me, but you don't. You know one persona, the one I put in front of all my friends, but you have no idea the things I've been through and what I'm running from."

"You're right. You made sure to push me away. It worked. I don't want to know you." I drill him with a cold, hard stare. "Stay out of my way, or I'll make sure Carson sticks to his word and kicks your ass to the curb."

I stalk off down the hall with Pierce's eyes glaring holes in the back of my head.

CHAPTER NINE

Pierce

T HAT WAS TORTURE.
   She hates me.
   Rightfully so.
But in my own defense, *she* kicked *me* out. Still, in hindsight, and seeing how much pain I caused her, I can admit I was scum. Don't know why she expected anything else…

But shit.

She still hates me. I just kind of assumed time would pass and she'd forget and we'd fuck. *Yeah, that ain't going to happen.* I'm trash in her eyes. I heard all the shit she said about me. The desire was strong for me to storm into that room and say fuck this shit, but I couldn't, so instead, I'm back home, in my safe haven and I'm throwing a goddamn pity party for myself once again. Fuck, today sucked. No way I'll be able to make it through the rest of community service as Lindsey Walker's punching bag.

No. Way.

Still in my clothes from the center, I pull out my paintbrushes and stand in front of the blank easel. I try to empty my mind, to not think of Lindsey, but her words replay over and over again, and before I know it I'm dripping with sweat, paint splattered everywhere. I'm completely and utterly lost in thought when I hear something from behind me and jump, almost knocking the painting over.

There standing in what should be my safe place from my family is Spencer. Why can't I ever just have peace?

"What the fuck are you doing here?" I fire.

"Making sure you haven't screwed up your life today."

"Well, can't you at least knock?" The mocking tone of my voice makes him set his jaw tight.

"I own the place. Didn't think I needed to," the smug bastard says. The look on his face makes me wonder how my fist would feel if I decked him.

Good.

It would feel damn good.

"Just 'cause you own the damn place doesn't mean you can just show up. Where are your manners?" I chide. "Don't you think the polite thing to do is see if you're wanted? And for the record"—I glue him with my stare—"you're not."

"Until you stop fucking up, you're my responsibility."

"For fuck's sake, I'm an adult. Leave me alone."

"Hmm, funny you should say that 'cause last I checked an 'adult' doesn't need his daddy to bail him out."

"Actually I do believe dear old dad was too busy to bail me out."

"Same shit, man. You're old enough to know better, yet here we are and yet again you fuck up, so no. No, I won't treat you like an adult. Not until you prove you can be one."

I glare at him. "Why do you even bother? There's no secret how you feel about me." My teeth clench. Why is he here? Why does he care? Swallowing hard, I try to keep my anger at bay.

"You don't know shit."

"Well, I know I don't want you here. I don't need you here—"

"Oh, isn't that rich," he interrupts me vehemently. "So what are you doing with your life then? You got a job?"

"You know what I'm doing."

"You started volunteering today." He stares at me intently as he strides around the room. I watch as Spencer stops to look at each painting on the wall before turning his attention back to me.

"So, if you know that, why are you here?" I glower.

"Consider it me checking up on my investment."

"Your investment?" I ask, but the moment the words leave my mouth I chastise myself for asking and caring what he means.

"I put a lot on the line reputation-wise to bail you out yet again. I'm double-checking you haven't messed that up too."

"Well, I haven't, so you can go."

"Not until you tell me what your next step is."

I look down then back up and shrug.

"Pierce." He sighs. "I don't give a shit if you choose to waste your life partying. I have my own issues with work I need to deal with. But it hurts Mom, so do something. Anything. Look at you."

"I paint." I wave the wet brush in my hand.

"Yeah, and even that's half-assed. You're not dedicated. You have no goals. The only thing you're good at is getting high and apparently fucking girls, but I'm telling you now, shape up or ship out."

Not wanting to hear anymore, I turn my back on him. It doesn't take a rocket scientist to know I'm done. Message came in loud and clear. I'm a huge disappointment to everyone.

When I hear the door close, I pick up my brush and fling it across the room. Paint splatters everywhere, the wood splintering into tiny pieces across the floor. Reaching into my pocket, I grab my phone and shoot off one text.

Me: Where's the party at?
Josie: Lit and then my place . . .
Me: Sounds like a plan.

Hours later and I'm at club Lit.

Lit is the hottest lounge in the city. The kind of place that costs a minimum of ten thousand dollars to get in. This isn't a dance club. This is a prestige playground for the rich and famous.

It's decadence and sin for the right price.

The booze is always flowing, and if you're jonesing for something stronger, it's only one rolled up dollar bill away.

From across the table, Josie is lining up a line of coke. Yeah, right in the middle of the fucking table, like she owns the place, but Lit is members only, so in truth, she kind of does.

She smiles up at me, a very flirtatious smile spreading across her face, and then winks. From this angle, I have ample view of her cleavage. She looks good. Not as good as Lindsey but good. A perfect distraction. As I study the outline of every curve she's displaying, my dick agrees. Maybe I should just take her to the bathroom and fuck her already. That will rid me of the crap memories of my day.

After she does her line, she reaches the bill out, but I shake my head. If I want to fuck her, I can't be getting coked up or I won't be able to get it up. She gives me a knowing look.

My gaze moves away from her and focuses on the bottle of Grey Goose. I pull it to my mouth and take a swig. As it burns my throat, I feel Josie take a seat on my lap, her hips grinding into my semi. She moves seductively to the beat of the music. I don't pay her much attention, though; I'm lost in the bottle. With each new swig, I come closer to oblivion. With every ounce of liquor that flows into my body, the pain from Spencer's visit dissipates.

Fuck.

Fuck.

Fuck.

Everything hurts. My body aches. Where the hell am I? Painfully I open my eyes and notice I'm in my bed. How the hell did I get home?

Damn everything hurts.

My head pounds in my skull like a jackhammer on a new construction site.

All of a sudden last night rushes by. The club, the booze, and Josie.

Shit, is she here?

Fuck, did I bring her home with me?

That would be bad. No way would I be able to get rid of her if I did. She'd totally read this as me wanting to get back with her and that is the last thing I want.

My right hand pats the side of the bed next to me, and I'm thankful to find it empty. Then, my phone vibrates.

Carson: Where are you? You were supposed to be here at 9am

Shit, it's nine twenty. I hop out of bed, ignoring the pain radiating from my body. I've never gotten dressed so fast in my life. Five minutes later I'm out the door. Not even showering, just brushing my teeth.

As soon as I get to Polaris, my first move is to head straight to Carson's office. Just as I'm about to knock, I sense her presence behind me.

"Are you fucking serious right now?"

I don't answer. I don't even turn around.

"You're pathetic. You're drunk."

"I'm not drunk," I fire over my shoulder.

"Maybe you aren't drunk still, but I can smell you from here, which leads me to believe you're hungover. Why are you here?"

"I need to be."

"We are all better off without you, especially these kids. Don't you think they've seen enough? They've had enough disappointment. You make me sick."

The need to object has me turning around, but by the time I do, she's already storming down the hall. My head pounds and the run-in with Lindsey is a bitter pill to swallow, but I still need to talk to Carson.

I knock.

"Come in."

With a tentative step, I enter. Carson looks up from his desk and straight at me. From the reclining position he's in, he repositions his body to lean toward me. His jaw sets as his head shakes one time. Enough to tell me how disappointed he is, enough to cut me down into a million broken pieces.

"Sit."

"Carson, I'm s—"

He raises his hand. "This is how it's going to go. You're going to listen, and you're going to listen good. You understand me?"

I nod.

"This is your come to Jesus moment. I'll do this one time." He stops speaking and his brows snap together. "One time." His pupils flare as he appraises my attention to him. When he's satisfied, he inclines his head. "I wasn't very different than you once."

My mouth drops. No way this man was like me. No one has their shit together more than him.

"Believe it or not, maybe worse. You get high and drunk, but you're not violent."

That's what he thinks.

"Trust me, I know," he says as if reading my mind. "I *was* volatile. Arrested multiple times in high school, the list was endless of my indiscretions, and then I met Mr. O'Brian. He was my mentor. He showed me there was another path, and yes, I still fucked up a bit, but eventually, I got my life back together, but it was a long road. You might not be violent, but you need help. Let me help you, Pierce. I know you're more than this."

His words knock the wind out of me. *Carson believes I can be more.*

Maybe he's right.

CHAPTER TEN

Lindsey

ANOTHER DAY.

Another damn day.

Normally, I'm excited to go to the center. The kids bring me joy. But not today. Today I'm not excited.

I need to come to terms with the fact Pierce Lancaster isn't going anywhere. Pierce has been "volunteering" at the club for a little over a week, but we haven't worked together again since the hangover incident. I keep thinking he'll somehow fuck up again and then he'll be gone, but every day that he's been scheduled over the past week, he's there with that damn smug-ass smirk on his face. He's the official bane of my existence. He drives me crazy.

I don't know what it is about him. I don't know if it's that he's so damn good-looking and sometimes I want to bash his head into the wall because he knows it or if it's because I want to hate him; I'm desperate to hate him, but instead I see him with these kids and I wonder how I could possibly hate him.

I need to hold my resolve close, even if it's false, even if it's an illusion, and even if the only person I'm fooling with this resolve is myself.

"Hi, Miss Lindsey," Toby says from across the room. Toby's the youngest member of the club, and from what I've heard, he's been with Carson since the beginning.

"Hey, Toby. Where is everyone?"

"Carson is teaching a few kids how to box, and I'm not sure where Pierce is."

Pierce. Can't he just go home already? My life would be so much easier if he were gone. *But why?* Why does his presence bother me so much? It's not as if I still want him. That ship sailed a long time ago. Sailed and sank. Pierce Lancaster is my very own Titanic. Sure, from the outside he's gorgeous, but no matter what happens, it's still destined to go down.

"I'm heading to the storage room. Will you be okay here by yourself?" He laughs, assuring me without words that just because he's the youngest here, it doesn't mean he can't fend for himself.

I step through the doorway and make it down the hall. Just as I'm opening the door to the storeroom, I collide with a hard body. My balance falters and I fear I'm going to fall.

Damn leg.

I brace for impact, but it never comes. Instead, arms wrap around me, pull me toward them and hold me close. I don't need to open my eyes to know who holds me. I recognize his smell.

Inhale.

Vanilla and cinnamon. A hint of peppermint, too. He's intoxicating, and I hate my traitorous body for softening at his touch.

"Let me go," I grit through clenched teeth and push off him. I refuse to look. I know the smug look in his eye will be there. For fuck's sake, I sniffed him.

I sniffed the enemy.

CHAPTER ELEVEN

Pierce

NOW THAT MY HEAD IS OUT OF MY ASS, THINGS HAVE gotten better for me.

Working at Polaris has been much better than I expected. The kids are great and the company even better. Although I doubt the lady in question would agree. If anything, her need to avoid me is almost laughable. I don't think anyone has ever wanted less to do with me than she does. It's actually quite entertaining.

After she sniffed me, well, that was a game changer. She can pretend all she wants, but she's not so immune to me as she pretends to be.

At first, getting her to acknowledge my existence was a challenge. Now it's a full-out obsession. Getting under her skin and breaking her resistance is a damn obsession of mine. That probably makes me a giant asshole.

I don't care.

Game on.

The thought makes me smile, and I'm so lost in thought that I legit walk straight into someone as I'm leaving the art store around the block from Polaris.

"Pierce?"

Speak of the devil. It's like my thoughts conjured her up.

How funny. "Well, hello, Lindsey," I drawl, and her eyes go wide.

"What are you . . . what are you doing here?" she mutters. Her face turns a warm shade of pink. She's cute when she's frazzled.

"Buying paint," I say so impassive that her mouth drops open.

"I mean *obviously* you are buying paint. But why?"

"Why are you buying paint?" I lift an eyebrow. I don't know why I'm busting her chops and not just answering but fucking with her is just too much fun and I love watching her squirm and blush.

"Carson asked me to pick some up." She places her hands on her hips and cocks her head. I want to smile so badly at her defiance, but instead, I bite it back and keep my face straight.

"So where are you off to now?" I ask, and by the way her sharp eyes bare into me it's obvious I'm the last person she'd ever offer information to.

Her lips pucker. "As if I'd tell you. You'd probably just follow me to drive me insane," she retorts with cold sarcasm.

"Or you can just ask me to go with you." I wink.

"Why would I do that?"

"Because maybe you're wrong about me."

"Hmm, let me see." She thinks for a minute and then opens her mouth. "Nope. Not wrong," she deadpans and then takes a step to the left to pass me. I'm not going to let her off that easy. I step to my right, thus blocking her departure.

"Hey, that's not fair. I have been on my best behavior the last week."

"Yeah, only one giant hangover."

"That was one time and I have been trying. Come on, Lindsey. You know I have been. Can't you admit there might be a chance you're wrong about me?"

"No." She shakes her head.

"Give me one shot to prove I'm not a total douche. I'm not asking for much . . . just lunch."

"No." This time she just blatantly rolls her eyes, and I can't help the chuckle that escapes. She's trying really hard to hate me and for some reason, I find it funny.

"What do you have to lose?"

"I'm not going to agree to eat lunch with you. This is my free time. Why would I spend my free time with you?"

"Don't you think you're being a bit petty? We're going to be seeing each other every day for the next few months, so shouldn't we make peace or something? Do you really hate me that much?"

"I don't hate you. I just don't care."

"If you don't care, what harm is it?" I reach into my pocket and pull out a quarter. "Here, fine. You don't want to agree, so how about we make a little wager? Heads you have lunch with me. Tails I let you go about your day."

"No chance."

"Scared?"

"I don't gamble, Pierce Lancaster, and offering that proves you haven't changed."

"Please," I whisper, and I don't know why I do, but I really want this. I really want to prove to Lindsey I can be more. I want her to believe in me like Carson does.

Something changed that day when Carson told me his story. The feeling I felt when Carson told me he believed in me was new. It inspired me. It breathed new life into me, and now that I've tasted the high from acceptance, I want Lindsey to see it too.

"Fine."

Her answer has me releasing the breath I didn't know I was holding. "Okay, here. You flip the coin."

She shakes her head as she takes the coin from me. Our fingers touch and I swear there's an electric current that pulses between us. I don't know what this feeling is, but it's there anyway.

"This is ridiculous," she mumbles under her breath.

"Yeah, it just might be, but if you don't, you know I'll just keep annoying you. Every day at work."

"This won't change anything. I'll flip your coin and if you win this one time, I'll take you up on your offer. After, when we're done and we'll be done. It will never happen again. You understand me. It won't change anything."

I want to say it might, but I don't. I just tip my head down.

"As you wish."

"Tails I win?"

"Yep." She moves her hand and flips the coin, covering it with her other hand to stop the motion. We both look down and then she raises it.

My lips spread into a deep grin. "Okay, lucky, what are you in the mood to eat?"

"Lucky? Why are you calling me lucky? I lost."

"Your loss is my gain, so in my eyes you're lucky."

She rolls her eyes. "Sushi. Next door. In. Out."

At her words, I lick my lips.

"Head out of the gutter, Lancaster."

"Never. It's so comfortable there."

Five minutes later, we're sitting across the table from each other. The waitress just took our orders, and now neither of us is speaking. The silence is awkward. Lindsey is fiddling with the top of her glass. Uncomfortably. I decide to rip the Band-Aid right off.

"Why do you hate me? I know I was a dick, but still—"

"I'd rather just not deal with you," she interrupts.

Well, that went well. "Can you at least try not to hate me?"

"No promises."

"Can you at least promise to not try to get me thrown out of Polaris?"

Her eyes go wide. "I . . ." She seems frazzled at my request.

"Listen, I get it, you hate me, you've made your feeling for me quite clear, but really, can you refrain from trying to get me fired or better yet, maybe watch what you say? Regardless of what you think about me, it sucks to hear someone talk shit about it. It's actually why . . ."

"Actually why what?"

"Nothing, forget about it."

"Is that why—oh my God. Is that why you got wasted? Why you were hungover?"

I shrug, not willing to admit my weakness but also not willing to deny the truth. I did hear her. And I did use it as an excuse to get fucked-up.

She opens her mouth to respond, either to apologize or to berate me. I'm not in the mood for either option, but luck is on my side. I'm saved by the waitress.

I've never been more happy for a spicy tuna roll.

CHAPTER TWELVE

Lindsey

As much as I want to keep a straight face and not let him get to me, I can't help but laugh at him. He's making a complete ass of himself. *The way he holds his chopsticks . . .*

"What? I never learned." He grins at me as the piece of spicy tuna falls to his plate at his crappy attempt to eat authentically.

"You are doing it all wrong."

"And you're an expert?" His left eyebrow rises.

"I am."

"Wait, seriously?"

"Well, I did live in Japan for six months."

He lifts a hand in the air. "Hold up. You lived in Japan? Come on, Lindsey. Tell me about it," he begs.

"I don't think–"

"Is it that hard to just put our shit aside? To stop hating me for one minute and just have fun?"

I guess I have nothing to lose. "Fine," I respond in a low voice, so low that he leans in and quirks up his brow.

"Fine?"

"Yes. Fine."

"Good." He smiles broadly. "Now tell me how you ended up in Japan?"

"Typical story . . . girl meets boy, boy's a DJ, girl follows boy to Japan for a show. Boy dumps girl." I shudder inwardly at the memory, ashamed of myself for being such an idiot to follow a boy to Japan. Pierce must sense my sullen mood because he makes another pitiful attempt of using chopsticks. I know what he's doing. He's trying to get me to laugh with his antics.

It works. Despite my best efforts, I'm laughing again as he tries, unsuccessfully, to grab a crab tempura roll this time. It's so hard to stop laughing, that he joins in and throws the chopstick on the table. Reaching across the table, he takes a roll with his fingers and dips into the soy sauce that sprays over the edge . . . *and is now all over his white T-shirt.*

"Dammit, serves me right for deciding to impress you."

"There's no reason to try to impress me."

"I just don't want you to hate me," he admits on a sigh.

With each moment that passes, some of the tension that has built between us dissipates. "I never really hated you, Pierce. I just don't like you." I wink. Truth is I don't like that he reminds me of a time before. That looking at Pierce is a constant reminder of what my life used to be. But I don't say any of that. Instead, I scrunch my nose and sigh.

"Pick up your chopstick."

He cocks his head but doesn't object. He holds them limply. None of his fingers are in the correct position.

"Your index finger . . ." I reach my hand out. "It's in the wrong position." He looks down and then moves. "Um, no. Like this." I pull the chopsticks from him, our fingers touching briefly. At the contact, his gaze meets mine and I inhale sharply. He thinks it's from frustration, but it's not. It's the way he looks at me, the way his skin feels against mine. I shake my head.

"Put your finger on top, bend at the knuckle, and then pinch the sticks together." He follows my directions and it's perfect.

61

"Good. Try again." He does and is rewarded by grabbing the spicy tuna and bringing it to his mouth. He groans as he swallows and I swear tingles run up my body.

"When things are hard to get, it makes everything taste better." He winks.

And I know he's not talking about lunch.

"What's for dessert?" The way his lips tip makes my knees weak.

"I don't eat dessert." It's lame, I know it, but I need to shut this conversation down. It's going in a direction I can't deal with. Dessert makes me think of all the wicked things . . .

"Of course you do. Everyone does."

"Not everyone eats dessert."

"Fine. You're right, not everyone does, but everyone wants it." He winks again, and now I'm one hundred percent sure he's talking about something entirely different. "What's your favorite? What's your guilty pleasure? Me, for example, I'd sell my soul for a dirty water dog."

My mouth drops open and I stifle a gag. "That is not dessert," I exclaim with disgust.

"Sure it is. You go out to dinner . . . you're walking home and you see the food cart for the dirty water dog, suddenly you're hungry again, so you get one . . . hence dessert. If it's eaten after dinner, it's dessert."

"I'm sorry but no. If I was walking down the street, hungry or not, I wouldn't eat a nasty hot dog from an even nastier street vendor."

"So what's your poison?"

I blow out a huff and roll my eyes, not wanting to answer but knowing full well he won't stop pestering me until I do. On a sigh, I tell him. "Macarons."

"Those little French things?"

"Yes, those little French things."

"Gross. They taste like perfume."

"Says the guy who eats processed pieces of God knows what type of meat."

"Don't forget the part where they sit in water all day." He grins, and a small dimple peeks out from his right cheek, making him look young.

"Disgusting, and not those ones. Yes, I like those, but my favorite are not the *'perfume ones.'* I like the fun flavors."

"Fun flavors?" he asks, leaning into the table. His interest plays on every beautiful feature of his face.

How can I think he looks beautiful? I hate him, *right*? Still staring at him, I remember he asked a question. *Flavors.* "Cotton candy and champagne."

"They make macarons that taste like champagne?" His eyes widen and he stares at me like I have grown three heads.

"That, and then some," I tease.

"Details. I need details of these wondrous pieces of cake."

"Sara's Bakery."

"Sara's Bakery?" He lifts an eyebrow.

"Yep."

"Is this piece of heaven here?"

I'm not sure where he is going with this line of questioning, but the nervous energy zipping through my limbs makes me tingle.

"Yep." I shrug, trying to keep my emotions level.

He scratches the scruff on his face and then motions to me.

"We need to go sometime."

The implication hangs in the air, and strangely enough, it's not so awful anymore and that thought is disturbing because I shouldn't want to spend time with him.

But I do.

———————— ◆ ◆ ————————

I'm sitting in the office of Polaris the next afternoon when I hear the door open. "Package for you." Xavier walks in.

"A package for me?"

"That's what Carson told me. So unless there is anyone else in Polaris named Lindsey Walker, I assume this is yours." He chuckles.

"Stop being a smart-ass." I laugh back.

I have no idea who would be sending me something, let alone why. I shuffle to the desk, rifling around until I find what I'm looking for: scissors. Slowly and carefully I cut through the tape, and then pull out a purple bag from the box. A purple cooler bag.

What the . . . ?

I pull it open and reach my hand inside. Shuffling around, I find the plastic edge of whatever is being cooled. With one pull it's out, and my mouth drops open. It's a twelve pack of macarons, and not just any macarons, but from Sara's Bakery.

Pierce.

Pierce did this.

Attached to the plastic container is a card. He bought me the macaron of the month box. I'm a freaking member of the macaron of the month club.

And a note: ***No one should go without dessert . . .***

He doesn't need to sign his name, I know it's him. Nor does he need to tell me what this means. The message comes in loud and clear.

"Miss Lindsey?" Xavier's voice pulls me out of my thoughts. "What's that?"

"Macarons, want some?"

He scrunches his nose. "What are they?"

"Little pieces of heaven," I respond.

"Well, in that case, yes."

"Great, come with me. Let's see who else is around and we'll have a macaron picnic."

"A picnic? Here?" Xavier looks at me as if I'm crazy, and I love the idea of a picnic even more now. These boys never do stuff like this. Things I take for granted, like eating macarons for no occasion at all other than a friend being funny.

A friend . . .

Is that what Pierce is? A friend? The idea doesn't seem so horrible right now. Maybe we could be friends. Maybe.

Once we find the other boys, we walk into the cafeteria. Grabbing plates and a knife, I set up shop and make everyone sit at a table in the cafeteria.

"Why are you cutting them into fours?"

"So we can all take a bite. Each macaron is a different flavor. How else are we going to have a macaron challenge?"

"Yes, how else indeed?" I hear from behind me. Turning my head over my shoulder, I see Pierce walking toward us. "Having a food challenge without me? Lucky, that is so not cool." His hands are on his hips, and he's posing in an overdramatic way to pretend he's angry.

"Didn't realize I had to invite you," I say in a coy voice, which makes him roll his eyes at me. "And stop calling me that."

"No can do, *Lucky*. And well, seeing as I brought the—"

"Thank you for that, by the way, but you didn't have to."

"I know, but I wanted to." His voice is sincere, and a series of butterflies take flight in my stomach at the sound.

Feeling flustered and flushed by the feelings taking root inside me at seeing Pierce, I blurt out, "Now let's start the voting. And *I guess* we can include you."

"Gee thanks." He shakes his head in a huff, but I can see the dimple. He's not fooling anyone.

The first purple macaron is cut into four equal pieces. The boys devour their bites, but I only nibble. "Hey, I never got a taste," Pierce exclaims.

"Oops." I smile innocently. "There's none left. Maybe next time."

Before I know it, he's leaning into me. Into my personal space, he's so close I'm dizzy. Our gazes are locked. My breath comes out ragged and harsh from being this close to him. *What is he doing?*

He answers my unspoken question by taking my hand in his. My heart hammers heavily in my chest as it lifts. The feel of his fingers on me is hot and heady, the memories that are imprinted on my mind resurfacing to the forefront of my brain. I remember everything.

We stare at each other.

Neither speaking.

The seconds pass, but it feels like everything is on pause as I wait to see what he will do. The boys talking in the background is a steady buzz against the pounding in my chest.

He lifts.

Thud.

Closer.

Thud.

His tongue juts out, and he swipes the tip of my finger where the cream from the filling has collected. Before I can think, he places it in his mouth and eats the rest.

"Ewwwww," rings out through the room. The sound of the boys gagging pulls me out of my haze.

"What are you doing?"

"Having dessert." He winks. His emerald green eyes twinkling with mischief.

He's too close. Too damn close. I remember what his lips feel like against my skin. Decadent. Like the first bite of a macaron. Sinful.

I need to get away.

Without a second thought, I stand from the table before announcing, "I'm going to wash my hands."

There was no sleep to be had last night.

None at all.

The last two days with Pierce has left me all types of confused.

On the one hand, I hate him. Okay, maybe not hate him, but dislike him immensely. He drives me insane. And yet, if I'm going to be truthful to myself, these last few days he wasn't that bad. Yes, he's a bit arrogant. And for sure he was a jerk in France, and if I'm being honest with myself, he's always been kind of a jerk for as long as I've known him. Take yesterday, for example, he was different, and I'm having a hard time reconciling the two versions. When I used to hang around him at the club scene, I thought his arrogance was sexy. Now, I don't. But what I do find sexy is someone who I can share a meal with, someone I can laugh with. Someone whose mind I enjoy just as much as his body.

I never thought Pierce had more to him. But two days ago he was funny. And yesterday he was sweet, buying macarons. *Shit.* I can't be thinking like this. Especially not now, not when I'm sure to bump into him at any minute.

On the way to the rec room to eat lunch, I hear cheers from the gymnasium. Curious about what the ruckus is, I walk in and stop short at what I see. Pierce is trying to shoot a basket with his shirt over his face. What the hell is he doing?

But holy wow.

With the shirt lifted over his head, it's not leaving much for the imagination. His abs are on full display, and if that weren't enough, his V is begging to be licked. God, he's hot. Why does he have to be so hot? It's not okay. No human being should be that hot.

A chorus of laughs, a round of cheers as he shoots and scores. The kids are going nuts. Jumping up and down and now, oh seriously? Now he's completely showboating. Dancing around the court as if he just took a three-point buzzer beater to win the game.

His crowd of boys goes wild and he loves every minute of being the center of attention. This is the sexiest thing I have ever seen. And the kids love him.

After his final obnoxious dance move, I roll my eyes and am about to turn my back and storm out of the room, when he removes his shirt completely and runs toward the boys, lifting Toby up and cheering.

And it's like the world has stopped.

I shake my head and turn around. I can't watch this. Can't allow this picture to melt my resolve of hatred. But they say curiosity killed that cat . . .

I turn back around and look right over to where Pierce is playing with Toby. An unfamiliar feeling weaves its way through me, and I realize it's a feeling I've never had in regard to Pierce before.

Jealousy.

I am jealous of Pierce Lancaster.

I have been here for three months and haven't gotten Toby to trust me, but here is the truth staring back at me. Even Toby is obsessed with Pierce. Toby who only likes Lynn, thinks Pierce walks on water. After only a few short weeks he's gotten to them in a way I haven't.

Just as I'm mentally berating myself, he chooses this exact moment to look up at me. *Damn it.* I'm caught like a deer in headlights staring, and worse, I'm probably still drooling. Placing my hands on my hips, I meet his stare. He smiles. I frown. He waves. I seethe. When he laughs, I throw my hands up in the air and storm out the door.

"Lindsey."

I hear his voice, but I refuse to stop. I try to pick up my pace, but I can't. My damn leg won't go any faster, and if I do, I'll probably end up falling head first on the floor, and with Pierce rapidly approaching, nothing could be worse.

"Wait, Lindsey."

I'm about to open the door to the rec room when he passes me on the right side quickly and opens the door for me.

"After you," he drawls.

And I swear I hiss at him.

"What's up your ass? Don't like a man to be chivalrous?"

"Nope."

"So you do?"

"Nope."

"That makes no sense. It's either you do or you don't."

I step through the door and look over my shoulder at him. "I do as long as it's not you."

He chuckles, shakes his head, and falls into step with me. "I thought we moved past this."

"Just because I allowed you to take me to lunch and let you participate in my macaron eating contest, doesn't mean we're besties, Pierce," I deadpan.

"But it doesn't mean we're enemies," he chides.

"That's debatable."

He holds his hands up. "You win."

AVA HARRISON

"And you see *I* could do this all day."

"Oh, I can tell, that's why I like you. You give as well as you can take. It's refreshing."

I don't respond. Instead, I walk to the refrigerator and grab my sandwich I made for lunch. Walking over to a table, I sit. Pierce takes the seat next to me. I glare at him. "Wasn't sushi enough? Do I really have to endure your company yet again today?"

His lips spread into the sexiest goddamn smile I've ever seen. It answers yes, and there's no way of changing his mind.

God, why does he have to make me so confused? It's awful that no matter how much I want to be indifferent to him, my body can't help but react to him.

I let out an annoyed groan. "Well, are you going to at least eat something or are you just going to stare?"

"Stare."

"Fine, have it your way, but I'm not talking to you. So just go on staring . . ."

"Oh, I will."

And he does. The whole meal, he doesn't speak, he doesn't eat, he just gives me a lopsided grin the entire time, and a part of me softens. Not a big part. But a small enough part that I'm worried. Because I can't let myself warm to him. Because if I do, there's no telling how much damage will come of it.

The day has dragged incredibly slowly since my lunch with Pierce today. The problem is my mood swings are driving me insane and all I can do is dwell on them. I'm so damn confused and I'm starting to think I'm also a little insane.

Hate him?

Dislike him?

Tolerate him?

Like him?

What the hell is going on with me? The four different emotions bounce around like a set of pool balls after you break. But the big question is, which one will the cue sink? With a shake of the head I stand from behind my desk and head out the door and walk into the rec room, my legs stop. *What's going on*?

There on the floor, sitting against the wall and only a few feet from the door, is Pierce, and next to him is Christopher. They appear deep in talk, fully engrossed.

Not wanting to interrupt them, I quietly make my way to the storage room, trying my damnedest to not make a sound. Pierce's gaze drifts over to me and our eyes lock.

"*Is everything okay*?" I mouth and he nods yes, but not before he responds without any sound "*fight with family*." That makes the blood in my body turn to ice. All of the kids have issues, but Christopher and Xavier more than most. That's one of the reasons they're friends, they understand each other and help each other out.

Christopher's head is down so he doesn't see me pass. He's talking into his hands, and muffled words pop through the silence. I can't make them out, but what I can make out is that he's hurting.

Emotionally hurting.

"I, of all people, understand, man. It might not look like it," I hear Pierce say, "but my family doesn't get me either. You can't . . ."

The wind is knocked out of me. I want to hate him, I do, but even I can see this is not the same guy from last year, let alone three months ago. Although every feature on his devastatingly handsome face is the same, it's what's underneath that's changed. He's subdued.

Different.

Behind the facade he's shown for so long, there's a sadness. One I know too well. It's in every comment, every look, and it makes me want to say he's not alone. That I understand. But those won't leave my lips because if I know anything about him or myself that would be too much. Instead, I make a silent vow to put the shit behind us aside and to show him through actions and what he needs most, friendship that there is another way.

A way that doesn't involve the next party.

A way that can make him happy.

CHAPTER THIRTEEN

Pierce

For some reason, I need her to want me, and the fact she won't is driving me insane.

I seek her out during the day like a stalker. I'm here even when I'm not scheduled to be. The need to see her has replaced all thoughts of going out, or partying, or being me.

Like now, for instance. I know she's in the cafeteria having her coffee. I don't need coffee. Hell, I don't even drink the stuff. But where do I find myself? In the damn cafeteria.

It's as if my feet have a mind of their own these days.

A delicious game of cat and mouse.

I can't get enough.

She's standing by the counter, the piping hot mug in her hands. Steam billows from the surface. Her lips purse and a puff of air escapes before she places the rim to her mouth to take a sip. She closes her eyes as the hot liquid courses down her throat, and I swear the way she drinks should be illegal, especially when kids are around. I can't help but step toward her. To close the distance between us.

When she opens her eyes, I'm there, right in front of her, staring down at her full, fuckable lips. "What are you—"

My hand lifts to her jaw and stops her words, touching her skin before lifting to brush the fullness of her mouth, of the skin

I so badly want to taste. "You had something on your face," I lie.

Her eyes widen and then narrow slightly, making my hand drop. She knows I'm lying, but I don't care. It was worth it.

"Please don't touch me," she whispers, her voice trembling, but not from fear. I've heard that tremble before, and fear was not present. All that's present is need and want. I move closer.

She's so close the scent of her perfume whispers in the air. She takes a step to the left to escape me, but so do I, not ready to let her go just yet. The dance we play continues. Another beat of an unsung song. One I intend to confront and she intends to hide from.

"Can't you just leave me alone?"

"No."

My words stun her, making her mouth hang agape. She furrows her brow, bites her lip. "Why?"

"I don't know."

I step closer until there's no distance between us. Until her chest rubs against my torso. Until I feel her heart beat against mine. I'm not sure why I'm doing this. I'm not sure why I'm torturing myself, and in turn, torturing her. I don't know what it is about her. I don't know why I can't get her out of my mind, why I can't stay away.

All I know is there's something about Lindsey Walker.

She's everything I can't have. She's all the rights I'll never have. She deserves better, but I can't find it in me to care and just stop. I continue to study her, waiting for something, for her to object to our proximity, for her to say something, to say anything. But she doesn't.

So I take the one chance I have and go for it.

I wrap my arms around her and pull her face to mine. There's no stopping me, not until I know what she tastes like. I crash my mouth to hers, nipping at her lower lip to coerce her open.

Her mouth parts of her own accord, letting me sweep inside and savor her.

She pushes away from me, her breasts heaving with exertion. "What the fuck! What gives you the right to kiss me like that?"

"You didn't seem to mind. Not when you were—"

"God, you make me so . . . so . . ."

"Shh," I coo. "Don't ruin it."

"This. What just happened? That can't happen again. I'm sure this is my fault. I'm giving you mixed signals, but I don't want you like that. Don't you understand that, Pierce? I don't want you. Friends maybe, but nothing more."

"Yes, you have already made your thoughts on me quite explicit," I mock.

"Don't pursue me," she hisses back.

"No promises, Lucky. When I want something, I go for it. And, Lindsey . . ."

"Yes?"

"I want you."

"You can't have me."

"That's what you think. But I know the truth. We're inevitable."

CHAPTER FOURTEEN

Lindsey

I ALMOST JUMP RIGHT OUT OF MY CHAIR WHEN MY PHONE rings from across the coffee table in front of me. I'm lost in thought, thinking about what happened today, trying desperately to pretend it didn't. Trying even more desperately to not read into it.

The phone rings again. Strange that someone is calling at this time. Looking up, I realize it's actually not so late. The clock on my computer says it's eight thirty p.m. In my former life, I wouldn't even be dressed yet. I'd be just getting out of the shower, pouring myself a glass of wine, and getting ready to go out for the night.

But that was then, this is now. And now eight p.m. is past my bedtime.

The phone continues to ring and I place my computer down on the table and reach for it. Amelia, my younger cousin.

My relationship with Amelia is funny. For years she hated me. I was kind of a bitch. But then after the accident, no matter how rude I was, how much I tried to push her away, she just wouldn't hear it. It's kind of crazy to think about now. I'm not sure why she kept trying with me. I certainly didn't deserve it, but I'm so glad I eventually softened and let her in.

More like begged her to forgive me.

"What up, cuz?" I answer.

"You in bed?" She knows me so well.

"Almost."

"You've become such a loser." She laughs.

"Takes one to know one," I reply, my words laced with humor.

"I'm coming over."

Hearing Amelia say she's coming over at this time has me standing from the couch.

"Everything okay?" I ask as I begin to pace the room.

"Yep. Just need to vent."

Her voice sounds tight and I know someone has made her angry. Amelia is usually so laid-back and carefree.

This can't be good.

"Well, come on by. I'm just doing some work, but I'm here."

"You work too damn much," she huffs in a dramatic pitch.

"It's work or party, or just have a pity party for myself. Which do you prefer?"

"You were totally intolerable with both the other outcomes. So I'll choose work." I laugh at that, and some of the tension I felt before has diminished. She still has her signature sense of humor, so it can't be that bad.

"You got your key?"

"I do."

"Okay, just let yourself in."

"Okay. Be there in thirty."

Amelia has been a godsend to me. When I was at my lowest and Olivia was in rehab, Amelia helped pick up the pieces of my broken spirit. I'm still not perfect, but I'm a lot better than I was. I'll never forget when I was finally out of the wheelchair after the initial accident and was made to use a cane. I was so damn depressed. Mortified to be seen in public like that. So Amelia did what she does best.

She was there for me.

There while I screamed. There while I cried. There when I was abusive to her. And still, her smile never faded. When I threw the cane against the wall, she barely batted an eyelash. Instead, she showed up the next day as if I hadn't kicked her out the one before. In her arm was a box. I still laugh thinking of that box. Her Bedazzler. And that's how I ended up with a crystal-studded cane, fit for a queen.

If Amelia is coming over tonight at eight thirty p.m. knowing I'm in pajamas, something is wrong. And I owe it to her, after all she's done for me, to be there for her too.

I keep myself busy as I wait. I have an idea for a business, a new venture that I'm passionate about. I want to figure out a way to help the kids but on a grander scale. So right now I'm spending my night researching business plans. I'm not sure exactly yet what I'm planning on doing for them, but what I want to make sure is that when I figure it out, I'm able to write up a plan and pitch it to my father.

Maybe then I'll get his attention.

Maybe if I'm like one of his many investments, he'll find time to talk to me too.

Doubt it.

As I'm researching the proper ways to create a pitch deck, I hear the familiar pitter-patter of Amelia's shoes hitting the wood floors in my apartment.

"I see you choose to work . . ."

"It was hit or miss for a while. I figured drowning myself in self-misery was not exactly a good plan for my evening."

"I'd say not."

I take her in. Her face looks paler than normal and she has dark shadows under her eyes.

"What's going on? You kind of look like shit."

"Geez, Linds, you reverting back to your old bitchy ways from before the accident? Because a little warning would be nice."

"I wasn't that bad," I whine.

"That's like saying a pet python is warm and cuddly," she deadpans.

"Har, har, har. You're cute. But seriously, what's going on?"

"My dad."

"Join the club." I pat the arm of the chair next to the one I'm sitting at. "Take a load off and spill it. What did dear old uncle do now?"

She sits and then proceeds to unburden all that's happened in her life since I last spoke to her. Her father's disappointment because her grades aren't good enough and her internship isn't good enough. Nothing is good enough.

Same song. Different verse.

Neither of us has good relationships with the Walker brothers. My dad is too busy for me, and hers is too busy ridiculing her.

In the end, when I finally opened up to her about my family problems, and she to me, we were forever bonded.

"I'm sorry. That sucks. But honestly, you're killing it. Your dad just sucks."

"He doesn't approve of my major. And the rest is a big waste of time because of that."

"One day you'll be the best designer ever and you'll make him eat his words." At that, she finally smiles.

"So what about you? What's the word on Pierce and Polaris? He gone yet?"

I bite my lip and then blush.

Amelia leans forward in her chair, her nose crinkling.

"Ummm, what was that for?"

"What was what?"

She narrows her eyes as her lips purse. "You just blushed," she responds candidly.

"Did not."

"Did too. Tell me. I need something juicy after my day."

"Fine. He might have tried to kiss me. Well, he did . . . um, kiss me."

"What? Stop. Back up. The beginning. Last I knew you hated him. And from everything you told me about the last few weeks, you made that point very clear to him that you hated him."

"I never hated him."

Her right brow lifts.

"Fine. I might have said that once or twice."

"Or fifty times."

"Okay, fine. I might have said it more times than I can count that I hated him, but I mean, well, I guess—"

"Spit it out."

"Grrr. Are you really going to make me say this?"

She nods.

"Imightnothatehim," I say quickly, all the words coming out in one word.

"And how did those words feel coming out of your mouth?"

"Like rat poison. Yeah."

"Rat poison might actually taste better."

"For sure," I groan.

"So what now?" She looks at me intently, and I let out a long, resounding sigh.

"Nothing. Like you said, I've made it very clear I'm not looking to have a repeat performance."

"But what about friends?"

"I have enough friends."

"You have two."

"You're real cute, you know?"

"I've been told that a few times . . ."

I really am lucky. To think if it wasn't for my accident I wouldn't have this. I wouldn't have her.

"Thanks," I say.

"For what?"

"For making me laugh."

"Shouldn't I be thanking you? I'm the one who came over here to bitch."

"I don't mean today. Thanks for everything. For not giving up on me. For helping me."

Her eyes go wide, and I swear she looks like she might cry, but instead, she shakes it off and gives me a small smile. "You've changed, Linds. You ever think maybe he has too?" We sit in silence for a minute, her unanswered question hanging in the air above us.

"Just give him a shot. Maybe if you just ask him what happened, you'll find out he's not so unlike you or me." She stands and gives me a kiss on the head. "Think about it."

"I will."

I spend the whole rest of the night and early morning replaying Amelia's words. *Give him a shot.*

"Earth to Lindsey," I hear from beside me pulling me from my persistent thoughts of what to do about Pierce.

"Umm, did you say something?"

"Yes. I said you're doing great, Lindsey. Your progress has been remarkable." Alison Ames beams a smile in my direction.

She's been my physical therapist since the accident. She's

witnessed me at my lowest and celebrated with me at my highest, and her encouragement has been a consistent factor in the improvements I've made over the past year. I smile widely at her words of support.

"I'm feeling good, Alison. I'm really feeling good. Do you think"—I bite my lip—"I can start running again?"

"Here's the deal, if and when you can walk two miles, I'll move you up to jogging. But only here. I don't want you walking two miles unless I can monitor you."

"Yeah, I can do that," I answer almost too fast, but I can't contain my excitement, the idea of eventually being able to run again is exhilarating.

"Only here," she repeats, her hand on her hip to get the message across.

"Got it. Starting now?"

She blows out a huff. "Fine. But slow. Starting speed is two."

Two is a turtle pace, but I don't say that, I'm just happy to be able to try. Once on the treadmill, I set the speed and start to walk. There's a bit of a discomfort in my tight muscle but not enough to stop me. Not now, when I'm so close to my desired goal. Thirty-five minutes later, I'm winded, huffing, and sweat is pouring off my body. My leg is so damn tight. I don't think I can make it. I'm almost there, so close the taste of victory hanging above me.

You can do it. Just push through the pain.

I resolve to make it no matter the consequences. Closing my eyes, I muster up all the energy inside me, but then the treadmill slows and my lids jut open.

Alison is staring at me. Her head cocked to the side, her lips pursed.

Shit.

"I think we're done for the day." She gives me a pointed look.

"It's obvious you're pushing yourself too hard. It will come, I promise, but you need to give your body more time to heal." The machine comes to a stop and she reaches out her hand to help me off. "Come on, I'll stretch you."

Together we walk to the table and five minutes later my leg is feeling a little looser.

"I think all the exercise you're getting at the center and here is paying off. But I need to stress, no pushing yourself. I want you to keep it up but make sure to not overdo it."

It's been the same conversation month after month. I want to go faster, and she continuously tries to slow me down. When I feel good I want to ride that high and today I'm feeling it. Even with my muscles tight, I want to keep going.

It's my late day for the center. On these days Carson comes in early and gets everything set up. When I walk in, I check the posted schedule and frown. My name and Pierce's are together at the basketball station—again. I'd hoped I'd be matched with someone else, but apparently not.

This is bad.

The temptations are too much when he's around. My body doesn't understand that he's bad for me.

Walking into the gym, Xavier's eyes light up when he sees me. "Miss Lindsey! Pierce volunteered for basketball again. Apparently, we didn't whoop on him hard enough." The other guys chuckle and I can't help but break a smile.

"Guess we're gonna have to do better then," I suggest.

Pierce grins. "The boys have decided since there are not enough players, you have to guard me," Pierce announces with a smug smile.

I frown.

"Thanks, guys," I groan, not loving this setup, but determined to roll with it for the boys' sake. They need to learn that sometimes we have to do things we don't want to do.

As I walk to my place, I vow to change my therapy hours and never come in late again. At least then I'll have one hundred percent control over how far away I get to stay from Pierce Lancaster. Alison's words ring loud and clear in my head: *Don't overdo it.* But I can't show weakness to these boys. They have to know they can overcome all obstacles. This is mine to overcome on a number of levels.

I square up to Pierce, getting in my defensive stance. He looks down at me, his forehead pinched with worry.

"Are you sure you can do this?" he whispers so the boys don't hear.

No, I'm not sure, but I don't tell him that. I'm actually one hundred percent sure I can't and I'm also pretty darn sure this is exactly what Alison was telling me not to do, but again I won't say that either. Instead, I stand up taller and puff out my chest in defiance.

"Get movin', Lancaster. We don't have all day," I goad.

He smiles widely at that before jetting to the left and effectively losing me. I go after him, albeit slowly, but eventually, I'm standing right in front of him, getting right up in his face, arms stretched above my head. I'm so close I can smell the perspiration mixed with his deodorant. As much as I don't want to admit it, the scent is intoxicating.

The boys must have already been playing because there's a sheen of sweat lining his forehead. He can't possibly be already sweating. He swipes it away while dribbling with his right hand, then makes a move and dribbles the ball underneath his leg.

Such a showoff.

I'm breathing heavily after the smallest movement. I barely even had to walk half the court and I'm ready to call it quits, but that's not going to happen.

Too much damn pride has me moving faster than I have in months to try to guard him.

Pierce loses me in a moment of weakness, shoots a layup, and scores a basket. The boys cheer and I moan in frustration. It still surprises me that Pierce Lancaster is actually athletic.

I thought the only sport he participates in is beer Olympics. I should know; I've been standing right next to him for years. Those days are over for me. But what about him? What does he do after he leaves here? Is he still hitting up the clubs until all hours of the morning? He couldn't possibly. If he were still doing that, he'd never make it here this early in the morning. I've been there and know how grim the mornings after are.

I need to stop being so judgmental. I want to hate Pierce, but I have to remind myself it's not his pastimes I hate. It's the way he treated me. I was no better in regard to the party life. I can't fault him for that. My brush with death helped me, and if not for that, I might still be doing the same things.

Taking the two steps I need to, I'm back in front of him, arms up in the air. Everything hurts, but instead of stopping, I push through the pain and back my approach again to block him.

"Linds, you're so cute, thinking you can actually stop me," Pierce badgers me.

"I'll do more than stop you. I'm going to steal the ball from you," I promise.

Don't do this, my inner voice screams. I can barely walk as is but wiping the smug look off his face sounds too good to me, so I do what I know I shouldn't, I try, more determined than ever to keep that promise. I won't push myself too hard. I'll just block him, no running.

He smirks, dribbling two times. Despite everything inside me screaming at me to stand still when I see my chance I take it. Consequences be damned. I swipe the ball out from under him, square up and shoot the ball. It hits the rim and goes around and around. There's a collective gasp as everyone watches. My hands are clenched and excitement courses through me. But at the last second, it falls out, not making the point.

"Better luck next time, sport."

I sneer, pissed I missed that shot. I go to square up with him again, but the muscles in my legs tighten painfully. I fall forward, clenching my calf.

Pierce comes to my side. "Lindsey, are you okay?"

"I'm fine," I snap, not wanting anyone to see this part of me. I'm tired of being in pain, tired of everyone looking at me with their sad eyes. I'm strong. I'm a survivor, and they'd do best to remember that.

"If you need to, go get some ice. We can work on drills," Pierce suggests.

"I said I'm fine." The words snap out of me, echoing off the high gym walls.

Pierce steps back, eyes wide. "You heard her, guys. On the line. We're going to work on some drills."

As they walk away, everything in me crumbles, all of the fight leaving my body. He's right, and Alison's words from earlier come back to me. *Don't overdo it.* Clearly, I have. I stand up straight and shake it off, then walk with a slight limp back to the office, where I spend the rest of the session hiding and licking my wounds.

A sound from the hallway has me looking up from my computer. I've been here for the last thirty minutes sulking and distracting myself working on a business plan. Ideas have been playing in my brain ever since I saw Olivia. The need to do more to help these kids runs through my mind day and night. But what? What should I do? I think about how Olivia is helping models, protecting them. That's what I want to do. I want to help girls. I want to help the boys too.

"Are you okay? I just wanted to check on you," Pierce says as he enters the office where I'm sitting.

"I'm fine," I hiss back, annoyed that he interrupted me, annoyed that he reminds me of what an idiot I made myself look like by hurting myself again. He keeps coming over. I want to tell him to leave, but he doesn't deserve my malice. It's not his fault I hurt myself.

He walks up to where my leg is propped on the desk. His hand reaches out and touches the material of my pants. My breath hitches. He's too close to me. He can't touch me like that. If he does . . .

"Let me see." He moves to lift the hem of my pants, but I can't let him. He can't see my scars. Not up close and personal like this.

"Stop. Don't touch me," I whisper, and he takes a step back.

"I didn't mean to upset you."

"I know, I'm just . . ." I bite my lip. "I'm fine. Don't worry about me."

He assesses me for a minute before he inclines his head down and then nods and walks away.

God I'm a bitch.

It's better this way.

You can't let him in.

Can you?

An hour later Carson is standing at my door. "Just a reminder that next week is the all-staff workshop. Make sure you put it in your calendar."

I don't look up from my papers. I simply tip my head down, telling him without words that I heard him.

"See you later, Lindsey," he calls from the doorway.

I start packing up my stuff to get home.

"Miss Lindsey? Can I talk to you?" Xavier says from the doorway. I look up and smile.

"Of course. Come in." I wave to the chair across from me. "Sit down."

He looks nervous, which makes my stomach turn. Something is wrong, I can feel it.

"I have some trouble going on at school and I need advice."

I frown, wondering where this could be going.

"What kind of trouble?" I ask, hoping to God it's not the kind that will land him in juvie. He's been one of the best turn-arounds I've seen since working here. The first day he came to the center he was all sorts of trouble, but the kid sitting across from me is a different person from that day and I hope to hell he isn't going backward.

"My older brother is a dealer for one of the gangs. He then, in turn, supplies drugs to smaller dealers at my school, but apparently, he stiffed the big dealer." His eyes are lowered to the desk, not looking at me.

"What does that have to do with you?"

"Nothing, but they want revenge and they see me as a way to get it." When he lifts his head, I can see how scared he is, and it breaks me. This is the problem for most of our kids. Even if they attempt to better their lives, their families have a way of pulling them back into trouble.

"Have you spoken to your principal or your teachers?"

"Yeah, but this isn't a new thing, Miss Lindsey. They hear the stuff every day, and they rarely ever do anything about it." His shoulders slouch forward and he hangs his head down.

I've heard the stories about inner-city schools. Teachers have their hands tied behind their backs most days. They're lucky to avoid gang violence, let alone take on every kid's issues individually. Our system has royally fucked these kids. There's no protection. No getting out without the help of our program and others like it.

"Maybe we should go to the police," I suggest.

"No," he says, surging to his feet. "That will make everything worse."

I figured that would be his answer. It always is with these kids. Getting the police involved will only bring the trouble right to his door. "I don't know how to help you if you're not willing to tell someone who'll do something about it."

"That's what I'm trying to tell you. Nobody will do anything about it and I'm scared."

My stomach drops at the sincerity and fear in his eyes. I come around the desk and, forgetting all about rules, bring Xavier into a tight hug. These boys have seen so much in their short lives and it makes me sick. No child should fear for their safety going to school, yet they do every day.

I feel helpless in this moment, knowing there's nothing I can do. This is why we need funding. This kind of center needs to transition to schools, to give kids who want to break away from those types of issues, a safe haven. Otherwise, we're sending them to the wolves every day.

"If they give you any more problems, please come see me, okay? I'll figure out something to help you. Whatever it takes."

"Thanks, Miss Lindsey," he says, hugging me once more and continuing to break my heart in the process.

I don't sleep that night, anxiety building for Xavier. The excruciating pain in my leg doesn't help the cause, and the thought of Pierce and the concern that played on his face, the way he came to me to help, what does it mean?

Nope, no sleep for me.

CHAPTER FIFTEEN

Pierce

It's got to suck to be in constant pain. I saw Lindsey's face today, and she definitely was hurting. I might not feel physical pain, but I do understand not wanting to appear weak. I never want to appear weak in front of my family. When they're around, an extra level of personal armor is needed. Kind of like Lindsey today. I don't fault her for snapping at me. If the roles were reversed, it would have been the same. I'd snap. How could you not?

Pride.

It's an ugly beast that likes to rear its head.

Regardless of the reason, it sucks to know I'm trying and she keeps pushing me away. It's fucking exhausting to keep at it. But I'm not willing to give up. Yeah, sure, the chances of us fucking again are slim even if she wants me, which was evident in the kiss, but right now I'd settle for friendship.

Sounds lame. But it's true. She's a cool girl, and to be honest, it's obvious we're more alike than I'd originally realized. It would be nice to have a friend. Even now it'd be a relief to have someone to keep distracted because a part of me is itching to go out and get fucked-up. Instead, I sit on my couch, pull out my vape and smoke some pot. It will certainly take the edge off the nervous energy coursing through me on wanting to break down

Lindsey's walls.

My apartment is eerie as fuck right now. It's dark out regardless of the time. It's not even five p.m., but a storm is brewing. The sky is pitch-black from the clouds hovering above the city, and at any moment it will open and pour torrential waters upon us. It's the perfect excuse I need to not go out and chase temptation.

I take a deep inhale. This would certainly piss off Carson and Lindsey. Lindsey more so, but she's not here and she'll never know. Getting high isn't what she'd deem a smart move for a "reformed party boy," but am I really reformed?

Each hit calms me to not care. Within the next thirty minutes, I'm high as fuck, loving life and not caring about any problem at all. My phone starts ringing beside me.

Josie.

Fucking Josie.

She's been calling nonstop since we went out and hooked up. Dumb move. Really dumb leading her on. Now I have to let her down easy, that I don't want her. She's not the girl I want. I want someone else. A fiery brunette who gives as hard as she takes. I really want Lindsey.

The thought has me sobering.

I don't just want friendship with her. No, the desire to sink into her again is what consumes my thoughts.

Fuck.

That's exactly what needs to be done. Feel her around me. Thrusting in and out of her tight body. Before I can think twice, I'm gripping myself in the palm of my right hand. Fisting myself from root to tip. My eyes slam shut and all I see is her. I'm so high it's almost as if she's actually here. Stroking me with her hand. Licking the tip. All the muscles in my body tighten. And then in a haze that threatens to knock me unconscious I come.

Well, shit. That sobered my ass up.

Looking at the clock, I realize it's now after seven. How much time had I lost already in drugs? Pot doesn't count. *Sure it does. Try telling Lindsey that.*

I shake off the thoughts and move to clean up the mess I've made. Now what do I do? Paint.

When all else fails, paint.

With a steady stride, I make my way into my studio, pull out a new canvas, and start to paint. I paint her. The girl is making my mind mush. She's tearing through my walls. I paint her until my hands are numb. Until my fingers want to bleed. I paint until all I feel is gone and I'm lost in my art. In my work. In my own broken mind and how I view everything.

When I'm done, I step back, sweat dripping off my brow.

It's beautiful

She's beautiful.

I grab her and then I place her away to dry. Hidden from the rest. She shouldn't be tainted by my other paintings.

I can barely keep my eyes open as I make my way to my bed. The phone rings again. This time it's Trey.

Voicemail.

I don't need that tonight. Not when her kiss lingers in my mind, the thought of her body around me still playing behind my lids.

Instead of getting in bed, I go back to my studio.

I need to paint again.

Tomorrow I'll win her over.

Tomorrow I'll do what I need to do.

CHAPTER SIXTEEN

Pierce

DIDN'T DO BETTER. INSTEAD, I'M SPRINTING INTO POLARIS, late.

Very late.

I should have called, but I'd fallen asleep in my studio painting all night and forgot to charge my phone. If that's not bad enough, I woke up so late today that it's actually noon.

It's not unlike me to wake at noon on the weekend, or after a night of partying, but recently, I've tried to be responsible. Other than the one mistake weeks ago I've been on time, worked hard, and kept my nose clean . . . pun intended. The worst part is it's damning how I look. When I walk into Carson's office, it's empty and I head to the gymnasium to see if he's there.

Just as I suspected, he is. He's stepped in to practice my drills since I'm not here. God, if it wasn't bad before now, I really feel like shit.

"Hey, man. Sorry I'm late. I-I . . ." What do I say? I fell asleep late. No matter the excuse, the damage is done. "I'm sorry. It won't happen again."

He looks me up and down and just shakes his head. It looks bad. It would take an idiot not to see I haven't showered. Haven't shaved. The scruff on my face is longer than normal, and I probably smell.

"You got this now?" he asks. "Is there any reason you'd need me to stay?" *Are you hungover, he's asking?*

"Nope. I'm good. Right as rain."

He narrows his eyes at me before deciding in his head that I'm either sober or not hungover enough to be a problem. The need and desire to defend myself is real, but weighing the options, I know staying quiet is my better bet.

"If you need me, holler." With that, he walks out the door and I'm left with Xavier, Christopher, and Marcus. We decide after running suicide drills to play a game of two on two.

Hours later I'm ready to leave, and I'm happy there was no incident after my late arrival. I expected Carson to pull me into his office eventually, but I was pleasantly surprised. Still, no matter the fact Carson never called me into his office, I know I need to talk to him. Squaring my shoulders, it's time to own my mistake. As my hand touches the knob to open the door, Lindsey's voice echoes through the hall.

"Classic Pierce. Always irresponsible and here I thought I was wrong. That maybe there was more to him than he let on, but I guess not. Maybe he should go, Carson."

My fist clenches.

What the actual fuck?

Something inside of me snaps. I thought we'd reached an accord. That maybe people would see me. The real me. That maybe Lindsey would see past the facade that was draped over me every day of my life. *But no.* Like everyone, she thinks I'm shit.

And I guess if everyone thinks that, it must be true.

Turning on my heel, I storm for the exit instead. Fuck this shit. By the time I land in my apartment I'm seething. By the time my phone rings I'm already drunk.

"Trey."

"What you doing?"

"Getting high." I laugh.

"Alone?"

"Yep."

"That's the definition of lame."

"Got a better idea?" After my day at Polaris, after hearing Lindsey bash me, I deserve a night off.

"You know it. Linc and I are going out."

"Tell me the deets. Where's the party at?"

"Same place as the last time I saw your lame ass."

"Cool. I'll be there."

He hangs up and I take another hit. This is probably a bad idea, but right now, as fucked-up in the head as I am, I can't find it in me to care.

Hours later, I'm high as a kite. Drunk off my ass and barely able to stand. Fuck. I need to go home.

Stumbling into the street, I hail a cab and get in. I see there's a text from Linc.

Linc: Where did you go?"

I try to type back a response, but every word comes out wrong, as I can barely see straight.

Me: mthe can

Linc: What?

Me: can

I try to type again and get annoyed and swipe through my contacts to hit his name.

"Too fucked to typpppe," I mumble out, the words sounding a mess.

"Pierce, is that you?"

Fuck.

I slam my finger down on the end button. That was not Linc. Looking back down, I see who I called. Oh fuck.

The phone rings back. Fuck. Did I really just tell Lindsey

how fucked-up I was? Now what? Shit, shit, shit.

Send to voicemail.

Ring.

Ring.

Ring.

Lindsey: Answer your phone

On the next ring, I answer.

"Are you okay?"

In my drunken state, her voice is calm, reassuring.

"I'm so—"

I'm about to say drunk when everything in my stomach comes up. Lack of food and too much vodka, it all comes back.

"Did you just throw up?"

I don't answer the driver, who's screaming obscenities in my ear.

"Get out. Get out."

The driver is pulling me out of the cab. Still clutching my phone in one hand, I hear Lindsey screaming.

"Where are you? Pierce!" she screams through the phone to get my attention.

"Don't know."

"Look for a street sign."

"I'm just going to rest here," I say as I get to the corner of the street.

"Pierce. Stay with me. Where are you?"

"Street. Corner."

"If you're on the corner, look up. Tell me what it says."

"Sixty-seventh, third."

"Okay, I'm coming for you."

"Close my eyes."

"No. Stay awake. I'll be there in five minutes."

"Okay," I mutter out as I close my eyes. Sleep wants to take over, but the world around me spins, forcing me to reopen them. No matter how hard I try they won't stay open. They flutter back shut.

Open.

Close.

Open.

Close.

CHAPTER SEVENTEEN

Lindsey

I'M A MESS. AN EMOTIONAL MESS.

Hearing Pierce has sent me into a downward spiral of feelings I don't understand. Concern, anger, nervousness, anxiousness. All the feelings are colliding against each other inside me and wreaking havoc to my nerve endings. I've never left my apartment so quickly. Well, at least not since the accident. Even my moves are faster than normal. The need to get to him, take care of him, *rescue him,* is fierce.

I'm no stranger to drunken binges, and he needs me. No one ever needs me, and no matter what my feelings are for him, I know I have to be there.

I'm in a cab before I can second-guess my decision.

Lucky for me, there was one right outside my building. I don't need to go far, only three avenues and a few blocks, but with my leg, my limp, my pain, it would take too long, and the way Pierce hung up . . .

Who knows what kind of trouble he can get into in that time?

So here I am nervously drumming my fingers on my legs as we hit every single red light in our path. Audible sighs pass through my lips, but nothing can make these minutes pass. It feels like a fucking eternity, even if it's only been five minutes.

My mind wanders as I wait for the light to change. How will I find him? Did he pass out? How will I bring him home?

Shit.

That thought cripples me right there on the spot.

The car starts to drive across the street, and in the far-left corner, I see a man sitting on the ground. Head down. Disheveled hair. His hands are in the dark locks and his body shudders.

Pierce.

That's got to be Pierce.

"If I throw in another twenty, on top of the ten-dollar fare to drive back to my apartment, will you wait?"

"You throw in a twenty and I'll help you get him into the car." His accent is thick, but the words still make me laugh.

"You got a deal."

The cab stops and he throws the hazards on. I hop out the back and together we both walk up to Pierce. His head is down still. He might be sleeping.

"Pierce."

His face slowly rises. His green eyes, normally crystal clear, are hazed over and won't focus.

"Pierce, we're going to put you in the cab. Can you get up?"

He mumbles something incoherent and lifts an arm but doesn't stand.

"Okay, we're going to have to lift him."

The driver looks at me, and I notice him looking down at my leg. Was I limping? How did he know? He gives me a tight smile. "I got it, miss."

It feels as if a serrated knife tears through my flesh at the notion that even this man knows I'm damaged. Broken.

I nod, not being able to speak from the vulnerability coursing through me. He takes Pierce to the cab, and I follow behind. His head drapes down and I'm sure he's sleeping now. Soft snores come out of his nose.

I pay the fare and the extra twenty when we arrive back. The driver basically drags Pierce's lifeless body to my doorman before my doorman can escort us up to the apartment.

"Right over there is fine, Robert," I say, pointing to the couch in the living room.

He guides him to the couch.

"Will you be needing any more help, miss?"

"No, I'm fine. You can leave."

He lifts an eyebrow, and I smile, inclining my head down in a gesture saying yes, I'm fine. We will be fine. With one last backward glance, he leaves.

Heading into the kitchen, I grab a bottle of water and sit next to Pierce on the couch. He must feel me sit because he snuggles closer until his head is resting on my lap.

"Lindsey," he mutters.

My fingers start to stroke his hair, lightly massaging the unruly strands. "I'm here. I got you," I coo.

"You're here?"

"I am."

"Noooo," he drawls out on a whisper. "You're not here. All a dream." His words are low, not clear at all, but I can still hear them, and they take my breath away.

I can't speak. I don't dare. I just continue to lightly touch him, through his hair, across his brow. He shudders at the sensation.

"All a dream. Lindsey wouldn't be here. Not with me. She's too perfect."

The word perfect makes me wince. *If he only knew the truth.* Like a phantom pain, my leg aches. But the throbbing in my scars doesn't stop my heart from beating faster in my chest.

Is he really saying this?

Is this real?

Or am I the one dreaming?

"She's everything," he whispers to himself. "Everything I'm not. Strong. Beautiful. Brave." He coughs, and I feel it will wake him from his haze and he'll stop speaking. But then he mutters, and I move my ear closer to his lips, so close his breath tickles my skin. "Not enough. She wouldn't be here," he mutters again to himself, and this time I feel the need to speak.

"I'm here."

"You're not here. You'll never be here." His voice holds so much pain.

Something inside me breaks. It's like a dam bursts. Every feeling I've ever felt in my own life of not being good enough floats to the surface. Every time I never felt enough beats down on me. My insecurities. My pain. It's all there, floating above me. The feelings he feels are tangible because I've lived them, I've breathed them, I am them. In this moment the wind is knocked out of my lungs, because right now with this beautiful broken man lying in my lap, I realize there's so much about Pierce he holds back, and although I can't condone his actions, his behavior, I understand it.

That understanding scares the hell out of me.

———————◆•◆———————

My legs ache, the muscles in my back even more. I lift my arms above my head to stretch and it's as if every single muscle has contracted and then snaps like a rubber band.

Light trickles in through my lids and they flutter open.

The couch.

We slept on the couch. Pierce's head is still in my lap from last night. Anger. Pure, unadulterated anger filters through every single molecule in my body.

He was drunk.

Probably high.

And now what?

There was a moment last night where I understood his desire to get wasted, but now, in the light of day, knowing that in a few hours he needs to be with children, I'm fuming.

"Wake up." I shake him.

He shuffles and lifts off me. "What am I—" He rubs his hands over his face, confused.

"Doing here? What are you doing here?" I stand up and glare down at him still sitting on the couch. "Hmm, let's see. You got drunk. You accidentally called me. Yeah, I'm not Linc. And then, if that wasn't bad enough, from what I could hear through your cell, you vomited and got yourself thrown out of a cab." I start to pace all while shooting him daggers with my eyes. "I'm telling you right here and right now, this shit ends *now*. Man the fuck up. You aren't a kid." He looks visibly wounded by my words, but I don't let that stop me. Instead, I stop my pacing and place my hand on my hip. "You're a fucking adult. Enough. You're not a bad guy, Pierce. No matter what you think. I know there's more, but I refuse to be a part of this self-destruction. I won't be your friend. Hell, keep this up, and I won't even acknowledge I know you. Do you understand?"

"Crystal."

"Good. 'Cause I'm tired, and believe it or not, I have a job and I didn't sleep, so if you can please see yourself out that'd be great 'cause I need to get ready to be a mentor to these kids."

He nods like a lost little boy, and a part of me wants to reach my hand out and comfort him, but I hold strong.

CHAPTER EIGHTEEN

Pierce

I'T'S OFFICIAL . . .

I'm a piece of shit.

If there was any doubt before, waking up with my head on Lindsey's lap and smelling like a urinal, officially answers the question. I'm despicable. My whole life I've let people down, and I've actually come to terms with it.

If it's already broken, why fix it? That's always been my motto, and in this case, I'm not talking about normal indiscretions. I'm talking about myself. I'm all types of fucked-up, and there's no reason to fix me. That's how I've always lived my life.

Until last night.

Well, actually this morning.

The look of disgust . . . Hell, I've never hated myself more than when I saw how pathetic I was reflected in Lindsey's eyes. Today, as the early morning sun beats down on me, causing a sweat to break out across my brow, I know that something has got to give. And that something is me.

With not much time to get home, shower, and get my shit together, I pick up my pace. The city is empty at this time of day. Only a soft hum from a few passing cars can be heard. It's quite peaceful.

With a fast clip, I weave my way through the streets, the

avenues, the blocks until I make it to my building. I don't stop to talk to Adam, the doorman of the building I live in. I've been here long enough that he knows the deal. I crashed with a girl. Except this time the norm doesn't stand. This time, I'm not basking in post-fuck bliss. Instead, I'm seething. Not at her. At me.

How was I so weak last night?

One comment.

That's all it took.

One small comment.

Today when she threw me out, she said I was better than this. And when she said it, for the first time I believed it. Maybe it was her voice. Maybe it was the sincerity there, but I believed that maybe, just maybe, I could be like her and get my shit together. Because honestly, the Lindsey I've grown to know in the last few weeks isn't pre-accident Lindsey, and that shows that anything is possible, even for a fuckup like me.

Within seconds of being in my apartment, I throw my clothes off and head into the shower, washing away the shit and grime—fuck, washing away the past. Maybe not all of it, but the part I can change.

I'm done.

There might not be something going on with Lindsey and me, but in the last few days, I've seen a glimmer of the chance that maybe one day we can be friends and I'm not willing to throw that away. So I shower and wash that shit off.

An hour later, I'm at Polaris. Two Advils and a bottle of electrolytes can fix any hangover that might kick in.

Each step brings me in one direction to seek her out. I don't know why, but I do, and when I find her standing in the hallway, my breath leaves my body, and all the words I want to say, all the apologies, die on my tongue.

She looks gorgeous. She doesn't look like a girl who slept sitting up on her couch because she was babysitting an asshole.

"Hey," I say.

She looks up and a scowl is present on her face.

"I'm sorry."

"I'm still mad at you," she hisses back. The fire in her voice makes me tense.

"I know."

"No, you don't. And I'm too tired to get into this now. I'm happy to see you're here, but I have to go." She turns on her heel and walks away.

Damn, that stung.

What did you expect? You were a complete douche.

She could have given you a chance to explain.

Explain what? She owes you nothing. Just because five minutes ago you chose to try to change, to grow the fuck up, doesn't mean she knows that.

My shoulders rise as a sigh leaves my mouth, and then I turn and head in the opposite direction, toward the gym. At least I can run off this energy.

Sweat out the pain.

When the door flings open, I'm happy to find that no one is there. The kids don't show up for a few hours, but usually another volunteer is here. Today it's quiet, and I welcome it. I start to run laps. Letting my mind clear. Running is almost as good as painting. Not quite, but almost.

All the pain drains away as the endorphins release and in this moment, like when I hold a paintbrush in my hand, I let it all slip away because in this moment, like when I paint . . .

Anything is possible.

CHAPTER NINETEEN

Lindsey

THE NEXT DAY I BARELY MAKE IT TO THE CENTER ON TIME. The lack of sleep the night before, and the concern and caring for Xavier, is slowly eating away at me. I'm in no mood for team building exercises, which is exactly what this day will consist of. But I put on my happy face and walk in, standing tall. I'm the last to arrive, and all eyes look at me as the door bangs open.

"Nice of you to join us, Lindsey," Carson jests from the front of the room.

I'm never late. In fact, I'm punctual to a fault. The way my hair is disheveled and with the dark circles under my eyes, I'm sure everyone in the room has one thousand and one guesses as to what I could have gotten into last night.

"All right, guys, let's get this day started. We have a fun day full of activities."

Everyone around the room groans, not loving the idea any more than I do.

"I've paired you all up with your partners for the day. They're posted on the door with the first station for each pair. Go ahead and get started. We'll meet back here for lunch." He claps his hands, and everyone is off and running.

I stay seated, figuring whoever my partner is will find me

soon enough. A couple of minutes later, Pierce is standing in front of me. I look up at him and frown. "You've got to be kidding me," I deadpan. "Does Carson hate me this much?" I drop my head to my arms on the desk.

Pierce chuckles. "Apparently, he hates me just as much. The last thing I want to do today is have daggers thrown at my back."

I smirk. "I'd rather set you on fire than throw daggers." We both laugh, the ridiculousness of this conversation entertaining us both. "What's the first station?" I ask, not really caring.

"Ten questions, which I assume is a spinoff of twenty questions."

Yep, Carson hates us.

We make our way to the station, dragging our feet. The last thing I want to do is play ten questions with Pierce Lancaster, yet the universe is against us, so here we sit. Reading the directions out loud, I say, "Flip the dice. The person with the highest number asks the questions first."

Without another word, Pierce picks up the dice and rolls, getting a four. He hands it over to me and I shake it in my palm a couple of times and let it roll across the desk. I roll a three. *Fabulous.*

"Ask away," I mumble.

He comes out swinging with his first question. "Why do you hate me?"

I laser a glare in his direction. "Do we really need to start with that?"

"My questions. Just answer."

"I hate you because you represent all the things of my past I'd rather forget."

"Question number two," he spouts off. "What is one thing about your past I represent that you hate?"

I groan. "The party lifestyle." It's all I offer.

"Why do I remind you of the party lifestyle?"

"Isn't that obvious, Pierce? You were the life of the party. Pierce Lancaster is synonymous with having a good time. Case in point, a few nights ago . . . " He seems to ignore my rant and just cocks his head and scrunches his nose as he thinks of another question to fire off. When a sinful smirk spreads across his face, I know I'm in trouble.

"Did you want to date me back then?"

I throw my head back. "I'm not answering that."

"These are my ten questions. I get to ask whatever I want and you have to answer. Now would be a good time."

"Yes," I say a little too loudly. "Back then I did very much want to date you."

"Why didn't you ever tell me?"

"Because I'm older, and I thought it might be strange because you're constantly surrounded by girls. I figured you wouldn't be interested."

"What about now?"

"What *about* now?" I say, frustrated by his line of questioning.

"Do you still like me?"

"I would think with all the sarcasm and insults I throw your way, it would be a good indicator the answer is no."

"What if I told you I'm done with it all? What if I said I think I could change? Would you give me a chance? I know you might not believe me after the other night, and I know it's no excuse, but hearing you talk to Carson, well, I was weak. But the thing is, I don't want to lose your friendship. I know I need to stop, that I need to change. Can't you give me a chance? Let me prove that I can?"

I consider him for a while. I've changed, so why couldn't Pierce? Am I interested in dating him? No. But could I give him a chance to be friends again?

"If you've changed, and I mean seriously changed, I could try to be your friend. But only friends, Pierce."

"Would you go to dinner with me so I can prove I'm different?"

"Are you asking me on a date? Because the answer is no."

"You said friends, Lindsey. I'm asking you as a friend to go to dinner so I can show you I've changed."

"Are you paying?"

He chuckles. "We're friends. Friends split the bill."

It's my turn to laugh. "Touché."

"Okay, my turn."

He narrows his eyes. "Are you trying to cheat me out of my ten questions?"

"No. You have more than exceeded your limit."

He grins. "All right then. Proceed."

I tap my finger to my chin, seriously considering thinking hard about what I want to ask Pierce Lancaster. "Why were you really arrested? What exactly did you do?"

His smile falls. "It's not really something I like to talk about, but since all is fair in ten questions, I will answer." He takes a deep breath. "I was driving a car full of people who had all been drinking and doing other drugs and a female passenger was getting"—his eyes shift away from me—"handsy."

My mouth drops open in mock shock.

"I told her to stop and she didn't. I swerved, and a cop was sitting in a parking lot right in time to see it."

I scrunch my nose, almost disappointed because the reason is so . . . boring. A woman getting playful in a car full of drunk and high party boys seems tame for that crowd.

"I'm surprised all she was getting was handsy."

He rolls his eyes, clearly not amused by my jab. "There were other people in the car. I'm not big into voyeurism."

"You're disgusting." I cringe, which gets a chuckle from him.

"Next question," he demands.

"What's the deal with you and your brothers?"

His face pales, not that I expect anything different. This question won't be easy for Pierce, but if this is my only time to glean the details, I'm going for it.

"Not going easy on me, I guess."

I shrug. "Like you said, all's fair in ten questions."

He takes a deep breath. "Since I was never expected to run Lancaster Holdings, I was basically ignored. My father didn't have time for me, and neither did my brothers. As a child, I harbored a lot of resentment and eventually turned to lashing out, which included alcohol and drugs."

"Did you like that lifestyle?" I ask, genuinely curious.

He purses his lips and his eyes narrow to slits. "No. If I'm being honest, I never liked it. It's a very lonely life. You're surrounded by people all night, but in the morning when you wake up, you're all alone again. When you need someone the most, there's no one."

I watch his face for any tell that he's putting me on. I don't find any. All I see is truth, and for the first time in a long time, the walls I've erected to keep Pierce out start to crumble.

"Why did you come to work here?" I go for an easier question, deciding to take it easy on him just this once.

"I had to do community service, and Carson reached out to me. It appears he has a very similar story to mine, and he's been able to reform. He believes I can, too, so he offered me the chance to fulfill my obligation while working to rebuild my life. I owe him a lot."

"Why are you being so honest with me?"

"I've nothing to hide, Lindsey. You of all people should know what it's like." He runs his hand through his hair, pulling at the root. "I can't explain it, but I guess I don't feel uncomfortable admitting my faults or showing you my weaknesses because I guess we're the same."

"What does that mean?" I say defensively.

"From what I gathered that night we got drunk—"

I cringe at his words. He gives me a tight, timid smile, a smile I can assume is saying sorry before he continues. "I have a feeling our childhoods were much the same, which is exactly why you found yourself in the same rut I was in."

He isn't wrong. My father was too busy running an oil empire to care much about what I was doing. My nightly soirées and run-ins with the law were all a cry for attention. Attention I never received. It left me a shell of a girl and bitter as hell. When Pierce compares his life to mine, I get it. Doesn't mean I like it, but I understand him a little better.

"Time is up," Carson yells through the room. "On to your next station."

"That's not fair," I grumble. "I didn't get in all my questions."

Pierce laughs.

"I suppose at that friend's dinner, I'll give you a couple more."

I roll my eyes. "Doubtful," I whine. "Where do we go next?"

Pierce looks over a sheet of paper.

"We have to build a fort with only the materials we can find in this room."

"A fort. Seriously?"

"So it says." He points to the paper as though it's the Bible.

We make our way to the station to get the full details of our task. On the desk are the directions outlining what we need to do. I read them out loud. "Each partner shall have three minutes to collect everything they can find around the room to help construct a fort. After three minutes you'll work as a team to construct the fort before time is called."

"So, a fort. All right then. Set the timer and let's start searching."

I set a timer on my phone and call out, "Go!" Pierce races off in a separate direction than me, letting me go to the station close by to limit my walking. I grab items I think make sense and head back to home base to drop them off before darting back out to search for more.

"One minute," Pierce calls across the room.

I watch as he jogs off for last-minute stuff, too. Finding a blanket, I grab it from him when he returns and then place it on the desk with all the other items.

"Time," I call.

A winded Pierce comes back carrying an umbrella.

"What do we have to work with?" I ask.

Pierce sifts through the pile and calls out what we have gathered. Three blankets, an umbrella, two large boxes, duct tape, four large blocks that look like oversized Lego, a packet of glow-in-the-dark stars, and a pad of stickers.

"What the hell, Pierce?" I snap, not entirely mad but a little confused. "In three minutes, I managed to get vital pieces to create a fort. You contributed an umbrella, a packet of stars and stickers, and one blanket?"

"Well, yeah. Oh, and this," he says, pulling a large Sharpie marker out of his back pocket.

I throw my hands in the air. Glad to see he went for the important stuff.

"Now what?" he asks, all boyish, disarming me and forcing my attitude to drop.

"We need to build this thing." My eyes scan the items. "We need to start with the floor. I suggest we use the blocks."

"The blocks? No way. That would be the most

uncomfortable fort ever."

My eyes narrow on him. "What would you know about forts?"

His eyes lower, hands going into his pockets while he rocks on his heels. "One of my nannies and I used to make forts when I was younger. It was one of my best memories."

The way his sad eyes tell the recollection guts me. A familiar empty feeling spreads within me. Memories of waking up to find that my parents were out of the country haunt me. The memories feel real, like I'm living through them all over again as tears well in my eyes, for the pain I felt, for the pain it appears he too has felt.

Was he really that neglected?

If so, we have so much more in common than I ever thought. My dad loved me, and he tried to spend time with me, but the busier work got, the less time he actually did. Through the years it became less and less.

"No blocks for the floor then. Got it. What would you suggest?"

Pierce chews on his lip, looking over our things.

"Let's use the blankets for the floor, and then those two boxes for the walls."

I try to envision what he's suggesting and finally decide to let him lead this and I'll gladly take orders. "Lead the way, captain."

He gets busy placing the blankets, creating a makeshift bed for a floor.

"What can I do?"

He thinks about it for a second and then directs me to hand him the cardboard boxes. "Can you break down the boxes so they are two large flat flaps?"

I try to picture where he's going with this, but so far, I'm

113

coming up blank.

"Hand me the tape, please."

Grabbing the tape, I watch as he tries to hold both pieces of cardboard up into a tent-like shape. It keeps collapsing on him and I can't help but laugh.

"What's so funny?"

"That's never going to work, just saying."

"You think you can do better?" His hands are on his hips and his eyes are slanted in question. I think he's going to prove me wrong when I can't come up with anything. Then brilliance hits. Our materials are in piles on desks. We can use anything in the room, and we have desks.

"Quick, help me with these. We're running out of time."

He quirks a brow but comes to my aid, positioning the desks to allow space for two bodies.

Overtop we lay one of the cardboard boxes. We use the other to drape down the back, leaving the front open. Crawling into the makeshift tent, we both get inside and tape the stars to the ceiling and then place the stickers on the walls for decoration. When it's all done, we both lie back.

"Not too shabby, Lucky."

"I've got to say, you were pretty quick on your feet, too. I have no idea how we could've done this without the stickers and stars."

Pierce laughs, turning toward me. "Seriously, I think if I didn't have you, I would've frozen out in the wilderness."

"Yes, this center is very wasteland-esque."

We both laugh at that, my stomach tightening from the exertion. It feels good. Better than I expected to be hanging with Pierce like this.

Staring up at the stars, I dare another question. "Pierce?"

"Yeah?"

"Would you give up all the money for a normal family?"

His hand brushes mine and tingles glide up my arm.

"Every time."

Blowing out a deep breath, I close my eyes and dream up what a normal family would even look like.

CHAPTER TWENTY

Pierce

"A GAUNTLET?" LINDSEY PRACTICALLY SCREECHES the question.

"Yep. It looks like we have to run a gauntlet against another team."

"Is he trying to kill us?"

Lindsey's dramatics have me covering my mouth to shield my grin. Today has been a test of wills, for sure. I didn't think I'd survive Lindsey's ten questions. She was a bulldog, and for some strange reason, I couldn't bring myself to lie to her.

Watching her over the past few days, I see how much she's hurting. The physical limitations her accident caused weigh on her, but she refuses to admit it. She'd rather suffer in silence than show any sort of weakness and it's admirable but crazy. Everyone has limitations and knowing them can help you surpass them. The harder she pushes, the longer it'll take her to be at her best. She's overdoing it.

"I'll be right back," I call to Lindsey, making my way over to Carson. Once Lindsey is preoccupied grabbing a glass of water in the fridge, I clear my throat to grab his attention.

"Hey, Pierce. How's it going?" Carson narrows his eyes as if he expects me to complain about my current situation.

"I'm concerned about the gauntlet for Lindsey."

"Did she send you over here?"

I shake my head. "Hell no. She'd cut off my balls if she knew I was saying something."

He chuckles, knowing damn well that my words are accurate. Lindsey doesn't mess around, and she's too proud to suggest such a thing.

"It's just that I've seen her struggle with her leg the past couple of days, and I don't want her getting hurt."

"I'll talk to her and make sure she's up for it," Carson says. I can imagine he's counting the many ways Lindsey will kill him for even suggesting she sit out, but someone has to try. I can't watch her get hurt. Not when I could have stopped it.

"Just . . . please don't bring me into it. We're finally at an understanding of sorts, and I don't want to go backward with her."

Carson's knowing smile tells me he planned this all along. I've got to hand it to the guy. He's a smooth criminal. "Noted. You better head back before she catches you talking to me."

I nod, heeding his words and jogging off while she's still preoccupied.

"You're back. Where were you?" Lindsey says offhandedly.

"Restroom," I lie. White lies are not the same as out-and-out lying, especially when used to not hurt someone—or in this case, piss someone off.

"While I was stretching, I read over the rules. It looks like I start first and then tag you in for the final lap. It's an obstacle course of sorts. We have to go to the gym."

"Should we head there now?" I ask.

"Yeah, the other team is probably waiting for us."

When we reach the gym, my concerns about Lindsey participating skyrocket. This place is set up in a very intricate obstacle course. Climbing, jumping, swinging—it will all be necessary.

"Do you think it's a good idea for you to do this?" I ask, not overthinking my words.

It was a mistake.

"What the hell does that mean?" she seethes. "First Carson, now you. I'm perfectly capable of doing this, Pierce. I'm not broken."

I wince, feeling the burn of her words to my bones. "I'm not saying that. I was just trying to help."

"Well, stop. I don't want your help."

With that she storms off, leaving me feeling like the world's biggest asshole. Was I wrong? Should I have left well enough alone?

No. It felt right. At the end of the day, she'll come around. If she can forgive me for fucking her and leaving her at one of her lowest points, she'll forgive me for having a heart and fucking caring.

And I do. God help me, but I care for Lindsey. The night of the engagement party it was as if a light switch went on. I always thought she was a cool girl, but she came across as self-centered. That night, however, I saw another side. She put my needs before her pride. If that wasn't enough, seeing her at the center, with these kids, that was the icing on the cake for me. I care about Lindsey Walker.

"Are you guys ready?" a guy named Trent asks. He's one of our competitors and sizing him up, I have to admit he might be the worst person to square off with. He's athletically built and I've seen him play basketball. White boy gets air. If that isn't bad enough She-ra, aka Marcie, strolls up beside him. We're fucked. It's team ex-partiers vs. team ballers.

"Yeah, man. Just give me a minute. I need to find Lindsey."

I round the corner and find her stretching.

"You ready? We're up against Trent and Marcie."

Her eyes widen. "Shit. That's some bad luck on our end."

I chuckle because it's accurate and kind of turning into our M.O. "We've got this." I extend my hand, helping her to her feet. "Let's smash it."

Lindsey lines up next to Marcie, looking stone-faced and ready to slay. She's always been a hard-ass, and although the only competition I've ever witnessed her partake in included chugging expensive alcohol, she always went balls to the wall. If there's one thing you can say about Lindsey, it's that she's no quitter.

"On your mark, get set, go," Trent calls out, and the girls are off. My mouth drops open with surprise at Lindsey jogging over to the course. It's not more than a few steps before she reaches it, but I'm still impressed.

They've made it over the wall of mats and around the large balls. Lindsey is killing it. Pride swells in my chest watching her. Not a year ago she couldn't even walk, and here she is competing in a gauntlet and holding her own.

Lindsey has always been attractive, with long brown hair and crystal blue eyes, but never more so than now. Her strength and courage are a force, and I have to admit she's driving me crazy in the best way. I've never wanted a relationship, and I typically run from anything close to it, but here in this moment, I want one.

With her.

You're not good enough.

I'm not, but I will be. I have work to do to prove it to her, but I'll do whatever it takes to be everything she deserves.

The women round the last corner for their final lap. It's a straight sprint. I yell her name, cheering her on. Her arms are pumping, and she has the lead on Marcie.

And that's when everything goes to hell.

I see it first in her face. The grimace can't be missed. Following that, I watch in horror as her leg buckles and she flies forward, slamming face first into the floor.

"Fuck," I yell, running toward her. "Are you okay?"

She doesn't say anything, but I can hear her sobs.

"Linds." My hand darts out to her shoulder.

"Don't touch me," she snaps, and I jerk back as though I've been slapped in the face. "Just leave me the fuck alone."

I know that right now not only is her leg hurting, but so is her pride. I won't leave her here like this.

"Pierce. What happened?" Carson says, running up behind me.

I turn around, looking at him. "I've got her. Can you please clear the room? Get everyone out of here."

His eyes narrow, and my back tenses. He better not give me a hard time. Lindsey is a proud person, and this has got to be killing her. The blood pumping through my veins speeds up as I wait for him to make his move. I'm ready to go to bat for her, just like she did for me once. If kicking everyone out is what needs to be done, so be it.

Time seems to stand still, but eventually he goes about emptying the gym.

A tight breath escapes me. The look on her face pains me. The anger she portrayed was nothing but a shield for wounded pride. Time will help, so I give Lindsey a few minutes to compose herself before I'll talk again.

When it's obvious that she's calmed down, I lower myself to be on eye level with her. She's not looking at me, though. Instead, she's focused on her leg, staring at it with distaste, hatred, and sadness. It breaks me. I can feel her pain in each ragged breath she takes.

"It's just you and me. Please, look at me. I want to know

you're physically all right."

A minute later, her head lifts, the tears in her eyes breaking me. "I'm so embarrassed, Pierce."

My shoulders sag. "There's nothing to be embarrassed about. You've been through something none of us has. You busted your ass out there. You should be proud. Fuck, I am."

She sniffles, swiping a tear from her cheek. "I don't want to face them, and to be honest, I don't think I can walk." That makes her cry again.

"Shhh." I rub her back, trying to soothe her. "I've got you."

"I feel like such a fucking idiot," she says through her tears.

"Stop. You're perfect, Linds. You seriously made me so proud today."

Her big eyes look up into mine and something happens. Something that almost brings me to my knees. Lindsey Walker makes me want to be a better man. Despite all the resistance, bickering, and pushing she did, I want her. I think I always have. No, I *know* I always have. It's why I pushed her away in Antibes. I wasn't ready to be who she needed. Who she deserved. But fuck if I won't be that person now.

"I'm going to carry you, okay?"

She nods.

"We'll go out the back. I'll get you in the car, and then I'll run back in to get our stuff and let Carson know. You won't have to see anyone." I lift her off the floor and into my arms.

"Thank you, Pierce," she says, penetrating me with her teary blue eyes. They're bluer than normal right now. It reminds me of Antibes, when they were so dark with lust I couldn't even make out their color. Now they shine like flawlessly cut sapphires. Beautiful. Mesmerizing. Perfect.

Funny how mood can change one's appearance so significantly. Or maybe it's just getting to know someone that makes them more beautiful. I'm lost in thought when she cuddles into my chest, shielding her face from onlookers, but I keep my promise. We remain unseen. It's the first of many I'll make, and it won't be the last one I keep. I'm claiming Lindsey as mine, whether she likes it or not.

CHAPTER TWENTY-ONE

Lindsey

"WHERE ARE WE GOING?" I say, my head leaning against him. I watch as other cars zoom past, feeling as if it's all in slow motion. The humiliation I feel presses down on me. I knew I was overdoing it. I should have stopped. I should have listened to my body. But my pride got the best of me. Stupid, stupid pride.

"I'm taking you home," Pierce says from beside me in the back seat of the cab.

I owe him so much. He was so caring, so gentle, when I didn't deserve it. He tried to tell me not to overdo it, but I wouldn't listen, and because of my stubbornness I fell flat on my face in front of everyone. The one thing I pride myself on more than anything is my independence, but I only managed to show weakness and stupidity. Pierce picked me up, grabbed my stuff, carried me outside, hailed a cab, and is now holding me cradled in his arms, allowing me to cry on his shoulders. For that, I will forever be grateful.

"Did you grab my purse? If not, I'm locked out." My voice is hollow, lifeless.

"I grabbed your purse, but we won't be needing your keys. I'm taking you to my home."

I sit up, head turning toward him. "Your home?"

He simply nods.

The rest of the ride is silent, neither of us speaking, both lost in our own thoughts. Mine, though, are dark. I'm not sure about his, but mine makes me feel ill. They make my heart beat too fast with humiliation. They make my stomach ache with pain. I try to not get lost in self-loathing of not being better, but instead, I stare out the window and let the city pass me by.

When we arrive, he offers to pick me up again, but I shrug him off. I can walk, well, I can limp, but still. Together we enter a large apartment building and are greeted by a smartly dressed man. "Hello, Mr. Lancaster," the gentleman calls.

Pierce smiles. "Hello, Adam."

The communication between the two is strange to me. Hearing Pierce referred to as Mr. Lancaster is the first oddity, but the professionalism he exudes also catches me off guard. The Pierce I know would be lax and youthful in his interactions. This man beside me is just that—a man.

He puts a key into the elevator and ushers me inside. *Of course he lives in the penthouse.* It's obvious as we continue to rise farther and farther, bypassing every floor. The elevator opens into a large loft.

I always thought of Pierce as a shallow child with no taste outside of tawdry and expensive. However, this space tells an entirely different story. Pierce is cultured and sophisticated. The décor is not flashy at all. It's understated and masculine. Great art adorns the walls and I'm taken aback. I would have never guessed.

"I'm sure the ladies love this place," I say offhandedly, trying to make a jab, but my words come out breathless, missing the mark.

He bites out a laugh. "They've never been here . . ."

"What?"

He shrugs as if this is no big deal. "It's true. I've never brought anyone home."

It's a very big deal. The picture I'd painted of Pierce Lancaster was so different. So incredibly inaccurate. I feel foolish and hypocritical. The truth is, I always loved the idea of Pierce, but this guy is so far beyond my reach. He's nothing like I thought he was. This version, the version I've seen at Polaris, the guy I've become friends with . . . this is a new Pierce. This man is everything any girl could ever want.

My stomach flips and flops, but a niggling voice in my head tells me that can't be true. He's got to be messing with me, right? Every night he was with a girl at the clubs. Am I really to believe he never brought a girl back here?

"Yeah, right," I say, calling him out.

He turns his head toward me, drilling me with an intense stare. "I'm serious, Lindsey. I'm not trying to tell you I didn't leave with girls, but they never came here."

My chest swells.

"My place has always been off-limits. Not even my friends have been here. I don't need that shit here. This is my place to get away from it all."

I don't blame him. This place is amazing. Opening it up to our old crowd would have ruined it. My father received bills totaling in the millions for damage caused by parties at my places. I cringe at the thought of how ridiculous I was back then before my accident. Back when I partied hard enough to make me forget my family shit. How completely and totally irresponsible. Those days are over, and I couldn't be happier for it.

"Thank you for bringing me here," I say, smiling. "Thank you for everything. What you did for me back there really means a lot." I lower my head, feeling self-conscious under his gaze.

"I just want you to be okay."

125

"But you didn't have to," I press, wanting him to know that what he did was no small gesture to me.

"You're my friend, I know you want to fight that fact, but we are friends. And as friends, I'd do anything for you. You know that, right?"

I nod, feeling it in my bones that he would do anything. Needing space and time to think, I walk to a painting hanging on the wall. It's vibrant and beautiful, and not as masculine as the other décor. This brings life to the place. I turn back to him.

"When did you move here?"

"This *amazing* apartment was given to me by *Spencer*." Condescendence drips off his voice. Each syllable spills more contempt. "He purchased it for me shortly after graduation."

"That was kind of him. One heck of a graduation present."

"It was his way of getting me out of my father's hair. I was a distraction. One the Lancasters couldn't afford."

I feel horrible for Pierce. It's clear he truly believes that. The isolation he must have felt all these years breaks me. He's the only one not involved in the family business.

"You can't possibly think they felt that way," I say, knowing what I've been told about Spencer and how important his family is to him.

"How else would I feel when my brother came to me one day and told me, 'Pierce, your antics are a distraction for Dad. I bought you an apartment so you'll have your own space. We're going to have a moving company move you over there. It's about time you have your own place, don't you think?'" He tries to imitate Spencer and it comes out ridiculous.

I don't mean to laugh, but I do. "We might have to work on your voice-overs."

At that, Pierce laughs. After a few moments of silence, I try again to help him see he might have it incorrect. "Has it ever occurred to you that maybe he thought both of you needed your space? At that point in time maybe it was better for you to get out of there. I don't know much about Spencer, but according to Olivia, he cares greatly about you and the family."

Pierce scoffs. "Spencer only cares about himself and that fucking hotel. I'd burn them all to the ground if I could."

His hostility is understandable to me. I've been there. I've felt the exact same way. I can't fault him for his feelings when he's been left to believe these things his entire life.

"So, you have no interest in going into the family business, I take it."

He laughs. "Hell no. The last thing I ever want to do is be a part of the family business." He sighs. "Just another way that shows I have nothing in common with any of my family."

"If not the family business, then what?" I ask, genuinely curious as to what he wants.

He looks at me shyly. "Honestly?"

I nod.

"I love to paint. I've always wanted to be an artist."

"Really?" I can't help but be surprised.

"Yeah. I actually painted all of those," he says, gesturing toward the painting I was just looking at and the others next to it. I jerk back, stunned.

"Y-You painted those?" *No way*, I think to myself. "Are you putting me on?" There's no way in hell Pierce painted these pictures. They are incredible. It would take a professional artist months to complete these.

"I did all of them in high school. It was my thing." He shrugs as if this is normal for a high schooler to do. "I love painting. There's something so relaxing about it."

"Pierce, you're seriously good," I say, walking up and examining another one. "Like, incredibly talented. I would imagine these are worth thousands of dollars. Why aren't you doing this?" I wave my hand across the room, motioning toward the wall of gorgeous custom paintings. I'd pay big money to commission one of these.

"There's no money in it. Besides, my dad thought it was ridiculous."

I balk at his lack of knowledge if he truly believes that. "He owns hotel chains. His hotels are known for their décor. Surely, he can't find art ridiculous considering it's a focal point in every one of his rooms. You could easily sell your stuff to the Lancaster."

"I never got the impression it would be an option," he says coldly.

"Well, have you ever asked? Have you ever showed them these?"

"No, I haven't, because it's not something they'd find a reliable career." He stalks off toward the back of the loft, clearly done with this conversation.

My shoulders sag in defeat for him. He's talented beyond belief, and the fact it's going unused sickens me. I'd kill to have a talent like his. But it's not my circus, not my monkeys. After all he's done for me today, the last thing I should do is push him.

"It's a really nice place, Pierce."

"You haven't even seen my TV yet." He grins.

I roll my eyes. Typical. Men and their TVs.

"Are you hungry?" he asks.

"I could eat something small," I admit.

"Popcorn and a movie?" He looks excited at the prospect, which makes me excited.

"Only if we can watch a rom-com."

"A what?" He scrunches his nose.

"A romantic comedy. You know, like *Sleepless In Seattle*."

"Not happening. I like you, Lucky, but not that much." He grins, winking at me.

"Compromise?" I pucker my lips.

"*The Heat*?" he suggests. "I'm totally willing to watch anything with Sandra Bullock."

"That I can get with."

Five minutes later we're cuddled underneath a blanket on a large sectional, popcorn in hand, watching *The Heat*. Pierce went all out to make me comfortable and it warms my insides.

The care he's shown me today is unparalleled. It makes me want to smash every last piece of the wall I've built around my heart. *Don't let him get too close*, the voice in the back of my head warns. I can't help but know she's right. I have to guard myself from him, but tonight it's just a movie and popcorn. What harm can there be in that?

The movie is hysterical, and both of us are laughing nonstop. Pierce's head is thrown back in laughter and I look at him, smiling wide. The carefree attitude he's sporting is something I've never seen on him. This is a whole other side to Pierce Lancaster. A side I could easily fall in love with.

I'm determined more than ever to keep true to my promise of friendship. I want to be close to him. I want to get to know him. There's no harm in friendship. No broken hearts in the end. Friendship I can do.

I snuggle into his shoulder and his arm comes around, pulling me even tighter into his body. The smell of aftershave and cologne twists my insides.

"Lindsey?"

"Yeah," I say on a whisper.

"Just making sure you didn't fall asleep."

I chuckle. "Don't worry. I'm not going to cramp your style and crash at your sacred bachelor pad."

"Oh, thank God. I was so concerned," he says, voice full of sarcasm.

"Nothing to fear."

"Not so fast. You still owe me," he says, and I just stare at him blankly, having no clue what he's talking about. "Friend date. I'm going to cash in on our friend date."

I sit up and look at him. "What?" I ask, confused.

"You know, you made me a promise. We're supposed to go on a friend date." His eyes widen. "I think that's gonna happen tomorrow."

"Oh, is it?"

He grins. "Yeah, it definitely is. I'll pick you up at seven."

A friend date. This is going to get interesting. The way Pierce stares into my eyes tells me he has anything but friendship on his mind. If I lean in just a little bit more, I could brush my lips against his. Perhaps his hand would come up and trail a line down my neck, making its way to my breast. From there . . .

No more.

This is just too much. Pierce Lancaster is dangerous to my heart, and I'm powerless to stop it.

CHAPTER TWENTY-TWO

Pierce

WHAT DID I DO?

I didn't think this through at all. Now that my apartment is quiet and no sounds can be heard other than the steady rhythm of the outside traffic below, it's dawning on me that this changes everything.

Or does it?

I've never really hung out with a girl before as *friends*. And that's what we're doing. Spending time together as friends.

It's a new concept, and to be honest, it's refreshing.

There's only one problem: what to do. It can't be romantic. It needs to show her a bit about me. Maybe open her eyes up to the fact there's more to me than what she believed for so long.

Last night showing her my studio was a huge step. I'm not sure she realizes how big the step was for me. No one knows I paint. Sure, Spencer has seen my studio, but he doesn't realize the magnitude of what painting means to me. He sees it as a passing hobby, but to me it's life.

It's the blood that runs through my veins. Painting is in every beat of my heart. It's what keeps me sane. It's . . . Me. Without it, I'm nothing, and the crazy part is my own brothers don't understand that.

She does.

I could hear it in the inhale of breath she took. I could see it when her eyes widened in disbelief. For the first time, the curtain was raised and she, Lindsey Walker, saw a glimmer of the real me, not the fake one I hide behind, and I loved it. I didn't understand how much it would move me, change me, but hearing her words, the way she looked at my paintings; at that moment I wanted her to know everything. I wanted her praise, her reassurance, and most of all her approval.

Fuck.

I want her.

She's not willing to open up to me yet, but she will, and for now, friendship will have to be enough.

I sit on my couch, kick my legs up, smug as shit at the turn of events, but then my stomach bottoms out, and the familiar feeling starts to creep in. *Will it be enough*? An anxious buzz penetrates my muscles, and I start to shake my leg. The itch. The uneasy energy. It's loud. Unnerving. It speaks to me of hiding.

Don't let her in.

You'll let her down.

My heart hammers. I know this feeling. Nothing good ever comes of this feeling. The ache is there. Lose yourself. Numb it. Shut it up. Find a distraction.

Pick up the phone . . .

My hand has a mind of its own. It reaches, it scrolls, it hovers over Trey . . .

Don't hit send.

I scroll back, the name Spencer staring back at me. I press without thinking.

"Pierce, I'm in the middle of something. If this isn't an emergency, I'm going to need to call you back."

The hunger intensifies. My mouth feels like quicksand. No words form.

"Pierce."

Say something. Ask for help. Tell him you need him.

"I'm fine."

"Okay, good. I got to run. I'll call you later."

Empty. An unbearable empty feeling is all I feel as my finger scrolls up to Trey's number again.

You can't. You're taking Lindsey out tomorrow. Be better than this.

I know what I need to do, but it's so damn hard. *"Let me help you."* Deep within me, I hear his words. *"Let me help you."*

Without thinking, I make the call.

"Carson, it's me, Pierce."

"Hey, buddy. Is everything okay?"

"No," I admit on a sigh. "Nothing's all right."

"Talk to me." There's no judgment, just concern. And with that, all the muscles in my back loosen at the thought.

"I don't even know where to start."

"Anywhere. Start anywhere. The fact you're calling is a huge step, so start wherever you're comfortable and I promise to listen."

And so I do.

I give him the synopsis of my war with Lindsey. I tell him of our past, the partying, Antibes. And then after I tell him about me taking her home. I don't tell him about the painting because right now, in my vulnerable state, that's too much. But I tell him about how I asked her to hang out tomorrow.

"Do you want more?" he finally asks when I stop speaking.

"I don't know."

"What are you afraid of? Right now you say you just want friendship, so what is it you fear?"

"What if I let her in, and what—what if it's not enough? What if I'm not enough?"

"Listen, man. I get it. But you can't live your life in fear. There are no guarantees in life. If that's what you're looking for, you'll always be lost. But what if you stop looking for the answer and just enjoy the journey? Lindsey might not be the end game for you, but what she can be is your friend, and if you value her and value herself, I know she'll always be there for you."

"So how do I do that?" I ask.

"Take down the walls. I know you did, briefly, but take them all down. You want to hide from your brothers, that's your pre-rogative, but take the friendship she offers. Let it build you up. What you did tonight, calling me, is a huge step. You could be getting high, but look, you called me. You should be proud of yourself. And tomorrow, show her this side of you 'cause I'm proud and she'll be proud too."

For the first time in a long time, I realize that maybe I do deserve it.

Maybe I do.

And if Lindsey is going to give me this opportunity, I won't fuck it up.

I'm done hiding.

I'm ready to see what can happen if I just let someone in.

CHAPTER TWENTY-THREE

Lindsey

"Wait. You stayed over there?" Olivia's voice rises in disbelief. It's almost comical.

"No. We just watched a movie and then I went home. Nothing happened, Olivia. I'm not going there again."

"Good, because he's not good for you, Linds. He's bad news, and he'll only drag you back down."

I don't know why, but I hate what she's saying about him. The Pierce I saw last night isn't that guy. Olivia only knows what Spencer tells her, and it pisses me off that he speaks so poorly of his brother.

"You know, Spencer should really try to get to know his brother. He's not anything that you've described. It's really sad how misinformed he is."

"Spencer hasn't said anything. In fact, Pierce has him completely snowed. No matter what kind of trouble the boy gets into and how much he drags his family down, Spencer always defends him. It's frustrating because he's spent so much time worrying about him, yet Pierce does nothing to change his situation."

"That's not true, Olivia," I seethe, trying hard not to sound cold, but failing miserably. "He's had a tough life and you're not really one with room to judge. It's fine for you to rehab your life, but Pierce can't? That's pretty hypocritical of you."

She sighs. "I don't want to fight with you, Lindsey. I've just been on the other end of those phone calls, and I know how much he's hurt Spencer. I'm sorry for being concerned about my fiancé."

She said she didn't want to fight. I should stop as I'm not going to win with her, but I can't. She's wrong this time. "When was the last time a phone call like that happened? When he was arrested?" I huff. "I'm telling you, Olivia. He's different."

She sighs. "I hope you're right, Lindsey. For Spencer's sake and for your own, because I can tell he's gotten under your skin. All I'm saying is, remember the things he's done in the past because I don't want to see you get hurt. Listen, I know I'm being harsh, but truth is, it's just too close to home. I was that destructive once. I saw how it not only affected my life but the people around me. It's hard for me to hear Spencer so upset. I know that sounds hypocritical seeing as how I landed myself in rehab, but I got help. I just wish Pierce would get help too."

The tension in my shoulders loosens. I know Olivia means well. She's not trying to be a bitch. She's just frustrated from the past, and I can understand. Trust me, of all people, I can understand how frustrating Pierce Lancaster can be. I hope I'm not wrong, but I really don't think I am.

"I miss you, Linds. When I come back in town, can we grab dinner?"

I smile, glad that we seem to be all right despite our argument. "Of course. I miss you, too. Go have fun in France. Send me pictures. Make me jealous."

She giggles. "You've got it."

We hang up the phone and I recall everything Olivia said. I don't regret standing up for Pierce. I truly believe he's a changed person. I hope he doesn't prove me wrong.

I spend the rest of the afternoon getting ready for our friend date. Pulling on a black shift dress and a pair of booties, I apply the last bit of makeup—a light layer of mascara, a touch of blush, and some lip gloss. Looking one last time in the mirror, I wince. What am I doing? My scar is showing. I can't believe I almost left without throwing on a pair of tights. Quickly, I reach into the drawer and place my foot into the black tights. The marks on my ankle scream at me to rip off the tights and crawl into my bed and cry. What would he say if he saw my scars?

Why does it matter? You're just friends.

Maybe I shouldn't go?

Call it off. Maybe Olivia is right.

Maybe he hasn't really changed.

Goddamn Olivia.

Grabbing my phone, I call Amelia. "I can't do this," I blurt out before she can even say hi.

"What are you talking about?"

"Friend date. I can't."

"Why the hell not?" she asks.

"Well, Olivia—"

"Stop right there, Linds," she cuts me off. "I really like Olivia, obviously, and I know she's your best friend, but her opinion of Pierce might be a little biased. She only hears one account, and that account is not the same one you are seeing. He might have changed. Give him a shot."

"It's not that," I admit on a sigh.

"Okay, so why don't you tell me the real story? What's really going on?"

"My leg."

"Your leg? I must be missing something. What's wrong with your leg?"

"My scars."

"No one sees your scars."

"That's 'cause I cover them," I deadpan.

"No, that's not what I meant. You are the only person who sees your scars. You know what we all see? We see a woman who went to hell and back, conquered odds, many could never dream of, and lived to be a better person. We don't see scars, we see a reminder that you lived."

I don't know what to say to that. Actually, her words give me a hard time trying to remember how to breathe.

But my lack of words doesn't stop Amelia from knowing what I need.

"You got this, Linds. Now hang up." She doesn't give me a chance to object before she hangs up.

She's right. I can do this. I lived.

The buzzer ringing through my apartment means I'm out of time. Hitting the intercom, I say, "Send him up." Then a few minutes later, I throw the door open. He's wearing a pair of black jeans and a black tee, with black motorcycle boots.

"This is . . . strange," I comment on our coordinated colors. "Were you spying on me?"

"Um, no. All black is hardly original." He winks.

"Should I change?" I grimace.

His eyes widen and he chuckles. "I think you look stunning. I don't want you to change."

I'm relieved to see he's not overly dressed himself.

"Ready to go?"

I nod, grabbing my clutch off the table. When I walk out the door, he puts his hand on the small of my back, sending shivers down my spine.

"Where're we going?" I ask to make conversation, needing to forget the way his hands on my body affect me.

"That is a surprise." He looks down at me, smiling wide.

The car ride is quiet, my nerves increasing with each mile driven. Why am I so nervous? *This is a friends date*, I remind myself. We pull up to his apartment building and I bite my lip, confused.

"Did you forget something?"

"No. Come with me," he says, opening my door and holding out his hand for me to take.

"Are you ordering me Chinese? Because this friend loves Chinese."

He chuckles. "I had something else in mind."

When we enter his apartment, one of the best smells invades my senses. "Are you making lasagna?"

He smiles. "It's almost done. I had my neighbor watch it for me."

"What neighbor?" I ask. He's on the top floor, so he doesn't have neighbors.

"Mrs. Millie Tilson. She's on the floor below me. She's in her early seventies and just had her first great-grandchild. She loves helping."

I smirk. "Making friends with all the ladies in the building?"

"Millie is more like my grandma."

The thought warms my heart. I'm glad he has someone like that.

Walking around the corner, everything inside me goes still. My limbs won't move as I take in the scene laid out in front of me. In the middle of the room is a round table set with fine white linen, an ornate candelabra, exquisite china, and what looks like heirloom silver flatware. My breath catches in my throat.

"You did this?" My head turns to see him rocking back and forth on his feet.

"I wanted to do something nice for you," he says shyly.

My heart swells. "Pierce, this is incredible. But you know, friends don't do this kind of stuff for friends, right?"

He chuckles. "Yeah, well, I was a dick to you in Antibes."

My stomach twists at the memory. Old feelings, deep-seated insecurities gnaw at every molecule in my psyche. I push them down; there's no place for those feelings here.

"I have a lot of making up to do if we're really going to be friends, Lindsey. I thought this would be a good start."

"A romantic dinner is a good start to a friendship?" I tease.

"An elegant home-cooked meal from one friend to another," he offers.

I nod. "You've done well, Lancaster. A point to you."

We sit down to eat, between bites we don't speak. The silence stretches between us.

Uncomfortably.

Begging for someone to break it.

I do.

"Tell me something funny," I blurt out, needing to kill the awkward tension that has descended upon us. He doesn't answer, and truth be told by the way his mouth gapes open, he must think I'm crazy. "Come on, tell me anything. Tell me something about you when you were a kid."

"When I was a kid . . ."

His mouth parts and I wait on bated breath for pieces of him he's about to gift me. It's like we're on the precipice of something, reaching toward the unknown. I should be scared of what this means to us but I'm not. I'm falling head first into the abyss. My eyes wide open. Eager for more.

"When I was young, around four years old, Spencer was fourteen and Grant was thirteen. We had a dog. Her name was Alexis. She was the cutest wheaten terrier you've ever seen." His lips part farther and he lets out a laugh.

The sound has my insides warming.

"What did they do," I press with excitement in my voice.

"One would hold me down, and the other would call out for Alexis to come lick me. They would hold me down for hours. Or maybe it was five minutes, but I just remember being soaked with dog saliva."

It's such a small moment, one he tucked away inside, so deep it was probably forgotten, but just hearing it, I understand him more. He loves his brothers. Looks up to his brothers. And all he wants is for them to love him back.

Like me.

He's so like me.

And, strangely enough, it comforts me.

Later that evening, Pierce drops me off at my place. He doesn't have to, I could have taken a cab, but he insists and a part of me melts.

"Thanks for tonight, Pierce. Dinner was amazing." I shuffle my feet. "The company wasn't too bad, either."

"I had a nice time, too. Friends?"

"Friends," I agree.

Pierce leans in and I hold my breath. He places a small kiss on my cheek, heating my insides. "Good night, Lindsey."

"Good night, Pierce."

I turn and enter my apartment. When the door is shut and locked, my back hits the wood and I slide to the floor. Tonight topped every night I've ever had with any man. Pierce could have taken me anywhere money could buy, but he made things special for me.

My walls are falling, and there's nothing I can do to stop it.

CHAPTER TWENTY-FOUR

Pierce

AS SOON AS THE DOOR SHUTS, ALL THE BREATH RUSHES out of my lungs in a whoosh.

This girl.

There aren't words to describe today. But I'm revved up. Excited.

I can't remember the last time I've been this stoked about anything. Or anyone. But there's something about Lindsey. It wasn't just that it was fun to be with her. It was easy.

Head in the clouds, I make my way out of her apartment building and start to walk to my place. I pull my phone out when I hit the pavement outside and hit the contact button.

"What's going on?" Carson answers.

"I just wanted to say thanks."

"So everything went good, I take it?" He laughs.

"Not like that, man, but you were right. I need a friend, and Lindsey is a good one to have."

"You got me too."

I welcome his words. Carson isn't as old as my brothers, but he's still a few years older than me and I do look up to him, so to know he's on my side makes me feel good.

"Now where're you off to?"

"I'm just going to go home."

"Good. Good choice."

I laugh. He's right. It is a good move. Truth is, it's the *only* move. I'm not willing to lose her and what this could be even if that is only friendship. I know she wasn't lying when she said she wouldn't put up with my shit, and the thrill isn't worth that risk.

"So what are you going to do on your day off?" he asks.

Closing my eyes, I think about it for a moment. What is my end game? If I'm being honest with myself, I want to see Lindsey. The revelation has me staggering. God, what's happening to me? It's like I opened up a damn floodgate and now I can't close it.

"I'm not sure. Out of curiosity . . ." I stop myself. God, I'm acting pathetic.

"She has the day off too." He chuckles, and I want to jump through the phone and thank him for not making me ask, but I try to play it cool.

"I didn't."

"Sure. Who you trying to kid, you or me?"

"Fine. Thanks for the info."

"No problem. Okay, man, got to go. Lynn is waiting for me, so you know . . ."

"Got it. Say no more. See you Monday. And thanks."

"No need, but you're welcome."

I place the phone back in my pocket and head home. Although fall is here, the air is still warm with lingering summer air, so instead of getting a cab, I decide to walk the ten blocks. That has to be long enough to clear my head, and then hopefully come up with the most kick-ass idea for tomorrow.

Five blocks in and I'm grasping at straws. What does she like? I realize I don't know very much about her, what makes her tick, or her hobbies. Maybe if I show her more about my passions, she'll tell me about hers. *Yeah, that's exactly what I'm going to do.* I'm going to take her to my favorite place in all of the city. I'm going to take her to the Met. I'm going to show her every painting that inspired me and that's embedded in my soul now.

For the first time I'm seeing straight and I'm excited for what's to come.

CHAPTER TWENTY-FIVE

Lindsey

MY PHONE RINGS BRIGHT AND EARLY, AND I GROAN IN response to the loud chime. Glancing at the clock, I question who on earth would be calling me at this hour.

"Hello?" My voice is groggy and full of sleep.

"What are you still doing in bed? It's a beautiful day. Get your ass up. We have places to be."

"Pierce?"

"Seriously, Lindsey. Get your ass out of bed and get dressed. I'm on my way to get you. We're going to the art museum." The line goes silent and I know he's hung up on me.

He can't be serious?

I jump out of bed and rush around, splashing water on my face to wake myself. I apply a little makeup and am just putting on my shoes when I hear his knock at the door. I open it with a blank face.

"Seriously? Nine a.m., Pierce?"

He grins. "I want to get there at the opening so we can avoid long lines. They have a new piece I've been dying to see."

His excitement is contagious, and I can't help but crack a smile. "All right, Picasso. Let's go." As I walk past, I grab the nape of his shirt, dragging him with me.

He's right. There are no lines at this time in the morning and we're able to easily walk from piece to piece and marvel for as long as we want. We're looking at an abstract modernistic piece I don't like at all.

"Not a fan," I admit.

"No? I think there's something beautiful about it," he muses.

"It looks like a preschooler painted a bunch of shapes and mixed them together."

"Or you could use your imagination. Step back and really take a look."

I narrow my eyes, but when I see he's not joking, I take a step back and really try to visualize what he sees. Tilting my head to the side, I "meh" out loud. He may be right that there's something beautiful about art, but it's the way he talks about it that's truly captivating.

"I really think you're missing your calling, Pierce. Very few people are born with the talent you possess, and I can tell you love it. Why aren't you pursuing it?"

He sighs. "Because I don't even know how to get started. It's something I've always just done for me. I don't know that anyone would be willing to pay for one of my pieces."

My mouth drops open. "You're an idiot."

He jerks back as if in shock.

"I would pay for one of your pieces, and not because I know you. We ran in a circle full of wealthy people who love expensive things. They would eat your stuff up in a heartbeat. But beyond that, you have connections to so many galleries and so many hotel chains. You just need to start painting."

"Maybe." He shrugs, seeming to consider what I'm suggesting.

"The best part is, if you're looking to do a hotel chain, you only need to create ten to twenty images and then have them printed on canvas. You could mass produce them and make a fortune. Do your custom pieces for the ultra-wealthy who will insist on having them."

He laughs as though I'm crazy.

"I'm serious, Pierce. You're really good."

He blushes, looking uncomfortable at my praise.

"I think you need to talk to your dad. Show him how good you are."

He crosses his arms over his chest, narrowing his eyes at me. "What about you? What is it you want to do with your life, Lindsey?"

I don't even have to think about it. I know. I've known since the second I walked into the boys' club. It was my calling to help youth.

"I love the center. I love the kids. I only wish we could help more. Girls need a center like it, too. Those on the streets have just as few opportunities as the boys."

"So, build one," he suggests as though it's the easiest thing to accomplish.

"It's not that simple. It's so much more. Take Xavier, for example. He's having trouble at school and I'm really worried about him, Pierce. The only way for him to get away is to get out of that school, but there's nowhere for him to go. Nowhere his mom can afford."

"So, what's the solution?" Pierce asks as if he believes I have this all figured out.

"I'd love to open up a boarding school for boys and girls on the street. Give them opportunities. The same we had. Help them with their résumés, all of that. Give them a fighting chance to make something of their lives."

Pierce looks at me. *Really* looks at me hard.

"I've actually . . ." I bite my lip. "I've actually been working on it already. I've even been working on getting a business plan together. Then I'll just need to find investors. I don't even know where to start."

"Call your dad, ask him to invest."

My stomach drops at the mention of my dad. "That's not gonna happen. I haven't spoken to him in a long time."

"Call him," he persists. "Give him a chance. I think if you work on a business plan and you show him how serious you are, he'll be proud."

"I don't know. I'll think about it." I won't. My dad doesn't understand anything that's not oil. He'd probably laugh at me.

"Stop that," Pierce demands.

"What?" I ask.

"Stop doubting yourself. You can do it. You're so smart, Lindsey. Those kids love you. Promise me you'll do it for them, if not for yourself."

"I promise I'll think about it."

He frowns but lets the conversation drop. We spend the rest of the afternoon wandering around the art museum, grabbing lunch, and just hanging out. I love having Pierce as a friend, but I also can't help but want more when he's like this, when he's so easy and free and open. These thoughts running through me are bad.

Really, really bad.

And yet, no matter how bad I know it is, no matter how hazardous it is to my heart, I'm not sure I want it to stop.

CHAPTER TWENTY-SIX

Pierce

I'T'S TOO DAMN QUIET.

It's well after three and yet here I am all alone 'cause I got stuck with computer duty. Obviously, I'm not always going to get sports, but computers? For fuck's sake, I'm an artist. What the heck do I know about computers?

No one knows you're an artist, though, so why would you be placed in the art department?

A part of me wants to tell Carson, let him in on this huge part of me. I mean, he's been so helpful. Why don't I?

'Cause you're so damn scared he'll look down at you, like your brothers did.

It's better this way.

If no one knows, no one can judge you.

No more sulking. Time for a distraction. A distraction in the form of a pretty brunette, with dark blue eyes and a small birthmark on her ear that every time I see, I want to lick . . .

Shit.

That was not the thought I meant to distract myself with, but now that I have, I wonder what she's doing. I pull out my phone and fire off a text.

Me: What you doing?

Lindsey: You're not supposed to use your phone at work.

Me: I'm bored.
Lindsey: Are you five?
Me: Entertain me.

From behind me, I hear the screeching sound of the door opening. "How did you know I was here?" I ask, turning to face her, but the sound of my words catches in my throat. She's wearing a white thermal, but it's tight and I swear it's see-through . . .

Does she know?

This can't be okay.

Fuck, is it getting hot in here?

"Don't you know by now? I know everything," she replies, and I need to shake my head to rid myself of the inappropriate images playing out in my mind.

"I'm starting to catch on," I answer too fast, but I'm still looking at the perfect outline of her breasts. She coughs and I know she's caught me staring. "Um, where are you supposed to be?"

"I'm in art. You really should tell Carson to put you in there. You'd be a lot better than me."

It's like this damn girl reads my mind. "Maybe next time I see him, I'll mention it," I mutter, knowing there's no chance I will.

"Pierce, there's nothing to be embarrassed about. You know that, right? Your work is really good."

"I'm not embarrassed."

She rolls her eyes. "Sure."

The sound of footsteps stops our conversation as Xavier walks in.

"Hey, man, you here for computers?" I beam, happy to have a distraction to just how hot Lindsey looks today.

"Um, actually I'm here to talk to Lindsey."

I look over at her and notice she has gone stiff. *What's that about*? "Everything okay?" I ask Lindsey, narrowing my eyes at her.

She looks over at Xavier and his face is pale. Her lip peeps up into a small, reassuring smile and nods before turning to me. "Nothing I can't handle."

"You sure?"

"Yeah." She moves to walk past me and I reach my hand out, my fingers touching the exposed skin of her wrist. She stops her pace and looks at me, her blue eyes looking concerned. "Are you sure you're okay?" I whisper so Xavier, who's already almost out of the door, doesn't hear me.

She bites her upper lip with her teeth and then inclines her head down. We stand there for a second, the heat of her skin searing the pads of my fingers with a burning want I didn't know was possible, but she breaks the trance without another word and leads Xavier out the door.

Leaving me alone yet again and this time more confused about her than I started.

———————•◆•———————

The day is slow.

Apparently not as many kids were here today and the ones who were didn't want to hang in the computer room. Carson is doing a boxing lesson, so most of the boys were there, leaving me a bit desperate for things to do. I take the time to research art galleries and agencies that offer representation. I'd never really thought about pursuing this as a career, but Lindsey's enthusiasm and praise has made me start to contemplate the idea. I have a lot to think about, but for the first time, the future doesn't seem so dim.

Hours later, I'm back in my apartment and my phone is

ringing off the hook with text after text. It's like every friend is trying to lure me out tonight. Even though I've been sober since the night Lindsey found me drunk and passed out on a street corner, doesn't mean the urge isn't there. How does the saying go . . .

Idle hands are the devil's workshop.

With every new text and plea, I find myself wanting to answer the call of debauchery and sin, so without a second thought, I rip my clothes off and take a cold shower, trying to freeze out the voices telling me to do things I know I shouldn't.

When the urges don't go away, I throw on sweats and a thermal and head straight out the door, my feet taking me to a location that shocks me. It looms in front of me. Dark and ominous, but what's inside is the opposite. What's inside is everything right. Everything I need right now. Inside is Lindsey.

She's like a siren luring me. I should turn around, not tempt fate. Respect the distance she wants to keep. But I can't. I want her. I want to be near her. She calms me, she gives me peace, and I want to bask in the feeling and never leave.

Without a second thought, I walk through the glass doors and straight to the doorman. "Pierce Lancaster, for Ms. Walker," I say.

He nods and picks up the phone sitting on his desk. "Hello, Ms. Walker. Yes, I have a Mr. Lancaster here to see you. Can I send him up? Okay. Thank you." He hangs up the phone and turns back to me. "Just sign this book and head on up to 15E."

After I sign my name, I head toward the elevator. In the silence, I wonder if I've made the right choice coming here. Maybe I should have called Carson instead. The truth is as much as we hung out in the past, I barely know Lindsey. Sure we've slept together and hung out a few times but coming here could be a bad idea. I'm still lost in thought when I see her peeking out of her door.

"What are you doing here?" Her eyes are wide as she speaks, and a tiny line creases between her brows. Her concern is evident in her features.

"Rough day. I needed to be away from that scene." I shrug.

She opens the door farther, and I step past her into the foyer. "I was just watching TV," she offers, probably to fill the awkward silence that's descended upon us.

"Do you mind?" I ask, turning to look at her.

She shakes her head and gives me a small smile, the first since seeing me, and my shoulders lift and then lower on an exhale.

Relief.

"Of course not. We can watch a movie. Come on." She leads me out of the foyer and I follow her into the living room where I plop down on the couch as if I own the place and take the clicker in my hand.

"Glad to see you made yourself right at home," she jokes.

"What do you want to watch?" Scrolling through the channels, it's obvious nothing is on, so it's going to be a Netflix kind of night.

"How about the new Avenger movie?"

"A girl after my own heart."

"I'll grab popcorn."

"Thanks." The inflection in my voice says I'm not referring to just the popcorn or the movie, but for the fact she's helping me. Her lips tip up, and a beautiful smile forms across her face. I can tell she wants to respond, but she just stares at me, her chest rising and falling steadily with all her unspoken words. After a beat, she turns and walks away, and I put the movie on. In the distance, I hear the familiar beep of the microwave and then she's coming back with a big bowl. She sits next to me, her body so close to mine that we're touching, and she tucks her legs so they are practically resting on my lap.

"Friends cuddle, right?" she asks.

No, they don't, but I don't say it. "Yeah, totally."

I let us both pretend we can do this. That there's nothing going on between us. I allow us to pretend ignorance, because deep down we both know, we'll never be friends.

We are destined for so much more.

CHAPTER TWENTY-SEVEN

Lindsey

S TRETCHING MY HANDS ABOVE MY HEAD, I STIFLE A yawn. I slept in today, but last night we were up late watching TV. We never actually talked about what set Pierce off, but I was happy he came to me. Him showing up at my place proves he's trying. The thought makes me happy in a way I didn't realize was possible. Until last night, I didn't realize how badly I wanted Pierce to succeed. How badly I wanted him to be clean. But when he showed up at my door, and he asked for my help, it was as if every last bit of resistance faded away. He was trying. He wanted to change. And I wanted him to as well. He needs to be clean for the sake of the kids.

Oh, who are you trying to kid? You wanted him to be clean for other reasons altogether. Selfish reasons. Because if he's clean, you have no reason to not like him, and you have no reason to not want to spend time with him. As friends.

The need to think of something other than the festering desire to check in with Pierce has me picking up my phone, but instead of calling him, I pull up my to-do list and start to bang out tasks I need to accomplish before work today. After about an hour of answering emails, I pull out my notepad and one item is still to be checked off.

Business plan, speak to Dad about it.

I can't put it off any longer at least I can't if I want signifi-cant money to help the kids. I have to call. My fingers shake as I search my contacts for the one man I had no intention of calling anytime soon but need to. My father knows my number, yet he never uses it. My pride has stopped me on a number of occasions and this time is no different. Pierce's plea for me to call has me finally hitting send.

It rings several times before I get his voicemail. I should hang up, but at the last minute, I decide to leave a message. The beep sounds, and I begin.

"Hi, Dad, it's Lindsey. I was just . . ." I sigh. "Listen, I need to talk to you. Can you please give me a call when you get a chance? Love you. Bye."

I end the call and enter the center where I'm nearly late for work. When I walk in, I'm happy to see Carson is already there and on top of things.

"Hey, Lindsey," Carson calls from the desk. "I have everything posted for you. You're gonna be running the art station today."

"Sounds great," I say, turning to leave.

"Hey, Lindsey," Carson calls to my back.

I turn to face him again.

"I've been thinking a lot about this and I want to say I'm sor-ry. I should've never let you compete in the gauntlet after every-thing you've been through. I feel really bad."

"Not your fault, Carson. And even if you had told me not to, I still would have done it."

"I believe that," he says, chuckling.

I look around the office and something dawns on me. The last time we were in here, I yelled at him about giving Pierce a shot. God, I was such a bitch.

"Pierce took good care of me. You were right about him, Carson."

He quirks his eyebrow. "How so?" His voice is curious.

"He's a good guy. He deserves a chance."

He nods. "I'm glad you agree."

"I'm sorry I jumped down your throat. I should've trusted you to know what you were doing. I won't doubt you again."

"You had your reasons, I'm sure. I'm glad everything is okay now."

"It is. It really is."

I turn to walk away before coming back in. "Hey, Carson?"

He looks back up at me.

"I recently came into the knowledge that Pierce is an extremely talented artist. You might want to have him run the art station at some point."

"Will do. Thanks for the tip."

I go set up my art room and get it ready for the boys. A few minutes later, they start piling in. Christopher, Rocky, and Jackson are not looking thrilled to be doing art today.

"Oh, come on, guys. Is it that bad that you get to hang out with me today?"

They all groan. "It's not you, Miss Lindsey, but I'd rather be playing basketball," Christopher says with a shrug.

"I get it, but it's always good to try your hand at new things."

They take their seats while I get them all set up and onto their projects. I lift my head and spy Pierce walking past the door. He stops and waves at me.

"I'm schooling them in basketball today."

I smile. "Yes, I saw that. Take it easy on them, would you?"

He grins. "Never, woman."

I chuckle.

The rest of the day passes slowly. I wonder how Pierce is doing with the guys at the basketball station. I kind of miss hanging with him if I'm being honest. No matter how much I complained about being placed with him in the beginning, at some point, everything changed.

I'm looking at my phone when it dings with a new email. I open it to see it's my bank and a large sum of money has been deposited. "What the hell?"

Christopher raises his head, lifting a brow at my language. *Sorry*, I mouth.

I pull up my bank app, log in, and scroll through until I see it was my dad. He has added a hundred thousand dollars to my account. It's his typical M.O. Whenever I call to talk to him, it's usually for money and it always ends with a deposit of a hundred thousand dollars. Enough to get me through the next couple of months, and it buys him time to avoid me.

Disappointment envelops me. I wasn't calling to complain or beg for drug money. I was calling because I wanted to talk to him. I wanted to make him proud. But none of that even matters. That he couldn't be bothered to call me hurts. Doesn't he want to hear my voice? Doesn't he miss me?

"Guys, I'll be right back. I need to use the restroom," I say, rushing out of the room. I'm trying to stave off the tears that will inevitably begin to flow. I make it to the bathroom before I let loose and a waterfall of tears drips down my cheeks at the loneliness I feel. My parents want nothing to do with me. I'm alone in this world. It's the simple truth.

I've been crying in here for five minutes before I look in the mirror to discover my face is blotchy and tear-stained. I do my best to wipe off the smudged mascara and dab my skin with cool water to take down the redness. It works marginally, but I need to get back to the boys.

Walking out of the bathroom, I collide with a familiar hard chest. Looking up into Pierce's worried face, I can't help it. I cry harder. He pulls me into an alcove, holding me tight and rubbing my back.

"Shhh. Lindsey, what's wrong?"

"My dad doesn't love me," I cry, suddenly feeling foolish and ridiculous. But I can't help that I'm breaking right here in Pierce's arms.

"What did he do?" His voice turns from worried to lethal.

"I called him to talk about the idea for the school, but he didn't answer. And instead of calling me back, he deposited money in my account."

"Buying you off," he growls under his breath, knowing far too well what that is. Moving to push away as embarrassment sets in from my outburst, he doesn't let go. "Let me hold you," he says, and I do. I let him in this moment. I need Pierce's strong arms, and I need to not be alone.

After my tears stop, I move to step away, but instead, Pierce keeps his arms around me. I look up to see what he's doing. Our eyes lock. We stand there, so close and frozen in place. The air crackling around is filled with tension. He moves closer to me, and I notice the green in his irises has disappeared, hidden behind larger black pupils. His body is so close to mine I can feel his chest expand with every breath he takes. He leans in, his mouth hovering over mine.

"We cannot do this," I whisper.

His mouth curls into a sinful smile. "We can." His words tickle my mouth, making my lids flutter shut at the sensation. Like a dream, his lips press against mine, softly, a whisper, as if it never happened, and a part of me fears if I open my eyes it didn't.

But a bigger part of me fears it did.

My lips part of their own accord, eliciting a groan from Pierce as his tongue presses into my mouth, moving slowly but with an urgency of wanting I have never experienced before. The kiss deepens until I'm dizzy. Until I'm confused. Until I no longer know why I'm pushing him away, but I am. Regardless of what my treacherous body wants, my hands have a mind of their own.

"We shouldn't have."

"Yeah, we should have." He smirks.

"Pierce." I step back, putting distance between us. "We're supposed to be friends. Friends don't kiss."

"Fine, friends don't kiss." He smiles, but I can tell this isn't over, and that scares me. Because we can't be more than just friends.

Can we?

CHAPTER TWENTY-EIGHT

Lindsey

BY THE TIME I ARRIVE HOME, I'VE CALMED DOWN ABOUT the deposit. It's not the first time my father has tried to buy me off, and quite frankly, I don't blame him. The only times I've called him in the past was when I wanted something, and those requests typically came with a large price tag. He was just getting a jumpstart.

The sad part is I was so looking forward to sharing my idea with him. I want him to know I'm no longer just sitting around collecting his paychecks. I found my purpose and I want to try again. And I want to work really hard to achieve it.

Sitting on my couch, I decide I need to do something about my father. I need to get through to him. I need him to understand me and see me. I won't be able to take this rejection again. Not if I want to keep my resolve and stay healthy. How easy it would be to fall back on my old ways.

I'm so thankful I found Pierce.

I'm so thankful for the way he held me, calmed me, took care of me.

After everything Pierce did for me, I have to admit my walls are crumbling fast. I find myself itching to be around him.

To kiss him again.

No. Just to talk.

It's more than that, though. In a short time, he's become a confidant, and I desperately need him tonight. I pick up my phone and send a quick text.

Me: Dinner at my place?

I sit here nervously twitching, watching the phone like a hawk, until I see the three little dots in a bubble, indicating he's writing back. I wait with bated breath until the words appear.

Pierce: On my way now. Better be good . . . JK!

I laugh. He knows me too well. At my house, it's always some sort of takeout, and tonight is no different. I want my form of comfort food, which includes extra cheese and pepperoni with a side of cheese sticks. I pull up the local pizza place in my contacts, place an order, and sit back and wait.

Why did I think this was a good idea? Asking him to come over for dinner is probably the dumbest idea I've ever had. We're in this weird limbo now where we're not really friends and we're certainly not dating.

So what are we?

And why are we doing this?

Because you want him, the voice inside me screams again and I try to shoo it away, but I can't.

I want him. I do. No matter how much I try to pretend that kiss meant nothing or that what's going on between us meant nothing. It does mean something. He's funny, smart, talented . . .

I'm fucked.

I shouldn't have invited him over. That's for sure. With a death grip, I hold my phone in my hand and think of how I can retract my invite only a minute after sending it.

Hey, Just kidding. I'm too scared to be alone with you now that I've realized that I like you, like really like you . . .

Nope, that won't work.

Maybe he'll come to his senses. I stare down at my phone,

willing it to ring.

It's fine. Everything will be fine. Just friends having dinner. Oh my God, why am I so nervous? It's just Pierce.

Who are you trying to kid? It's not *just* Pierce.

Twenty minutes later, there's a knock on my door. Swinging it open, my breath hitches. Pierce in a navy-blue Henley, jeans, and tennis shoes, has my mouth practically watering. Pierce doesn't need to go all out to impress. He is magnificent. I step aside, ushering him in.

"So, what's on the menu tonight?"

"Pizza," I say with a shrug.

"Seriously?"

"Is that okay?" I suddenly feel self-conscious. Maybe he doesn't like pizza. I never thought to ask. Or maybe he's disappointed after all the effort he put in the other night.

"Pizza is awesome. I've been craving it."

I bite my lip, happy that something so small can make him so happy. It's funny. In our pasts, pizza would not have happened with the friends we kept. Late night parties, yes . . . but a casual night with the most excitement being what toppings to order on our takeout, not so much. Our lifestyles were so different then. These days, the little things truly make us happier than all the extravagant parties and restaurants from our previous lives. At least that's true for me. But I think the same could be said for Pierce. And even though I live in a condo that costs more per month than most people make in five years—and is paid for by my father—we're just two normal people trying to make something of ourselves.

"I have something for you," I say, shuffling my feet. When I got home, I'd wanted to dive into something, anything, to take my mind off my dad. I have plenty of things I could still work on with my own center, but I wanted to do something for Pierce.

"I did some research and found information on how to start selling your work. I pulled up a directory of all the galleries, different agents, anything I could find. It's sitting in a manila folder on my desk. Let me grab it," I say, walking over to the desk. I grab the folder from its current place and hold it against my chest before I extend it out to him.

He looks at the manila folder questioningly before taking it. His smile tells me he appreciates the gesture. Whether he plans to actually follow up on any of it or not is the million-dollar question. "This is really cool of you. Thanks for doing this."

I shrug. "It was no big deal. I really think you need to do something with your art."

"I'll look through this later and see what I can find." He pulls me into a hug. I squeeze back.

Ten minutes later the pizza is here and we dive in, each piling our plates high, not caring about looking like gluttonous pigs in front of the other. This is what's so great. I don't have to be anyone else in front of Pierce. The front I put on for years can be dropped and I can just be me—a silly, insecure, lonely girl.

After we eat, we sidle up next to each other on the couch, browsing Netflix. "What's it going to be?"

"You pick," he says, sounding close to sleep.

I surf through until I find a good rom-com. Just when I think Pierce is conked out, he puts his arm around me. I'm sitting too close to him for my own good, the smell of his aftershave doing things to me it shouldn't. As the movie progresses, a sexually charged scene comes on and I cannot stop squirming.

"Lindsey," he whispers in my ear. "I thought you wanted to be just friends. You really should move your hand away from my leg. Unless . . ." There's mischief in his voice.

I look down and notice my hand is awfully close to *him*. My cheeks heat as my fingers brush against the material of his pants. Looking up, our eyes connect, and his darken. Of all the reasons we shouldn't, I can't think of one of them right now. So, without a second thought, I lean up.

"Friendship is overrated." I crush my lips to his.

He kisses me with an intensity I've never felt before, like the world begins and ends with me. Like I'm everything, and with each caress of his mouth against mine, I believe it.

He draws my tongue deeper into his mouth, and I lose myself completely. This is more than a kiss. This is him taking possession of all that I am, all that I want, all that I feel, and I let him chase away all rational thoughts. Allowing him to own me with the heat of his mouth on mine, until we collide in a frenzy of passion lighting a fuse that makes us both burn.

We're a fury of hands and legs as we seal our lips together. We can't get enough.

His tongue sweeps inside my mouth.

His teeth nip at my lower lip.

I moan at the roughness of his kiss. If possible, as the seconds pass, each of us grows hungrier until we finally pull apart, both out of breath and panting for more. I look at him. My heart hammers in my chest at what I want.

I want him in my mouth.

The thought shocks me, but everything about this encounter is shocking. Moving down, I position myself between his thighs and then peer up at him. There's a slight ache in my leg from the position, but not enough to stop my need to do this.

"What are you doing?" He hisses at the sound of his zipper being lowered. A primal groan emanates through the room as my fingers pull him out.

"Playing," I respond. I'm met with a chuckle.

"Have at it." He leans back, giving me better access.

With my right hand, I grasp his hard length. His hips jut forward, his body quivering beneath. Feeling him come undone has me acting adventurous and wanton. Now in my mouth, I pick up the tempo of my hand, stroking his base even faster, all while licking and sucking the tip. After a few minutes, I feel Pierce try to pull out of my mouth, but the desire to taste him, all of him, has me holding steady until he finds his release. Once he's done, I move to get up, but his right hand reaches down and stops me.

"And where do you think you're going?" His voice is raspy as he brackets his arms around me. Tightening his grip, he pulls me toward him and I fall onto his torso. "My turn," he grates, and who am I to object?

He flips me over and hovers above me. Lifting my shirt, his rough hands trail patterns on my skin, starting at my navel and working downward, unzipping my pants and then pulling them down far enough around my knees so he traps me within them like a rope, but at the same time, I have enough wiggle room to spread my legs.

My thighs part in offering, begging him to feast on me. There's a look in Pierce's eyes I've never seen before. Hunger. Desperation. He exhales against me, his breath tickling my flesh. The feel of his tongue is next, lapping away at my damp skin. With each swipe of his tongue, he tightens his hold around me. Soon I'm soaring over the edge, rising to a crescendo until I'm shaking and convulsing and finding bliss.

We lie quietly, slowly coming back from heaven. After a minute, I sigh contentedly. "That was amazing."

"It was."

"So, you know this changes everything," he says with an impassive shrug.

"Why? What do you mean?" My words come out too fast and it makes him laugh.

"I don't want to share you," he replies.

"I think I should be more concerned about you. No one wants me."

"You really think that? You have no idea how men look at you, do you?" The confusion in his voice is evident. He really doesn't understand. But he hasn't seen my marks. The lights are always off. He can't see how damaged I am. He has no idea the looks I got right after it happened. How I thought it would be okay to bare my leg in a short skirt that first fall and the gawks I received because I did. I vowed never to make that mistake again.

"I used to."

"Well, it's true, they all want you, and I don't want to share." His voice takes on a possessive tone and I roll my eyes at him. He's being ridiculous.

"So, what does that mean?"

"I want to see where this goes. Let's give this a try."

His words take me aback. There's no way Pierce would want to be in a relationship with me, is there? All those years he never wanted me, now he does? It makes no sense. *Unless . . .*

Unless all he wants is sex.

By the way he stares at me, it's not just sex he's asking for and I swear my heart starts to pound rapidly in my chest as if I'm about to go into cardiac arrest. Pierce Lancaster wants to be with me. As the idea takes root inside me, so does the pitter-patter against my breastbone.

I want this.

I want him.

But can I trust him enough? Or will he break me more than I'm already broken?

"I don't know if I can. Right now you're clean, but I can't be with you—"

"I won't let you down."

He says it, and he means it, but for how long?

How long before he sees me, all of me, and realizes I'm not enough?

CHAPTER TWENTY-NINE

Lindsey

R EGARDLESS OF THE DOUBT THAT LINGERS IN MY bloodstream, I'm still walking around on cloud nine from last night. Our relationship—if you can call it that—has moved to the next level. I thought at this point I'd be kicking myself for caving, but honestly, every day he surprises me more. I have a perma-smile on my face as I walk through the halls of the Polaris Boys Club.

Rounding the corner, I almost collide with Xavier. When I step back, I gasp. His eye is black and blue and swollen shut. My hands come to my mouth. "What happened?" I question, fearing I already know the answer.

Xavier averts his gaze. "N-Nothing, Miss Lindsey. I-I fell."

"Bullshit."

I don't even care about my language. Now he's lying to me? Does he think I don't know? He turns to walk away, but I grab his arm. In the process, his sleeve lifts up, and I see cuts lining his arm. I pull him back toward me, push up his sleeve farther, and anger seeps into my bloodstream. Whoever did this to him, I'm going to find them. I don't care what part of the hood they're in.

"Don't lie to me. Tell me why this happened."

"I can't," he whispers.

I step closer, until I'm standing directly in front of him, and his gaze drops to the floor.

"I can't tell you, Miss Lindsey. Please don't make me."

"To protect you I need to know."

"I promise, I'm fine."

"I know you aren't telling me the truth. Please talk to me. You can trust me."

"But can I? Will you tell Carson? Will you tell Pierce? Because unless you promise me . . ."

"You know I can't do that. Xavier, if you're in trouble, if you are being harmed, I'm legally bound to report it. If I don't and something happens . . ." My words trail off. If something happens to him, it wouldn't matter if I got in trouble. All that matters is I failed him. And I'd never forgive myself for that.

"Fine," he says, sounding completely defeated. "I was wrong to think I meant something more than your rules. You're just like everyone else," he fires back, anger and frustration evident in his voice.

I know I shouldn't. I know that if anyone finds out, I will lose my job and worse, I know if something goes wrong, the consequences of my actions are limitless, but hearing the desperation and the torment in his voice is too much for me, because before I can stop myself the words spill out of my mouth.

"Tell me. I promise I won't tell. Tell me who did this and what is going on. You can trust me. I'll help you . . . no matter what."

"My brother," he admits. "He owes a gang fifty thousand dollars, and this is their warning. He has a week to come up with the money, or else they're coming for me."

I drop his arm. My hand comes to my forehead, and I begin pacing, all the while envisioning the million ways I can find these pathetic cowards and make them pay. And then it hits me:

my dad has just sent me a sum of money I don't need.

I turn back to Xavier. "I have the money. I'll make the payment. You let the idiots know." And with that, I sealed the last nail to my coffin. If anyone finds out, my dreams of helping children, my dreams of a boarding school are done.

He begins to cry, and my anger turns to concern for him. He's such a strong, proud kid. I know how hard this has to be for him to show weakness in front of me. I pull him into my arms.

"Shh, it's okay," I coo to get him to calm down. "I've got you. I'll take care of this, I promise." I mean every word of it. Financially speaking, I will help him. I would help any of these boys.

He steps back, wiping a tear roughly from his eyes. "I can't have you do this, Miss Lindsey. It's not fair to you."

I put my hands on my hips. "And it's fair that you're getting dragged into this? It's fair that your brother has put you in this position? No. You have a future, Xavier. You can make something of yourself. I don't care what your brother got into, but you're not following his path. You're going on with your life, and you're going to prove that you are not him. Do you understand me?"

He nods.

"That's all I want. I don't want you to repay me. I don't want you to thank me. I want you to prove to me I didn't make a mistake by helping you out. Promise me you'll work harder and you'll make something of yourself."

He nods again. "I won't let you down."

"That's my boy. Now get to your station. I'll pull out the money and get it to you in a couple of days."

He pulls me in for one final hug. I pat his back and send him on his way, then go directly to Carson's office. I know what I need to do. Three brisk knocks on the door and he calls out for me to come in.

"What's going on?" Carson asks, looking up from his stack of papers.

"What would I have to do to start a boarding school for these kids?"

"A boarding school?" He wrinkles his forehead.

"This place is great, Carson, and what you've started here is amazing, but it's not enough. Sending those kids off to the public schools, with all the violence and gangs? It's only a matter of time before they either get pulled into it or severely hurt. Their families can't afford to send them to private schools. But what if we could start a boarding school and offer scholarships for some of these kids to attend?"

He places his pen down. "Did something happen?"

"No," I lie, not wanting to drag Carson into the mess with Xavier. "I want to make a bigger difference. I want somewhere girls from bad neighborhoods can have an escape, too. There has to be a way to work with the state to provide such services. Isn't there government assistance available? Or private donations, maybe? What would I have to do?" My voice hitches, the desperation oozing off of me.

"It's a big undertaking, Lindsey. The money it would take to run something that big is frankly in the hundreds of millions. I can't begin to tell you how much work it was getting this center going."

"Money isn't an object, Carson, and I have all the time in the world." The truth of the matter is, my circle has billions running through it. My father alone could afford to fund damn near the entire thing. Carson looks skeptical.

"I'm serious. I want this, and I want it sooner rather than later. I'll do whatever it takes."

He smiles. "Let me start digging some stuff up from the state.

I'll see what I can do."

I smile, turning to walk away.

"Lindsey," Carson calls.

I turn back around.

"I'm proud of you. You've come a long way from the girl I first met. You're going to make your family proud."

"Thank you," I say.

We'll see.

CHAPTER THIRTY

Lindsey

'M SITTING ON PIERCE'S COUCH, RELAYING THE DETAILS OF my talk with Carson. My hands are flying around animatedly as we discuss all of my ideas. His eyes are wide, but a smile remains on his face the entire time. When I'm done, he just sits there quietly. I grow uncomfortable, wondering if he thinks I'm crazy.

"Say something," I push, wanting to know his true thoughts on my idea.

He shakes his head. "I'm speechless," he admits. "The thought you've put into this . . . Lindsey, it's incredible. If you can pull this off, it will be huge. Those boys at that center need this. They need you. And I love the idea that it will be co-ed. You're right, girls need the same opportunities."

I bob my head, eager for his feedback.

"So, what do I need to do to invest?" he asks, and I jerk back.

"W-what? Invest? Are you serious?"

"Why wouldn't I? It's amazing. I have money from my trust."

"Pierce, I don't know what to say." It's my turn to be speechless.

"How about two hundred and fifty thousand dollars?"

My eyes bug out. "Two hundred and fifty thousand? Are you kidding me?"

"Nope."

"Seriously?"

He chuckles. "You keep asking me this and I keep telling you, I'm dead serious." He smiles.

"Pierce, you don't know how much that means to me. It's huge."

He bends down, kissing my cheek. "I believe in you."

I'm overwhelmed with emotion. Touched by the fact Pierce believes in me. "I can't thank you enough."

"I'm doing it for you, Lindsey, but I'm also doing it for the boys. Rocky, Christopher, Xavier, all of them. They all deserve these chances. I think between my contacts and yours, we can really make this happen." He begins to pace. "We need to work on a business plan."

"We? You want to help?"

He continues to bowl me over with his generosity.

"Of course. This is important, Lindsey. I'm all in."

We spend the next hour doing our own research on funds available through the state. We've compiled a folder of information for me to sort through over the next week with tons of applications and phone numbers of agencies I'll need to start reaching out to. I'll compare them to what Carson finds, and we should have a good start. In the meantime, I need to look for a place to build the boarding school. Or better yet, find a building that can accommodate such an undertaking.

"You know, Jamie Ryan is a venture-capitalist, and this is exactly what he invests in. Hang on. Let me call him," Pierce says.

I'm familiar with the name. He's a former NBA player who came from Compton. It's been his life's mission to help kids get off the streets. I sit, my knee bouncing up and down rapidly enough for pain to shoot through my skin. Is this man serious?

"Hey, man. How's it going? . . . Yeah, it's all good, it happens. . .

No, I actually called for something else. My girlfriend is trying to start a boarding school for inner-city kids."

His girlfriend? My body heats and my cheeks warm. Is that what I am? Even though he said he wanted me all to himself, I still doubted him, but hearing him call me his girlfriend . . .

I'm at a loss for words.

Hearing the words changes everything about last night. I can't deny that I love the idea, *but wow*, I didn't realize that's what I was.

"Yeah, it's great, man. She's thought about everything. It's going to be co-ed, year-round that does seminars and works on all academic areas. It'll also help them plan a future . . . Sure did. I invested two hundred and fifty thousand." He chuckles. "Not all of us can be NBA superstars. I'm running down my list of people I thought would be interested. Can I count you in? . . . Solid. I will get all the information over to you ASAP . . . Later, man."

He secured more money.

"He's in for three million." A slow grin spreads across his face while the air rushes out of me.

"Three million?" I squeak.

He nods and fist pumps the air.

"Oh my God, Pierce."

I throw my arms around him and pull him into the longest, hardest kiss I've ever been part of. After several minutes, we pull apart.

"It's a great idea and really needed, Lindsey. You could change so many kids' lives. It'll be hard for people not to see that. This is only the beginning."

Those words are so loaded. *Only the beginning.* Only the beginning for the boarding school, but also the beginning of us, because in this moment, I don't want anything but him. All of him. Every second of the day. Our pasts do not define us, and

I'm tired of not living my best life. I'm all in with him.

Lifting up to my tiptoes, I kiss his jaw and then his mouth. "Make love to me," I whisper against his lips. He doesn't answer, just sweeps me into his arms and makes his way into the bedroom. He places me softly on the bed.

"Turn off the lights," I say.

He gives me a puzzled look, but then he nods and obeys. I'm thankful he didn't question me. Tonight has been too wonderful to bog myself down with insecurities. Or worse, pity. The idea of him seeing my scars, of him seeing the puckered skin from my accident, is too much right now. I just want to enjoy him.

Once the light is off, he moves back over to me. Slowly he undresses both of us until we're naked. Then he lies on the bed while sheathing himself with a condom. I crawl on top of him and slowly lower myself until he's fully encased in my body. Though dark in the room, his eyes shine brightly at me, filled with so many emotions, my body heats. I rise and then lower myself, taking him deeper and deeper with each movement of my body. I keep up the pace, finding a rhythm somewhere between lust and love. But the more I watch him, the more I witness my own feelings reflecting back at me from his eyes, the more my movements become erratic, showing him with my body how I feel.

I'm coming undone but strong arms bracket around me, keeping me grounded to him, sealing his lips on mine, promising without words that he'll never let me go.

CHAPTER THIRTY-ONE

Pierce

"Hey, are you busy? I wanted to talk to you about something," I say as I enter Carson's office and sit down in the chair in front of his desk. He looks up at me and sets his pen down.

"Sure what's going on?" he asks.

"Thanks for your help," I mumble back as my fingers tap on the table.

"No problem. It's no big deal."

I shake my head adamantly at him. "Nah. It *is* a big deal, at least to me. I know you know my brothers, obviously, and you could have easily just brushed me off as another fuck up. But you didn't. And I'll forever appreciate that."

His blue eyes bear the semblance of something at my words, maybe pride. "I can't say I know all about it, but from someone who fucked up a lot, I try to never listen to what others say. All that matters to me is the now, not the past, and right now I'm proud. You've been doing great, and the boys love you."

I'm startled by his words, taken aback, and I don't know how to respond. I'm robbed of my words and a silence descends on us. All I can do is stare. *He is proud.* The confirmation of what I thought has knocked the wind out of me.

"You okay?" he asks.

"Yeah. Thanks, man. They mean a lot to me too. So, there's something I wanted to discuss with you."

"Have at it." He leans forward onto his desk to rest his chin in his hand. Giving me the stage to speak.

"Lindsey has this great idea, for a boarding school. A place where kids can go to be safe."

"Yeah, I know. I gave her some info to get in touch with the state."

"So, the thing is, she's working day and night on this and I want to help."

"Okay, what do you have in mind?" he says as he studies me.

"I was thinking we could do a fundraiser of some sort. Something with the boys to raise money. The kids can do maybe a telethon or something."

"Hmm I love it"—he bobs his head—"but it needs to be more."

I look around the room and my gaze collides with Carson's running gear in the corner. "What about a run of some sort?"

"Yes, great idea," he exclaims, and by the way his lips spread across his face I know he really does.

"Figured you would," I say, nodding to the sneakers, and he chuckles.

"Do you want to plan the logistics?"

"I think I'll let Lindsey do that."

At my words, Carson's forehead creases and then he nods. "She's lucky to have you as a friend." But as the smirk he can't suppress peeks out across his face, it's obvious he knows we are so much more.

CHAPTER THIRTY-TWO

Lindsey

EARLY MORNING LIGHT STREAMS IN THROUGH THE drapes in my bedroom, blinding me as I rub furiously at my eyes.

Is it morning already?

How did morning come so fast? Didn't I just fall asleep? No, apparently not, as my sleep laced eyes open reluctantly. I'm so tired it hurts. I guess that's to be expected when you can't sleep. The week has passed, but Pierce's words still hang over me even days later. He's right. I need to talk to my father, ask him to invest, but this time I need to go see him, face-to-face and tell him about my idea.

Maybe then he'll notice you. Maybe then he'll pay attention and when he hears how much time and thought you put into this, he'll be proud. Last night I tossed and turned, trying to think of what to say to my father. Hours later, and only a handful of *z*'s under my belt, I still haven't thought of anything. But what I do know is that I need to take the day off from work and I need to call and make sure they aren't short-staffed.

Determined I can't put off seeing my father any longer, I reach for my phone and scroll through the contacts until I find the number.

On the third ring, Carson answers. "Hey, Carson," I say into the receiver.

"Hey. Everything okay?" he asks, which doesn't surprise me. I never call the center.

"I hate to do this to you, but I have someplace I need to be today. Please tell me you're not short-staffed."

"I've got plenty of help today, but what's going on? You're worrying me."

"I'm good. It's nothing bad. I-I just need to confront some-one." A nervous laugh bubbles through my mouth. "Wish me luck."

"Lindsey, you don't need luck. If anyone gets stuff done, it's you. When you walked in this door all those months ago, you could barely walk without a cane. Now look at you. When was the last time you needed assistance? Every week you grow stronger and stronger. You managed to survive something most wouldn't. You managed to hold your head high no matter the circumstance. Whatever this is, whatever you have to face, I have no doubt you'll conquer it and come out on top."

"Thank you. I can't tell you how much I needed to hear that right now."

"Happy to be of service." He chuckles. "Okay, go do what you have to do. I'll talk to you later. If you need me, remember I'm always here."

"Thanks, Carson. I'll touch base later."

I hang up, walk into my closet, and throw on a pair of black pants, a white blouse, and a blazer. I might not want to talk to my father, but at least I'll look the part marching into his Park Avenue office. After I'm dressed, I proceed to sit in front of the mirror for what seems like an hour, conjuring up the right fa-cade to present to my father.

I need to conquer this hurdle.

Now, two hours later, I'm ready to see him. Presenting

myself to Jeffery Walker, aka Dad, is like stepping on a battle-field the morning before a war; you never know how the battle will turn out. You'll probably suffer many casualties, but you're there anyway.

I walk right past his assistant without acknowledging her. I hear her call out my name and try to stop me, but I'm already flinging his office door open.

There he is, looking superior as always, sitting behind his obnoxiously ostentatious desk in his ridiculous office with the floor-to-ceiling windows. I might have grown up with a silver spoon in my mouth, but Jeffery Walker's office is a whole new level of opulent. From the top floor of a building he owns, he runs the world, or at least the world of oil. One would expect him to work in Texas, but who needs to do that when he can fly there for a meeting in his own jet . . . one of the many in his fleet.

Dad might have made his billions in oil, but he likes to pre-tend he's old New York money, like a Rockefeller or something. I don't know who he's trying to fool, but he made sure growing up I'd never have a hint of an accent. That I always sounded like the upper crust of society. I imagine this is because he, in fact, isn't old money at all. Rather, he was raised in a small house, in a small town, and just happened to strike it rich.

Sometimes, looking around, I wonder if he's happy. Or whether we'd be better off with less. Maybe then he'd care?

He looks up and his eyes widen at my presence. There's no question he's been caught off guard and he's not happy. His sec-retary will get an earful, that's for sure. I can't even feel bad for surprising him. After all the times he's put me off, he deserves it. I do feel a little regret for his assistant, but not enough to not have done it.

"I'm done!" I scream at him, acting completely unhinged.

His brow rises and confusion plays across his face. Each line and wrinkle begs me to clarify what I'm done with. "The fact you don't know is pathetic."

"Lindsey, I can see you're upset. Why don't you sit down and tell me what's going on?"

"Don't patronize me, Dad. Sending me money; not calling me; pretending for one minute that you care, then ignoring me again in the next. Stop. Don't pretend anymore. I'm sick of it. I'm sick of this bullshit," I hiss. "But most of all, I'm sick of you thinking you can buy me off. I don't want your damn money."

"What do you want?"

"I want my dad. I want my father. I don't want you to send me money. I want you to talk to me. I want you and Mom to be a part of my life. When I woke up in the hospital that day, I thought I finally had it. Seeing Mom cry, seeing you cry, I thought that would change everything, but has it? Where have you been?" A tear slips down my cheek. I try to fight them back, but instead, a sob falls from my lips. "Where have you been?"

"I've been here the whole time, I haven't gone anywhere."

"But that's the thing. Sending me money. No questions asked, that's not what I want. I want to help these kids. I want to invest my money to help them and I want you to talk to me about it, strategize with me about it. Come up with ideas with me on a Sunday night. I want dinner with you and Mom. I want for us to discuss my hopes and my dreams, my aspirations. I want you to tell me what's going on in your day. I just want to be normal. Working at the center has made me realize I'm no different than these kids. Sure, I have money, but I still lack guidance. Still lack love."

"Your mom and I—"

"I know you love me. I do. Truly I do. I know you love me in your own way, but I need more. And to be honest, if you can't give me that, I don't know where we go from here."

He sits and thinks for a minute, pulling his hands through his hair. He looks visibly shaken. *Good.* Maybe now he sees me. He takes a deep breath. "I'm so sorry. I never knew. What can I do? How can I fix this?"

"Just be here. Be here for me," I whisper. Tired.

"I will. I'll be here. I'll do better," he promises. We sit in silence. I'm not sure how long, but eventually he looks up from his deep thought.

"Starting now." He sits up taller, places his hands on his desk, and cocks his head. "Talk to me. Tell me what I can do to help? I know you want to help these kids. What can I do?"

And for the first time since I've been in this office, hell, for the first time in a long time, I feel genuine hope. I see us at the crossroad of something important and know we're headed in the right direction.

I proceed to tell him all about my plans and he vows to help me. I leave his office with a plan in motion. Together we'll find a location. He'll help with the funds. He'll be there for me. He'll be there for everything.

When I arrive at Pierce's doorstep, I fall into his arms, emotionally spent but also relieved from my talk with my dad. He holds me for a minute before looking into my eyes.

"Not that I'm complaining, but what brought that about?"

"Good day."

His hand caresses the swell of my breast, trailing down to the hollow of my belly. "Care to elaborate?"

"In a minute. First, tell me about yours."

"I spoke to Carson today."

"You did? About what? Is everything okay?"

Pierce places a hand on my arm and rubs up and down in a comforting manner.

"Everything is better than okay. I hope you don't mind, but I know you told him about your plans, and your wanting to raise money for the kids and he was so excited, that he wanted to plan something too. He wants in. He wants to offer you all his help. I suggested a fundraiser. Something with the kids and he loved the idea."

Without giving him a chance to finish, I lift up on my tiptoes and kiss him. Next thing I know he's pushing me back against the wall. His lips press deeper into mine and his hand runs up the side of my torso, stopping right below my breast. When he swipes a finger over my nipple, my body becomes electrified with need, eliciting a mewl from me. At the sound, his kiss becomes hungrier. Then he pulls away and his mouth trails soft kisses on my flesh. With each press of his lips to my skin, I lose myself to him until I'm unable to control myself any longer. I lower my hand to his pants and press it against him. He's rock-hard beneath the fabric.

His mouth is back on mine, our tongues colliding at a frantic rate. We're desperate for each other. He pulls us to the floor, placing his body behind me, neither of us caring that the cold tile bites at our skin. The chill does nothing to alleviate the heat burning inside me—inside *us*. His hand tugs my pants down to my knees, and then he pushes gently on my back, forcing me to lean on my elbows on all fours as he spreads my legs.

The sound of the ripping of the condom wrapper has me desperate, panting, and squirming for him to touch me, but instead, it feels like an eternity passes as I wait. Then it happens.

He thrusts.

In . . .

Then out.

In . . .

Then out.

The sensation is too much as he slams inside me.

The feeling that's building is unreal.

Unearthly. A possession.

Our bodies come together in sweet perfection.

A primal intensity grows between us until we're both on the brink of an eruption.

Building.

Building.

When I feel his body shudder within me, I fall over the edge. We lie on the floor, sated. His hand tickles me.

"No way, Lindsey." He tickles in earnest. "No way are you getting away with telling me nothing. If I have to, I'll tickle it out of you."

And as I fall into a fit of giggles, I know he's telling the truth, so I turn onto my back and swat his hands away. "Okay. Okay. I'll tell you. But I need to eat first."

"Good girl. What to feed you . . .?" He raises his brow suggestively.

"Food, Pierce. Food. Like the kind you find in the fridge. Or better yet, pantry. What do you have?"

"Not a whole lot of anything, actually."

I stand, pull my pants back up, and make my way into his kitchen. Opening the cupboard doors, I rummage around. It's slim pickings, but that's okay. I'm used to empty cabinets in my apartment.

"Sorry about that. Grocery day comes tomorrow." He laughs.

"Well, we have two choices. We can order in, or we can eat peanut butter and jelly sandwiches."

"My call is on sandwiches *if* you make them naked."

I roll my eyes at him but start to make one anyway even though I'm not naked. Five minutes later, I've made two sandwiches and wave them in the air at him as I wink suggestively.

I take a bite and he gives me his signature smirk. It's as if this snack has become foreplay. The thought makes me laugh. Only with Pierce.

"Perfection. Now tell me about today," he says as he lifts the sandwich to his mouth.

"I saw my dad today," I deadpan.

His hand stops moving and he turns toward me. His eyes find mine, his gaze steady, waiting for me to go on. When I don't, he places his meal back on his plate and prompts me. "And?"

"It was actually good."

"Must be nice," he mutters under his breath.

"Surprisingly, it was. You should try it sometime."

"Yeah, I'll take a pass on that."

I take his hands in mine. "No, really, you should. I can't tell you how much of a weight has been lifted off my shoulders. For so many years, I've held onto so much animosity. Animosity that was never needed. If I had just been upfront about how I felt years ago, I would've saved myself so much time and heartbreak. I was too scared, Pierce. Scared of rejection. Scared of not being enough. But for what? Don't be like me. Don't waste another day."

"That's easy for you to say."

I push back, separating us. "Easy for me to say? You have no idea about my life, Pierce. You think I don't know what it's like to be last? To feel unwanted? I spent my whole life feeling like this. I understand how you feel. All I'm saying is you don't need to waste another day feeling this way. You can change this. You can change."

"I can't."

"You can. You're just too scared, and I understand that, but there's nothing to be scared of. Just try."

"I don't know if I can."

"Will you . . . will you at least think about it? For me?"

"Yes." He gets up and then proceeds to lift me into his arms.

"Where are you taking me?"

"To bed, obviously."

"Didn't we just do that?"

"I mean to bed, bed. You're sleeping over."

"I am?"

"Yeah."

"Do I have a choice in the matter? Maybe I have someplace I need to be tonight. Or better yet, maybe I have someplace I need to be tomorrow." I smirk at him. "Ever think about that?" I stick out my tongue.

"Nope. What I say goes and you're staying. End of story."

I roll my eyes at him and he pulls me closer, nuzzling his mouth to my ear.

"I want you next to me when I wake up."

Those words make me shut up and melt in his embrace.

CHAPTER THIRTY-THREE

Pierce

For the first time in a long time, I sleep. I don't just sleep through the night, I sleep peacefully. It's crazy how you take the small things for granted. How energized you feel after not spending the night worrying. How invigorated you feel when you finally feel comfort. I know why. It's Lindsey. She's why I feel this way. Lindsey does this for me.

I turn my head and look at where she's lying, her arm draped across my chest, her hair fanned across the white pillow. The contrast between her dark locks and the pristine pillow is striking. A familiar urge to paint her takes root inside me, and I can't help but smile at the thought. It's been a while since I've wanted to paint something as simple as beauty, but that's what she is inside and out. She is beautiful. The best part, the part that makes her genuine, is that she has no idea how fucking gorgeous she is. She's like a ray of sunshine that has come and brightened my life. Like that first glimpse of spring after a long winter.

I could do this every day.

Holy shit.

I could do this every day. This could be my life. I could wake up in the middle of the night and Lindsey would be in my bed. Sounds pretty fucking perfect to me.

With a reach of my hand, I run it down the curve of her hip.

Even in her sleep, she inches toward me, seeking my heat. A thought crosses my mind. I could take her now. I could lose myself in her. And I should.

She moans as my hand trails lower. She's like a cat in heat. It makes me chuckle. "What are you doing?" she says, her voice still laced with sleep.

"Trying to have my way with you," I respond nonchalantly.

"Try all you like, but first can I eat?"

As if on cue, I hear her stomach rumble.

"Yeah, yeah, yeah," I chide, all while making my path lower.

"Wait. Seriously, what time is it?" she asks. I pull my gaze away from her and look at the clock.

"Oh, shit. It's after nine. Looks like breakfast will have to wait."

She stretches her arms above her head and shakes off any remaining sleep. "How did I not wake up?"

I shrug. "Guess I relaxed you."

"More like exhausted me."

"Yeah, probably more that." Standing, I make my way over to the closet and grab her one of my robes. When I return to the bed, I hand it to her. She smiles in appreciation.

"You were pretty insatiable," she says as she puts it on and stands in front of me.

"Speaking of insatiable . . ." I pull her until our lips are hovering over one another. But instead of kissing her, I lower my head and place my lips on the soft skin on her neck and trail my tongue down her flesh. She swats at me.

"Will you stop that? We're going to be late."

"Fine," I say begrudgingly. "Let's get dressed." I walk back to the closet and grab some clothes, but when I return, her back is to me and she's no longer in my robe. My gaze sweeps over her perfect ass.

Fuck.

My dick gets hard and a groan escapes. Turning her head over her shoulder, she rolls her eyes.

"None of that." She walks off toward the bathroom and I can't help but watch. "Go shower."

"Shouldn't we shower together, conserve water?" Now, that's a good idea.

"No." Her tone is short and I wonder why, but instead of asking, I just walk into the bathroom and turn the water on. Lindsey's been weird about being naked with me, not sure why as her body is banging, but to each their own. *I guess.*

Thirty minutes later, we're finally dressed and we head out the door, stopping at Starbucks to grab a coffee to go for her. Fifteen minutes later, we walk into Polaris.

Yeah, I could get used to this.

I turn to Lindsey. "You need to speak to Carson. I told him a little about it already when we spoke, but I think you should speak to him today about it too."

"Should I?"

"Of course you should. This is your baby. If you feel passionately enough about it to speak to your father, of course, you need to talk to Carson and make sure it happens."

She thinks for a minute before nodding. "Yeah, I'll go find him now."

I take her hand and squeeze it once. "I'm proud of you, Lindsey. Her lips spread into a smile. I'm proud of her. I wish I could be more like her.

Maybe one day I can.

CHAPTER THIRTY-FOUR

Lindsey

"Hey, guys." Carson smiles as we walk into his office. "I can't tell you how excited I am for this fundraiser. What a fabulous idea, Lindsey."

"Oh, I can't take credit for it. This idea was Pierce's. And yours, I hear."

It certainly wasn't mine. When he pitched me the fun run idea, I didn't tell Pierce how much it hurt to know I wouldn't be able to participate. It stung deep to the bone, though, every scar across my leg feeling singed with pain. I smile anyway, because no matter my objections to the idea, it was a fabulous one.

"You guys did good." I wink.

"All him." Carson points over at him and gives me a look. I know he's silently telling me, *I told you so*. I bob my head and tell him back without words, *you were right*.

"It might've been my idea, but this is all you," Pierce says, as he takes my hand and puts it on his lap. Carson's eyes widen as he stares at us.

"So, is this a new thing?" he asks while looking at our entwined hands.

"New, but a long time coming," Pierce replies, and at that Carson lets out a full and boisterous laugh. I can't help but join in.

"Okay, let's talk about the fundraiser. Any ideas?" Carson says.

"I'm going to defer to you since this was your idea," I answer, looking at Pierce.

"Well, I've been thinking a lot about it, and I think the best idea would be to have the kids run, as well as the adults. Adults will have to buy in, and I'm thinking the kids will need to be sponsored."

Carson nods at Pierce's suggestion.

"I have a long list of potential donors."

"Me too," Carson says. "I've collected a ton of names. Plus, I have all our past donors, including the ones who haven't donated since we started the place. I think we should aim for the first week of November."

"Will that give us enough time?" Pierce asks.

"Yeah, totally. During the next few weeks, we can divide and conquer. I'll prepare the details. The kids can reach out to the potential donors with us. That way they feel involved. We can also reach out to some of my contacts in marketing and publicity."

"That's a great idea. And I do have some money we can—"

"No, Lindsey," Carson cuts me off. "There's no need for you to give anything else. I'm sure we can get the marketing done for free. Bridget Lancaster does marketing. Maybe she'll volunteer."

At the sound of her last name, the muscles in Pierce's hand tighten around me, cutting off my circulation.

"It's a great idea." I look over at Pierce and squeeze him twice.

He furrows his brow while he lets go. He's still grinding his teeth with unspoken words.

This makes him uncomfortable. Maybe even angry. I can read Pierce pretty well, and he's definitely not happy. Bridget is married to his brother Grant, so he obviously doesn't want her involved due to his strained relationship with his family. I wait for him to protest. To object. But he doesn't. He keeps quiet, and that selfless move makes me fall for him even more.

"So, where should we start?" I finally say, needing to break the silence before it becomes obvious to Carson that there's an issue.

"Let's look at the list, divide it, and we'll each start working on our part. I'll reach out to Bridget also. Pierce will reach out to some of his contacts. Lindsey, you'll work with the kids to get donations. Sound good?"

"Sounds great."

"With the weather, we only have a few weeks to set this up. We're going to have to work really hard. We can't risk an early snow. You can never tell what'll happen in November."

He's right. In New York anything is possible.

CHAPTER THIRTY-FIVE

Pierce

LINDSEY IS WORKING ON LOGISTICS FOR THE RUN, SO I'M just lying on my couch looking at the papers she brought over a few weeks ago when the phone rings.

The name glaring back at me startles me. Spencer.

That's a name I wasn't expecting. Sure he checks in, but honestly, ninety percent of the time, he sends a text.

"Hello?" I answer.

"Your presence is requested at dinner," he offers up in his usual condescending tone. It drips off him. It's funny because even if he's not trying, he still exudes arrogance. I guess that's an occupational hazard for being a big shot CEO. No matter what you say, you make it sound like everyone is inferior to you.

"Hello to you too, Spencer." I roll his name over my tongue in the same stuck-up fashion in which he issued the invitation. I know the saying kill them with kindness, but in this case, it's more like reap what you sow. He wants to be a stuck-up ass, so I can act like one too.

"Mom wants you there, so I expect you there," he hisses, obviously not finding my tone funny.

"Well, I'd hate to let you down."

He doesn't respond to my sarcastic quip, but his lack of response is answer enough . . .

I already let him down.

Three hours later I find myself pulling my Range Rover into The Lancaster compound. It looks exactly like it did the last time I was here, last year. When my father had a heart attack.

I imagine the welcome I'll receive tonight will be just as friendly as when Spencer gave me all his thoughts on not showing up at the hospital to see Dad.

"Get your pathetic ass over here," he hissed into my voicemail. *"You're a disgrace. Even Grant showed up. Even fucking Grant is here. You're an embarrassment to the Lancaster name."*

I was out of the country . . .

Truth, I don't remember where the fuck I was. I was in the middle of a bender somewhere. Out of the country. Not checking my phone. By the time I turned it on, I had over ten messages ranging from concern to full-on death threats from Spencer and more surprisingly Grant, who at the time was hated almost as much as me. Eventually, I showed up.

That was beginning of the end for big brother and me.

I let myself in, using the key I have always had but seldom use. Walking through my childhood home, I'm still taken aback by the sheer immensity of the space. Vaulted ceilings and priceless art lead me to where I hear voices. My mind becomes lost in the vastness, memories hitting me like a tsunami. A vision of myself as a young child, I'd fallen asleep in the room under the window where a large armoire used to be back then. I was playing hide and seek with Spencer and Grant at the time, but they must have given up looking. When my parents finally found me, they were so relieved and wouldn't stop hugging me. I remember the feeling of being loved and secure and comforted. How different things became since then.

Now there is no armoire, and no hugs to be had.

"He lives . . ." Spencer says as I walk in through the large archway leading into the living room. Olivia swats at him and he shrugs as if he has no idea why she's giving him a hard time.

"Pierce, darling you're here." My mom's voice sounds far away and lost in thought. She looks at me with an unfocused haze and unshed tears. Sad and confused. Both emotions making me feel uneasy to hear and see them. I know I haven't been perfect but why don't they understand? I stayed away because I *had* to. Because I could never live under the shadow they all cast down upon me. Being the forgotten child is incomprehensible to them. Harder than any of them could ever fathom because while they were jetting off, living their lives, I was raised by a nanny. And when I begged for attention, I got money deposited into my account.

I think that's why I feel so connected to Lindsey. She gets it. She gets me. She knows what it's like to be swept under the rug because everyone is too busy living their own damn lives to see you.

"Hey." I look over to see Grant, Bridget, and my niece Isabella looking out the window in the corner of the room. Bridget walks over to me, holding Isabella's hand. "Do you remember your uncle?"

"No," her soft voice replies.

"That's not a surprise," Spencer says under his breath. I hear him, but I don't turn toward him, I have no intention of giving him the satisfaction of knowing I'm bothered.

My dad is sitting in the burgundy and gold ornate wing chair next to my mom's. He looks paler then I remember, not as strong or scary as the big powerful man I grew up fearing and being in awe of at the same time. "Dad." I nod in his direction. When he doesn't get up, just looks at me with narrowed eyes, I wonder why I'm even here. No one wants me here, that's obvious, and I'm not sure why I should stay.

Thankfully, I'm saved by the bell as a member of my parents' domestic staff informs us that dinner is served. God, how pretentious is this? Why can't they just hang in the kitchen while dinner is prepared, *like a normal family*?

Nope, not The Lancasters. I guess if you employ a staff of five to make sure your immense household runs smoothly, a *figurative* bell is still rung for dinner . . .

Together we all head to the formal dining room.

The meal is tedious.

No one speaks to me. No one asks me what I'm doing. All they do is talk about the expansion of The Lancaster and The L.

I stare at the grandfather clock for one whole hour, listening to the hand moving painfully slow.

Tick.

Tock.

Tick.

Tock.

Then it happens. Someone finally acknowledges the big elephant in the room, and the reason I'm here. And that someone is my father.

"So tell us, what are you planning on doing once your time is over at Polaris?" my father asks.

"I haven't really thought about that yet—"

"Don't you think you should? Don't you think you should have a game plan?" Spencer cuts in.

"Why don't I just make this easier on all of us? Why don't you tell me what I can do to fit into your damn bubble?" I snap, fed up with this evening. At my outburst, Grant stands and turns to Bridget and inclines his head down. Silently saying they are leaving. He scoops Isabella into his arms and the three exit the room. As soon as they are gone, my father crosses his arms in front of his chest as his mouth opens.

"Don't speak to your brother like that," he chimes in. "He's only asking what we are all wondering. Do you have a game plan? Do you have any idea how you're going to support yourself?"

"Support myself?" I ask. My trust will support me . . . won't it?

Spencer must notice my conclusion because he speaks instead of my father, his arms hitting the table to lean in. *Shit.* He means business. This can't possibly be good.

"There is a stipulation in the trust that *if* you are deemed incompetent . . ." Spencer's words trail off with the desired attention, letting me come to the life-changing conclusion by myself.

My heart thumps hard in my chest as my stomach drops. "I get nothing?" I don't understand what is going on. How did this happen? How did I not know?

"If—"

"Let me get this straight." I stand pushing away from the table and looking directly at my father. "If Prince-Mother-Fucker-Spencer deems me unfit, I get nothing."

My mother gasps at my outburst before biting her lip and motioning for me to sit back in the chair. "Pierce, please," my mother says.

"No, I won't sit. Is this shit real, Dad?"

"We're only doing what we think is best," he responds.

"Are you for real? Are you fucking for real right now?"

"Do not speak in front of your mother that way."

"So *this* is why I was asked here. This is why you are all here, like a goddamn intervention. 'Shape up or ship out.'" I air quote. "Do what you want me to do or lose everything. Good to fucking know." I jerk my head in Spencer's direction. "Wow"—my hands tightened into fists as I stare him down—"you really do have delusions of grandeur." I turn my back to them, my mom speaking behind me begging me to stay.

But I'm already gone.

CHAPTER THIRTY-SIX

Pierce

A T FIRST, I'M TOO ANGRY TO DRIVE. I'M ALL OVER THE damn place in my mind. Thank fuck I get back to the city safely because I barely remember the ride.

When I pull into the city, I wonder where I should go.

Lindsey.

I pick up the phone and call her: voicemail.

Fuck.

She must be still out to dinner with Amelia.

Looking down at the clock I see it's already ten. Where the hell has the night gone? Too much anger is inside me to go home. Too many emotions swirling in my lungs, choking me, has me picking up the phone and calling Linc.

"Where you at?"

"Pre-game. My place."

"I'll be there."

Ten minutes later, I'm riding the elevator up to Linc's apartment. When I walk into his place, he pulls me into a hug, slapping my back. "Bro, where you been? It's been too damn long."

"Busy with volunteering." I shrug.

"You're still doing that shit? Tough break."

A part of me wants to say it's your damn fault I'm in this mess, but I was the driver. I should have known better. "You're telling me."

"Well, you're here now. So let's fucking party! Tequila, vodka
. . . both?"

"Tequila."

Next thing I know, extra chilled glasses are being passed
around and all the guys are taking shots. I haven't hung out with
them for weeks, but it's like old times. Like I haven't missed a
beat. However, with every drink a desire inside me intensifies,
it's like a dam is breaking, pouring out and spilling over every
surface.

"Anyone got any blow?" With the fresh booze flooding my
blood and all my inhibitions fading away, the words pop out of
my mouth before I can take them back.

"Nah, not yet. About to hit up my guy though. You want in?"

Do I want in? "Hell, yeah."

After sending a series of texts, Linc pats me on the back.
"Time to head out. My guy is meeting me at Lit and he's got an
eight ball with your name on it."

"Let's go."

Once at the club, Linc looks at his phone and smiles broadly.
He tips back his drink and then stalks off to the corner of the
room by the bathroom. He's talking to someone, but in the dark
space, I can't make out who it is. All I see are his eyes reflecting
against the dim light peeking out from the bathroom door as it
flings open.

Dark. Sinister. That must be his guy.

I lift the glass up one more time and let the burn sting as it
goes down.

I'm drunk.

I'm so drunk, the room is spinning and I can barely
stand. Linc is back already and I'm too fucked up to realize that
he's already laid out the coke on the table. The line is spread

long, in the wide open, for everyone to see and no one says a word. *Got to love the security at Lit.*

"You're up first, man," Linc says as he hands me a freshly rolled up hundred-dollar bill. Benjamin Franklin peeks up where it's folded over. *Go big or go home, I guess.*

I take the bill and lean down. I'm a live wire of nervous energy the closer I get. One hand lifts to close the opposite nostril and on instinct, my eyes close. My movements halt and bile collects in my throat as a feeling of hate, of hating myself, floods my system.

I'm pathetic.

I'm weak.

Just do it. If you do it, you'll feel strong.

Against the backdrop of my lids that are still closed, I see her reflection: Lindsey.

Her smile.

Her eyes.

Her lips part. She looks at me.

With pride.

She looks at me like I'm her knight in shining armor.

As if the suns rises and sets when I'm around.

She looks at me like I'm everything.

As if I make her happy.

As if I can be so much more.

My eyes fling open. The white powder so close if I inhale I'll be high. What am I doing? I can't do this . . .

I hate myself for being so weak.

"*You aren't weak.*" Her voice plays in my ear. I can hear it. Clear as day. "*You haven't done it yet. Walk away.*"

In the same moment, I hear Spencer . . . "*You have no plans. What are you doing with your life?*"

I try to shake away the opposing voices in my ear: the angel and the demon.

The muscles in my back tighten.

The dark voice inside me is winning over.

I'm about to resume my position when the bill is snatched from my hand. "You snooze you lose, bro."

A round of chuckles are had at my expense as Linc leans forward and takes the line intended for me. He leans up, a Cheshire grin on his face as he inhales deeply. "Shit," he exhales as he pulls back holding one nostril and sucking in.

I stare at him half in contempt and half in appreciation for taking my choice off the table. I'm contemplating what to do next. Should I line up another one? Lose myself in the oblivion?

Looking up I turn to ask for the bag when I notice . . .

Seizing.

His body falls to the floor.

"Get up." I roll his body, shaking it violently. His eyes won't open. "Fucking wake up!"

"Shit, someone needs to call nine-one-one!"

A frenzy of people . . .

The music stopping . . .

The paramedics rushing in . . .

Then the cops.

He's pronounced dead on the spot.

I'm numb.

I'm hurting.

I hate myself.

Questions are asked, so many questions:

Who bought the drugs? Linc bought the drugs.

Did anyone see the drug dealer? No. Well, not really. Just his eyes. Black eyes. Dark as the night. They haunt me.

But it's not just his eyes that haunt me. It's them. *All of them.* I can feel their eyes, all of them staring at me. Probably hating me as much as I hate myself. The line was for me. I should be dead.

It should have been me.

"Want to share a cab?" Trey asks, pulling me out of my sordid thoughts. Looking up, I notice that the club has finally emptied and it's just us standing where the body of our friend used to be.

"Nah, I'm good."

Trey's expression stills and grows serious. His brows knit together. "You shouldn't be alone." His voice sounds tired.

"I won't be alone." Broke and hoarse, splintered pieces, fractured glass. That's how I feel. As if I'm a picture frame that's been beaten by a hammer, and all that's left are shards.

He bows his head and then his shoulders lift before he turns. We begin to walk out together in disbelief, the reality of the situation finally falling on top of me. I can feel my hands shake. When I'm outside, the air hits my face bringing me out of my daze.

Trembling, I pull out my phone, praying she'll answer this time.

"I need you."

———————•✦•———————

I fall when I see her. To the ground, knees hitting the wood floor beneath me. I'm tired, so fucking tired. My head tips down and a harrowing feeling spreads across my chest. And when she kneels beside me, I lose it. Everything I was holding back pours out of me in silent screams and tear-stained cheeks. The feeling of her hand on my back tells me she's got me, and I welcome it, *to know someone finally does.* If she hurts in this position, she doesn't say so. Instead, she stays on the ground with me for what seems like an endless amount of time as I cry. I can't remember the last time I've cried.

Years . . .

When I can finally breathe again, she stands and reaches her hand down to help me up. A small movement, but monumental. This girl, Lindsey Walker, is lifting me up and it means everything.

When we are in her room, she points to the bed and I get in, she gets in beside me.

"Tell me what happened?"

"Linc," I whisper. "My friend. He died."

She pulls me into her embrace again. "I'm so sorry."

"It should have been me," I confess.

She moves away and sits up, looking down at me. "I don't understand."

I know what I'm about to tell her might make her angry. Fuck, she might leave me, but she deserves to know the kind of man she is with.

"I had a bad night," I try to explain. But it doesn't matter the rationale, I know I was weak. I know I was wrong. "I made a mistake." My voice cracks and I hate that I have to do this.

She reaches out and takes my hand, her soft fingers trailing on my skin. "Talk to me. Tell me what happened."

Inhale.

Exhale.

"I saw my family. It was bad. In a moment of weakness, I got drunk, made bad decisions, and well . . . I almost got fucked-up." I don't need to clarify. Lindsey was in the scene for years. She knows what I mean when I say, "got fucked-up."

Her eyes widen as her face noticeably pales. When I don't continue, she squeezes my hand, telling me without words that no matter what, she's here for me. She's not going anywhere.

The gesture is enough for me to find the words that have gotten lodged in my throat.

"The line . . ." I pause and swallow. "The line was for me. I was supposed to take the first line." My heart thumps erratically in my chest over my confession as I wait for her to respond, as I wait for her to finally see me for the fuckup I am and tell me she's done.

The room is quiet. The only sound comes from our breathing. My declaration hangs in the air, suffocating me with the silence that follows.

"Why didn't you?" she finally whispers.

"Because of you. I didn't because of you. I stopped . . . for you."

"You can't stop for me. You need to stop for you."

"I have." I let my head fall forward into my hands. She moves in and hugs me, softly coos in my ear. Rubbing circles on my back.

"That should have been me."

"I know it."

She knows it.

I know it.

Everyone knows it.

A man is dead because of me.

And I hate myself.

CHAPTER THIRTY-SEVEN

Pierce

THE NEXT MORNING COMES, AN AWKWARD FEELING TAKES root in my psyche. I lost my shit yesterday with Lindsey.

She saw me cry.

Fuck she saw me weep like a baby.

She held me. Rocked me.

Now in the early light of day, I still feel numb. I've always tried so hard to keep walls up. To not let anyone in for fear of the devastation they could cause, but this girl has officially eradicated them all. Blew them the fuck up. Broke every damn resistance I had.

Now what do I do?

Let her in, a voice nags in my head.

And if she sees what's really inside you? How broken you are.

Let her in.

I push the thought away with a loud grown. It's unwelcome right now.

———————◆◆———————

The brisk morning air sends a chill down my spine. Three days have passed.

Three long sleepless days.

I'm still numb. Today is worse than normal because of where I am: standing in front of a row of tombstones. Lindsey wanted to be here, but I told her I wanted to do this alone. But now, standing here, I know I need her. This is unbearable.

The pastor is speaking, but through the sobs all around me, I can't hear his words. Linc was too young to die. He shouldn't have died. *It should have been you.* My heartbeat is too fast. It feels like I'm dying. Like I should be buried alongside him.

He shouldn't have died, the words scream again, my whole body shaking with a suppressed sob that I won't let escape my mouth. The pain inside me burns like an inferno. One lone tear leaks from my eye and my fingers lift quickly to push it away.

I can't fall apart.

I won't.

With a deep inhale, I push it down, allowing the blaze to fade away into ice.

I'm completely numb by the time I arrive at Lindsey's. I'd fired one text to her:

I need you.

I seem to be sending that text often these days, but it's true. I need her warmth, her strength. I need her protection for the baser needs I can't control when I'm like this. I need everything she has to offer.

And she lets me.

She lets me walk into her apartment. I don't even knock. She lets me kiss her. I don't even say hello.

I just consume.

Take.

Take.

Take until I exploit all her resources. Until I'm so spent, I finally fall asleep.

The days pass.

I can't rid myself of this feeling. Luckily, Lindsey has called Carson and explained what was going on. She took some time off to be with me. She hasn't left my side. Not since I left the funeral, a shell of the man I normally am. Broken. She holds me and comforts me. She talks to me when I can't sleep, which is often. And when I do finally fall asleep from my body's exhaustion, it's fleeting, tossing and turning until the early morning hours. Until the sun peeks through the drapes, letting me know a new day has begun.

Again here I am: another night, another nightmare. My body lies in bed and the darkness tries to consume me, my thoughts move faster than I can take.

Flash.

Flash.

Flash.

Sleep eludes in a series of visions behind my closed lids.

Linc.

His face.

His body convulsing.

Him talking to the man in the corner.

Dark eyes, the color of death. They look up and catch me watching. They gleam wicked, a smirk on his face.

Dark eyes . . .

I wake, but the haze of the nightmare lingers.

Another day. Another night where I know sleep won't come. How could it? My eyes won't even close. They know if they do

I'll be plagued with visions.

Why won't they go away?

Why can't I make them stop?

I can't take this anymore.

It needs to stop.

———————•◆•———————

Sleepless nights and endless torment.

I need to refuel.

I need to sleep.

I can't.

The dark of the night haunts me.

The fear of insomnia is my constant companion.

In the middle of the night, without a word, I kiss her on her cheek and leave. As the memories dance in my vision, it feels like ice fills my blood. It blossoms in my chest. Suffocating me. Making it hard to breathe. I need to expel this broken feeling inside me, so I do, the only way I know how.

I paint.

I lift up my paintbrush and pour all that is in me onto the canvas. It feels like every nerve ending inside me is snapping. Like shattered glass. The shards tear me apart, ripping me up, severing me completely.

By the time the light ebbs into the room, signifying that the night has passed, I ache. Everything inside me aches, and my vision is spotty from the lack of sleep. But tonight, a painting stares back at me that's different from the rest of the series of paintings I've been making.

Today, looking back at me are dark eyes. Eyes so black they remind me of obsidian. They stare at me, causing a chill to run up my spine. They're all that I remember from that night.

Something that tastes like copper floods my mouth.

Blood.

With quick steps, I head to the bathroom and open my mouth. Without realizing it, I'd bitten my inner cheek. Still staring in the mirror, I hear the buzzer ring.

Who could be here?

My hand hits the intercom. "Mr. Lancaster, Lindsey Walker is here, sir."

"Send her up."

I open the door wide. Dark circles and disheveled hair show me she's worried. She bites her lip, concern evident on her face.

"You left." She chews on her bottom lip.

"I had to," I respond as I rake my hand through my hair.

She steps past me and starts toward my bedroom and I follow her. Once inside, she sits on my bed and looks up at me. "Do you want to talk about it?"

"No."

To that, she nods and then shakes her head. "I think you should speak to someone. You need to forgive yourself. These nightmares. This not sleeping. It's killing you."

"I don't think I can."

"You can." She smiles with assurance, and for the first time in the last week, I allow myself to believe it.

"Okay."

"What can I do to help?"

I shrug.

"Let me hold you."

"I'm not one of your boys."

She gives me a soft smile. "Aren't you though? Come here."

I move closer and place my head on her chest. Slowly she runs her fingers through my hair lulling me to bed. Taking care of me. Giving me what I need.

I listen to her breathe, calm, the even cadences of each inhale and exhale. It doesn't take long, but eventually, the corded muscles in my body relax.

And sleep finally comes.

"Thanks for last night."

I kiss her slowly. I kiss her passionately. I tell her with a million unspoken words and with the swipe of my tongue how I feel about her, about what she means to me.

She tells me back.

We pour everything that we have into each other.

We strip off our clothes and she lets me love her the only way I know how.

The next day I have an appointment with a Dr. Montgomery. Apparently, he is affiliated with the hospital and his specialty is grief. I don't know what will come of this. *Maybe nothing.* But if I can move forward . . .

Surprisingly, last night was the first time I slept the *whole* night since Linc died. As if the idea of finally voicing my thoughts and feeling today had calmed me.

I walk through the door to his office, my gaze skating across the reception space in front of me. It's surprisingly warm and inviting, with artwork and comfy chairs set up in an intimate fashion. In the corner of the room is a mahogany desk with an older woman sitting behind it. The whole set up is in complete contrast to the front facade of the intimidating skyscraper this office is located in.

"I have an appointment with Dr. Montgomery."

"Please have a seat, and the doctor will be right out," she responds with a warm smile.

I'm staring at my phone when I hear my name being called. I look up and am met with a man who appears older than me, I'd say mid-thirties and wearing a crisp navy suit. My breathing becomes ragged as I cross the room and follow him down the hall and into what must be his office.

"If you want, you can sit on the couch, or the chair?"

I choose the couch. It's red and velvet and looks inviting. Dr. Montgomery takes a seat across the coffee table and then leans forward.

"So, Pierce, what's going on?"

"I can't sleep."

"Can't sleep? Or don't want to sleep?"

"Both."

He nods. "I've worked with many patients who have suffered through nightmares. Often, I've found there is a catalyst. Has something happened?"

"My friend died and I'm having nightmares," I blurt out, my back muscles loosening a fraction, just from unloading this onto him.

"I'm sorry to hear that. This all must be very hard on you." His voice is calm and reassuring. Telling me without words that I can trust him, and I do.

"It is, but it's the nights that are killing me. I can't sleep. I can't close my eyes. I just can't." My hands run through my hair, frustrated, tired.

"Tell me what you dream?"

"The nightmare is always the same."

He picks up a pen and scribbles on his notepad.

"I see him leaning forward. I see him taking the line, I see him dying. Over and over again. I see the eyes. Dark black eyes. I want to stop him. Tell him to not buy the drugs, not for me. It's my fault."

"It's only natural to feel responsible."

"He bought them for me. It's because of me that he's dead. I killed my friend."

"It is not your fault." He lets his words soak in. "You are not responsible for any one's behavior, only your own. You need to forgive yourself."

"How do I do that?" I mumble.

"Only you can answer that. But I think the first step is recognition."

"I have so many regrets, I'm drowning in them. If . . . if I had just done the line myself . . . If I didn't call him to go out."

"You can't say 'if,' you don't know what would have happened, Pierce. You need to move forward. Forgive yourself."

Over the next few weeks, I do what I do best. I throw myself into painting. I throw myself into organizing the run. I throw myself into everything so I don't think.

The only time I allow myself to think of what I lost, of what almost was my fate, is at night. Alone, with my brushes. That's when I bleed.

I bleed my soul into my work.

There's only a few days before the run, and I dread the phone call I have to make. I don't necessarily have to invite Spencer to the run, but this is for Lindsey and having him there means more money for the kids. There is also a place inside me, that I don't like to admit, wants him there to see me run. To see the work I did to help set this up. I hit send and before I can answer he speaks.

"I'm sorry about your friend. Olivia spoke to Lindsey and she told me your friend died of a drug overdose." His words level me. I'm speechless. "I can't imagine what you're going through. I can't say I'm not surprised though—"

"Are you serious right now?" I snarl into the phone, not able to control my rage from what I'm hearing. I'm a live wire that's just been lit, ready to explode. "My goddamn friend is dead and all you can say is you're not surprised."

"Pierce, calm down. I didn't mean it like that."

"Oh, and how exactly did you mean it?"

"I just think that maybe seeing this, acting like this will open your eyes to the way you've been acting."

"Oh, that's fucking rich."

"Meaning?"

"I'm pretty sure you know exactly what I mean."

"I don't think I do."

"Your fiancée. Or did you forget?"

"Stop right there before you say something that you can't take back. Olivia made her mistakes, but she strives to be better." *Unlike you.* That's what he's really saying and I've had enough.

"That's the sad part. You, up there on your pedestal, you have no idea what us mere mortals do."

"I know you still don't have a plan," he huffs.

My fists clench, turning white as my nails bite into the skin of my palm.

"I'm done." I inhale a sharp breath. "You want to see the worst in me . . . then fine." I exhale.

"I want you to grow up and succeed."

"There's no talking to you."

I hang up.

He doesn't call me back.

That's when I realize I never asked him to come.

Doesn't matter anyway, he wouldn't have.

Not worth his precious time.

The thought is sour in my stomach. There was a time before, where I might have reached for the bottle. But that's the thing I have changed.

That was the one thing that Spencer is right about, watching my friend die was the rude awakening I needed.

Ironic that Spencer is too blind or stubborn to know that.

I stalk out of my studio. I can't let him get to me. Dr. Montgomery said I need to focus on my catalyst and redirect.

Find what makes me happy, painting and Lindsey.

Creating.

So I decide to let her in. She's been asking me about my process. Showing her is exactly what I need now to make me happy. With the fun run in two days, I can't be like this. The nightmares are better. Almost completely gone. I'm coming to terms with my roles and what was out of my hands. I've come too far in this month to allow Spencer to bring me down.

CHAPTER THIRTY-EIGHT

Pierce

"**G**ET YOUR SNEAKERS ON. WE'RE GOING FOR A walk," I say, giving no additional information.

Lindsey's brow rises, but she doesn't fight me, and that's what I like. She doesn't ask any questions. She doesn't need to know what we're doing and if it's something she wants. She trusts me. And she's always willing to try something new. There's something so incredibly real about her.

Based on my experiences—and hers as well—I'd expect her to be like every other girl from my past: shallow, self-centered, and whiny. All the things I'm accustomed to from my history with girls. Lindsey used to be one of them, but she's nothing like that now.

She's down to earth, caring, and so willing to jump right in—even if it sounds like work—and have fun. Her perseverance and determination—despite the setbacks from her accident—are incredible. Lindsey isn't the person I always thought she was.

It's easy to get sucked into the party lifestyle, especially when you have more money than you know what to do with it, but it's so much harder to get out of it. Painting has always helped me from not falling into the total abyss of addiction. When life gets to be too much, I take a step back and see the broken people around me. Others have it so much worse than I do. That helps me to channel the anger and apply it to something else—something beautiful.

"Are you going to tell me where we're going?" Lindsey asks, looking out the window.

"Nope. It's a surprise."

The truth is, it's nothing big. She might very well be disappointed, but this is my life, the one I hide from everyone else, and I want to let her in. I've never been more inspired in my life, and right now I want her to see a glimpse of my world.

Before I paint I like to find inspiration and the best way to do it is to observe the city.

Observing is my process. Nothing is better than watching an onlooker's reaction to the different intricacies of the city. A tourist taking in the many homeless men, women, and children during what I'd imagine is their first visit to the city. Their responses ranging from disgust to sadness are so raw. It's in those moments I find inspiration. And New York is full of interesting people with stories I can only dream up. I watch the homeless, listen to the conversations of desperate housewives and bored husbands, and every time, something comes from it. If I'm being honest, it helps me to see I'm not the only broken person in this big world.

Our first stop is going to be to the Bethesda Fountain. There's always such a mix of cultural and socioeconomic people there. I wonder what Lindsey's reaction will be. Surely, she's been there before. Will she be underwhelmed?

"Pierce? Did you hear me?"

My head turns to her. "I'm sorry. What did you say?"

Her eyes widen, and a smile graces her lips. "You seem excited. Will you tell me what we're doing?"

Since we're almost there, I don't see a reason to hide it from her anymore. I stop in my tracks, looking at her and rocking back and forth on my feet. "I want to show you my process for painting."

Her eyes widen marginally. "You do?"

She seems surprised by this. I'm very private about my painting and she knows this, but if I wanted to share it with anyone, she has to know it would be her.

I nod. "I wanna share this with you for all the support you've shown me."

A smile spreads across her face. "Tell me everything," she says, grabbing my hand and walking us forward. There's a skip to her step that wasn't there before. She's excited, which only makes me more excited.

"Typically, I just walk and never know where I'm going to end up. There are so many places in this city to find inspiration, but today, we're going to go to the Bethesda Fountain. It's one of my favorite places."

Moments later we're standing in front of the fountain. I've seen it a million times, so my focus is entirely on Lindsey. Tingles work their way down my spine as I watch her eyes widen and her mouth hang slack. Surely Lindsay Walker can't be in awe of such a mundane thing. I pull out my small sketchpad and begin to capture her in this moment, hoping she doesn't turn away, because I want to remember this second forever.

"For all the years I've lived in the city and walked by this fountain, I've never once stopped," she admits without looking away. "It's beautiful."

She's beautiful.

Her reaction is more than I could have ever hoped for. Someone with the world at her fingertips would typically turn their nose up to the fountain. She doesn't. It doesn't matter how much she had growing up. She can still appreciate something beautiful.

We spend the next half hour sitting on the fountain ledge and watching people as they pass by us. Smartly dressed men and women walk hastily to what I imagine are their high-paying jobs. The man in front of me stops to check his watch. From this angle, it looks like an Audemars Piguet—expensive. I bet he works on Wall Street, making deals on the daily, and at night he goes home to his overdone wife, riddled with plastic surgery and long, painted nails. They fight, he leaves and heads to his mistress. The man checks his phone and a smile graces his lips. Yep, it's his mistress.

This is what I like about the city. These people can be whoever I want them to be.

"Look," Lindsey says, poking me in the side. A carriage drives by and a man and woman sit snuggly inside, looking cozy and in love.

I look at her with a raised brow. "You've never been on a carriage ride?" Not that I have. In fact, I've done very little touristy things within my own city.

"No," she says. "When would I have done that?"

When you live in the city, things that tourists enjoy are things we take for granted. I don't want to do that anymore. I want to enjoy life and everything it has to offer. I've seen the inside of just about every club in this city, but now I want to enjoy more.

"Let's go," I say, pulling her up and toward the horse-drawn carriage. Once sitting, we make our way along the park. We tour the city pretending we're tourists, allowing him to point out different architecture and places of relevance. A lot of it is unknown to me, and I internally mark the places I want to explore myself. I have no doubt they will all provide loads of inspiration.

Lindsey leans into my side, placing a kiss on my neck. "Thank you," she says. "I like this."

I do too. There's something so normal about this. Something

right. When we're done, we head back to the fountain for one last look.

"Excuse me, miss, will you take our picture?" a woman asks Lindsey.

She smiles, taking the phone from the woman and helping to line up the group. Every one of them smiles widely, clearly enjoying their time in New York. When she's done, she hands the phone back and comes to stand next to me.

"What next?" she asks.

"We can check out another place. I have a ton of them all over this city."

"What if we found a new place?" she suggests.

"That's even better."

She goes to turn around, but her foot snags on a raised portion of the base of the structure. Her eyes widen as she stumbles backward. My hand shoots out to grab her, but I'm too late. Water splashes all around her. People stop to point and stare. I want to push them all away, shield her from embarrassment. I'm waiting for her to begin crying or yelling or anything but what she does next. She throws her head back and laughs with abandon. She stays rooted in the cold water, laughing with not a care in the world. I join her. The scene is so ridiculous.

"Come on," I say, holding out my hand to help her out.

She takes it, continuing to laugh despite her shaking body. The cold air does nothing to help. I take off my hoodie and pull it down over her small frame. She takes a step and winces.

"What's wrong?" I ask.

"N-Nothing," she lies.

I can tell by the way her face has gone pale and the crinkles around her eyes are deepening, she's in pain. "Lindsey, talk to me."

"My leg. It's tight. I did something to it."

"Let's get out of here and get you someplace warm," I say, wrapping my arms around her shaking shoulders.

"No. I want you to get your inspiration. After everything you've been through, you deserve to find something that makes you happy."

Despite the fact she's soaking wet and has hurt her leg, she's concerned about me.

This woman continuously surprises me.

"You make me happy." I smile. "Plus, I have plenty of that. Don't worry."

Leaning down, I capture her chattering lips. Everything and everyone around us disappears and all I can focus on is the woman in my arms.

The need to get her home is overwhelming.

I lift her off the ground and carry her to the cab, not wanting her to put any pressure on her leg. Once inside the cab, I pull Lindsey tightly into my arms, where she snuggles against me. She's soaking through my sweatshirt, the cold turning her lips blue. I do my best to keep her as warm as possible until we're back at my place. We barely get through the door before my lips are back on hers.

"We need to get you warm," I say, walking her toward my bathroom. Setting her down, I turn on the water, allowing it to run warm. I want to take care of her. If she'll let me. "Let me wash you."

Lindsey's back straightens. I know before she speaks, she's shutting me out. "I—no. Not with the lights on. I can't, Pierce."

As much as I want to fight her, want to make her share her broken pieces with me, after everything I showed her of my own pain after Linc died, I don't push. It's been a hard day. "Let me make it better for you," I say, heading toward my cabinets to find some candles. I place them around the bathroom, so they'll give us enough light to see, but not enough that she'd feel uncomfortable. Switching the overhead light off, the candles reflect off the walls but give very minimal light. It's romantic.

"Will this work?" I question.

She nods. "Yes."

"Come here," I command. She obeys. "Hands up." Once her hands are over her head, I pull the wet sweatshirt from her body. My hands go around to her back, unclasping her bra and letting it fall to the floor. Walking her backward into the steamy shower, taking it nice and slow so as not to irritate her leg further. Her hands come up to my cheeks, bringing my lips toward hers. Our kiss ignites a fire within me and she's feeding the flames with every nip of her teeth. A groan breaks through and more than ever, I need all of her clothes off.

"Lindsey, let me see you. All of you," I beg.

She stays still, looking around at the near darkness that envelops us. Surely, she can see that whatever she wants to hide, she can in here. I'm not trying to rush her. I only want what she'll give. I'll take her scraps willingly.

She lowers her pants, stepping out of them and discarding them in the corner of my shower. I know she stands naked in front of me and my breath hitches.

"Turn, I'm going to wash you." Dumping shampoo in my palm, I rub my hands together and apply it to her scalp, massaging in the lavender scented shampoo. Her shoulders rise and fall, and little sighs of contentment escape her lips. All her noises are making me harder every second. I need her. It's a desperate feeling.

I spin her around and kiss her with everything I have. All the passion and frustration go into this kiss. Lindsey is my kryptonite, and I'm afraid I won't recover.

Her hands run down my back, leaving goose bumps in their

wake. It occurs to me I'm standing in the shower with my boxer shorts on, soaking wet. I pull away from her, lowering my pants to the ground. I can hardly make out her expression, but I don't miss the intake of breath. I toss the soaked boxers into the corner and pull her back into me, searing her with more kisses.

The day with Lindsey was incredible. She's incredible. Every moment I'm with her I fall harder and faster. I want to spend every moment with her, just like this, but more importantly, I want her to be okay. She took a hard fall today.

"Let me wash you," I say roughly.

Without a word, she turns around, handing me the soap bottle. She allows me to rub my hands up and down her back, washing her. My hands slide lower until I'm cradling her ass in my hands. Kneading and massaging, I get a rise out of the noises she makes.

She needs more.

I want more.

So I take it.

My mouth is rough against her as I continue to explore her body with my hands, every whimper pressing me on. My hands are at her entrance and the heat radiating off her is an aphrodisiac better than anything else. This woman is everything.

"Please," she begs.

She doesn't have to say what she wants. I know. And tonight is about her. I'll give her anything she wants. With one arm tethering her to me to support her, the other sets off to torment and tease her until she's begging me.

One finger glides in and then another. Her head lulls back on a moan. My other hand comes up to cup her breast, pulling and tugging so she loses her mind. And she does. It's not long before she's calling out and collapsing into my arms.

I finish washing her and then dry her off and carry her to my bed. We fall in together, tired and content. I'll never tire of this. Lindsey is my game changer, my reason to be better. Together we're unstoppable. I only hope the high I'm feeling now isn't followed by the low I'm accustomed to.

I wouldn't survive the loss of her.

CHAPTER THIRTY-NINE

Lindsey

'M ON CLOUD NINE. LAST NIGHT WITH PIERCE WAS everything. He was gentle and caring. His tenderness toward me made my heart swell. He didn't push me to see my scars. Instead, he made accommodations so I'd feel comfortable.

I wanted to stay with him all day, but today is physical therapy and Alison will be ready to kick my ass in gear. With the fun run tomorrow, it's what's best. I want to get out there and participate. I want to show Pierce I'm strong. As much as I need his strength, he needs mine too. I can be that person for him.

I walk through the door and Alison's waiting for me. "Why are you limping?" she asks with a frown.

"I'm fine. I tripped is all."

She narrows her eyes as though she's seeing right through my act. If I'm being honest, it hurts like hell. "Come sit down and let me take a look," she demands.

I want to argue, but with Alison, it's pointless. She's a dog with a bone when she wants something. So, I acquiescence. She lifts my pant leg and huffs.

"Your ankle is black and blue. What the hell happened?" she scolds.

"I told you. I tripped."

"That was one hell of a trip. You know you can't do this stuff,

Lindsey. Your screws were removed only a few months ago. You're lucky you don't have to use the cane anymore. If you keep this up, you'll have to go back to it."

I'm pissed. The last thing I need is Alison making me feel worse. Yet, she's doing a damn good job of that.

"Let's stop talking about this and just get on with things. Tomorrow's the fun run and I want to be ready to go."

Alison frowns, hands coming to rest atop both of her hips. "You can't honestly think you're going to be able to run tomorrow?"

"I walked your two miles. I'm ready to jog." I grit my teeth.

Fuck yes, I'm running. This is an event to raise money for my boarding school. Hell will freeze before I sit this one out. I'm not weak and she can't make me be. I'll push hard today, and I'll be ready.

"I hate to be the bearer of bad news, but that's not happening." Her voice is hard, reprimanding. "You cannot run. I have to remind you again; your pins just came out a little over three months ago. That, and you have been pushing yourself way too hard. You're setting your goals to unrealistic expectations. Let's not forget how you came in here after that gauntlet at work. No. End of story. You won't push yourself. We will keep up our exercises and when you are ready—"

"Stop!" I yell in frustration. Alison has been such a great coach through all of this. She's tough, but she's always been gentle with my feelings. Why is she being so cruel? "Why are you doing this?"

"I'm not trying to hurt you, Lindsey. That's exactly why I'm telling you this. I don't want you to hurt yourself. And now, after yesterday's setback, it's not a good idea."

"I have been running my entire life, Alison. I can do this," I say with conviction, but I know she's right. I hate it and it's starting to turn my stomach, but there's no denying I'm not ready. I hate feeling less than. I hate feeling not whole, and after this accident, that's exactly how I've felt. It's taken away my independence and made me feel small.

"I don't wanna talk about tomorrow. I just wanna do what I came here to do."

Alison sighs, and her hand comes to rest on my shoulder. "Lindsey, I don't want to hold you back, but I also want you to do things the right way. If you push it, you'll get hurt, which will just slow up all of your progress. If you work on things slow and steady, you'll be back to yourself in no time. But you have to do it the right way and you can't push it."

"But this is my race. How will it look if I sit it out?"

"The fun run is a great cause and they need you there to oversee. Let the participants run and you worry about building awareness," she suggests.

I slink out of her grasp, not wanting to talk about this anymore. What will Pierce think? What will that say to the boys? I'm feeling lost and the need to shut down is heavy on me.

We go to our first station, which is just some light stretching. Alison takes my ankle in her hand and slowly bends it forward. I cry out in pain.

"That hurts?" she says with a raised brow.

I nod. She starts manipulating my ankle and with every turn, I wince.

"You're going to need some ice and to rest today," she says.

"No. It's going to be fine. Let's do this." I start to stand, but Alison stops me.

"No, Lindsey. It's not fine. You have to ice and rest. There's no arguing. We won't be doing anything else today."

I want to cry. Tears threaten to fall, but I push them back, unwilling to let Alison see me weak. She's already seen me at my lowest and I don't need her to think this is another major set-back. Last time I got to feeling sorry for myself, I skipped therapy for a week, opting to stay in bed and sulk. I won't do that again. It added an extra two weeks of having to use the cane. That's never happening again.

"Fine." I give in, not seeing another choice. "Let's get ice on this so I can get the fuck out of here."

Alison's sad eyes only manage to piss me off. At this point she'd usually be her hard-ass self, telling me to stop moping, but for some reason, this time she doesn't do that. I want to ask her what's up, but the truth is I don't think I can handle her issues today with mine. It's taking every ounce of strength I have not to go off the rails. No, I'll let her deal with her own issues. Today, I'm going to try my hardest not to fall victim to my own.

CHAPTER FORTY

Pierce

W HEN LINDSAY GOT TO MY PLACE, I COULD TELL BY the way she wouldn't make eye contact with me that something was wrong. I tried for the first half hour to pull it out of her, but I was met with a wall of brick and mortar. I know she had therapy today with Alison. Could something have happened? Lindsey is so strong—too strong for her own good sometimes. She pushes herself too hard.

"What would you like to do?" I ask, trying to buffer the situation. She doesn't even look at me, the anger radiating off her like a live wire.

"Let's just watch TV," she says with a huff.

"Okayyyyy," I draw, frustration building at her attitude.

I turn on something funny, hoping to lighten the mood, but ten minutes into it, Lindsey hasn't uttered a word or even cracked a smile. She's sitting slouched down on my couch with her arms crossed over her chest, staring straight ahead. I scoot toward her, pulling her into my side, and she still doesn't move.

"Talk to me, please," I beg, acting like a pussy for feeling awkward in my own fucking house. "I'm tired of the strangeness, the hostility. I don't like it when you're like this. I'm the king of putting up walls and I'm finding I hate it when it's done back to me."

"I'm fine, Pierce. Let's just watch the damn show."

I jerk back at her tone, my unease quickly turning to anger. I can only take so much of this before my own temper gives way. She's making me feel like I've done something wrong and it's starting to grate on me.

"You're clearly not fine. Did I do something? Because you're acting like I did."

"Jesus, no. Not everything is about you, Pierce."

"What the fuck, Lindsey? What's going on with you?"

"I'm stressed out. I have a lot on my plate. The fun run is tomorrow, and I'm tired. I should probably go home."

"Yeah, maybe you should," I spit, wanting to throw something. "If the fun run was going to be too much for you to handle, why did you take it on?"

"I didn't say it's too much. I said I have a lot going on."

"My point exactly, Lindsey. You're already juggling so much. No one would blame you if you just took a step back."

Her face grows red. "Take a step back?" Her voice rises. "I've taken enough steps backward, Pierce. This is something I'm doing for me and nobody else," she says, seething. I should drop it, but I can't help but poke the bear.

"That's funny. I thought you were doing it for the boys at the center?"

If it's possible, a vein in Lindsey's throat pops out in anger. "You know I am," she fumes. "Don't even start with me."

I throw my hands up in the air. "Start with you? You're the one who came to my house picking a fight when I've done nothing. What the fuck have I done to make you treat me like this?"

"Everything," she screams. "You're a constant reminder of my past and everything I've lost."

And there it is.

The elephant in the room.

The slap in the fucking face that only Lindsey could deliver.

It always comes back to my past.

To the drugs.

All my own self-loathing comes to the surface, making it very hard to remain calm. If there's one thing Lindsay can bring out in me, it's the old temper. I've tried hard to repress it, but I can't stay quiet and take her verbal beating anymore.

"If you want to leave, leave. I'm done being your punching bag."

"You want me to leave? Fine. I'm out." She stands, gathering her stuff, getting ready to go. I grab her arm and she pulls it roughly out of my grasp. "Don't touch me," she barks, leering at me with a glare that punches me in the gut.

"Why are you doing this?" I need her as much as I need my next breath, but I can't help but feel like she's pushing me away.

"I'm not doing this, you are," she says, throwing it back in my face.

I quickly pull her into my chest, hugging her tightly, as she hits and wiggles and tries to get loose.

"Let me go. Let me go," she says, beating her fist against my chest.

"Take it out on me. Do whatever you need to, but you're not leaving here like this," I yell, hoping to get through that thick skull of hers.

"But you just told me—"

"I don't give a damn about what I said. I was wrong and I'm not letting you go." My voice leaves no room for objection and eventually she goes slack in my arms, sobs wracking her body.

"Shh," I coo, patting her back gently. We stay like this for a couple of minutes, me allowing her to get out whatever it is she's been holding in. After a couple of minutes, I push her away lightly so I can see her face. "Tell me what I can do to help."

A tear slides down her cheek, and I sweep it away. "I'm just tired, Pierce. Tired of feeling like this and tired of not being me. I want things to be back to the way they were."

My brow rises in question. Lindsey has come so far from those days. The thought of her being caught up in that life again makes me physically sick. She's too good for that—for me.

"Not the drinking and the partying, Pierce, but physically I want to be all right."

I frown. She has no idea how amazing she is. No other girl I know would have fought this hard to bounce back. The things she's done at Polaris are life-changing for those boys. She gives them a role model many of them don't have.

"You have no idea how incredible you are. The strength you show through all of this is something most girls I know would never have. They'd fold into themselves and throw pity parties."

She sniffs. "Like I am right now?"

"You're having a bad moment, but you'll get over it."

"I'm just tired. I really do need to go home. Tomorrow is a big day."

I don't want her to leave. Not like this. I've been here before and nothing good comes from being down. I want to protect her from herself. She's stronger.

"Stay here with me," I beg, not wanting her to leave on these terms.

"We're fine, Pierce. Everything is fine, but I really need to get a good night's sleep, and tonight I think it's gonna happen in my own bed."

My arms drop to my sides, knowing I've lost the fight. When Lindsey has something in her head, there's no persuading her. She's bullheaded like that.

"I'll see you tomorrow," she says, leaning in and placing a small kiss on my lips.

I kiss her back, but the passion is absent from this kiss. No matter how much she says we're okay I can't help but feel like we're anything but.

CHAPTER FORTY-ONE

Lindsey

WE WALK SIDE BY SIDE IN WHAT MUST BE THE MOST exceptionally beautiful November day in New York. Regardless of the strain between Pierce and me today, I have to admit all the stars have aligned for us. We got lucky. It's the perfect day for our fun run fundraiser. The temperature of the air is a brisk fifty-nine degrees. Today's the day that, in a former life, I would've walked from my Upper East Side apartment all the way to the Village. It's warm enough that I'm only wearing a long-sleeved hoody and ankle-length running leggings. Leggings specifically bought to cover my scars. I'm wearing sneakers as well, but they're just for show, as is my running outfit. I'll obviously not be running today, and it makes my heart twist a little in my chest.

We make it to East Sixth Street. That's where Carson has arranged with the city to hold the run. East River Park track is the perfect location. With children involved, we needed a secure location and it's closed off enough to be safe.

When we enter and step onto the track, I see the children. *Our Polaris children.* I spot Christopher, Xavier, Toby. I spy Lynn and Carson in the far corner, and Bridget speaking to a news cameraman. She did a great job. Not only did she do everything super fast with regards to marketing, but she also had a publicist friend help us. The turnout is fantastic for the fun run, and we've already raised a ton of money from just sponsorship of the kids, almost three hundred fifty thousand dollars, which is much more than I expected. I wonder how much we'll make from adult buy-in today. There was no specific amount to run, and there wasn't a specific donation amount for a child to run, but many contributed well above what we expected. Pierce did an amazing job.

I squeeze his hand. "You did this," I say.

"It was all you, babe."

"Hardly."

"It's going to get even better." He smirks and I'm taken aback by how sweet and calm he is. As if nothing happened yesterday. I expel a long exhale and try to let out all my pent-up anxiety. When my shoulders start to relax, I finally ask him what he's talking about.

"How can it get better than raising almost three hundred fifty thousand dollars?"

"Well . . . by the end of the day, we'll be closer to four hundred thousand dollars."

I squint at him through the early morning sun gleaming in my eyes. "Why?"

"Well, I'm running, and I got a few people to join in last-minute, too. They all said they'd match my donation of twenty thousand dollars."

My stomach bottoms out. He did this for me. After everything, he did this for me. For the first time since we woke up today, I smile, and then as the amount of money sinks in, I laugh. "Pierce, you can't donate more money. Are you kidding?"

"Nothing you can say to stop me. I am and that's final." He crosses his hand in front of his chest as if to say there's no arguing with him.

"But twenty thousand? You already donated two hundred fifty thousand dollars."

"I guess you're right. I'll make it fifty thousand dollars. Got to keep the number even."

I roll my eyes. There's nothing to dissuade him once he's got his mind made up, so I don't even bother to try.

When we get to the running track, Amelia runs up to me and throws her hands around my neck. "Give them a chance," she whispers in my ear. "They're trying. If you need me I'll be at registration." After she jogs off, Pierce and I are left standing together looking up at my parents. He squeezes my hand, and within his tightened grasp, I know everything will be okay. Regardless of the strain on our relationship these past few days, he understands how stressful seeing them today could be, but also that them being here means more than words can say. So I let my lips part into a welcoming smile, allowing them to know it's okay, that they can come talk to me.

Together, they walk up to us.

"Hey." I shift my weight nervously, and I notice my mother has unshed tears in her eyes. I'm taken aback. Pierce extends his hand and introduces himself.

"It's a pleasure to meet you," my father responds for both of them before he addresses me. "We are so proud of you, Lindsey."

"We are," my mother agrees, wiping away a stray tear that has fallen. "Thank you for inviting us."

"I'm happy you could both make it."

"We wouldn't miss it." The tone in my father's voice is sincere, and I know from the bottom of my heart after our last talk that my father means it. They wouldn't miss it. "I also brought some friends." He smiles as he points to registration. "Some big donors."

"Are you serious?"

"There's nothing I wouldn't do for you. I wanted you to know that."

"You guys being here . . ." I turn to my mother and reach my hand out. She encases my free hand in hers. "It means the world to me. Thank you."

We stand and make small talk for a minute before they have to go. They couldn't stay for the event, but it doesn't matter. They came.

They came.

As soon as we're alone again, a girl comes jogging up to Pierce, throwing her arms around him. All the muscles in my body become tense.

"Oh my God, Pierce. This is fantastic. I'm so happy you invited me. Look at the kids, they're so cute," she whines, and her voice grates on me.

Who is she? And why does she have her hands on *my* boyfriend?

"Hey, Josie. Thanks for coming," he says to the blonde pawing at him.

"As if I'd miss it."

I step forward and stretch out my hand. "Hi, nice to meet you." It's only then that Pierce remembers me.

"Oh, I'm so sorry. Josie, this is Lindsey. Lindsey, Josie." He doesn't say I'm his girlfriend and suddenly I feel lightheaded. My weak legs threaten to crumble under the weight of my insecurities.

"Nice to meet you," she says, then turns back to Pierce. "I've missed you. Where have you been? It's been months. Not since the night we got arrested. No, that's not true. We went out that night . . ." She drawls out the word with implication as she giggles.

Just as he's about to answer, Carson walks up. "Hey, guys, the run's about to start."

Pierce turns to me. "I'll be right back."

I stare at him, dumbfounded. The night he got arrested? *This is the girl who got handsy?* And what did she mean that night? What night? Recently? Did he cheat on me?

Anger swells within me, and something stronger.

Jealousy.

An unfathomable jealousy.

She's gorgeous.

Fit. And also, most importantly . . . not broken.

I know I shouldn't ask, but I can't keep my damn mouth shut. The need to torture myself and find out more about her twists in my gut. "It's so nice of you to come," I say to her.

"Of course. I'd do anything for Pierce."

I bet you would.

"So . . ." I try to fill the awkward silence while being a glutton for punishment at the same time. *Real smart idea.* "Have you known Pierce for a long time?"

"Are you kidding?" She laughs, and her voice is like a dagger slicing and shredding everything inside of me. "Pierce and I dated all through high school," she admits in triumph.

I feel sick. My heart aches as if it's been pulled out from my chest and wrung out onto the pavement beneath my feet. The words she just said start to replay over and over again, like a recording skipping on repeat, and then a realization dawns on me . . .

He was arrested because his ex was getting handsy. And if that wasn't bad enough, now she's here, in front of me, flaunting how perfect she is. The worst part is he called her. No, the worst part is she's drop dead gorgeous and he called *her.*

All my insecurities work their way through me, cutting and wounding me like a serrated knife. Digging into my flesh until I bleed. Pierce runs back over.

"Come on, Josie," he says and together they jog away.

Stabbing pain.

From the outside, I stand unfazed, a fake smile on my face, but on the inside, I break and crack. Invisible pieces of my soul smash to the floor as I watch them. Both beautiful. Both fit. Not broken. Not mangled.

Like me.

CHAPTER FORTY-TWO

Pierce

WITH EACH STRIDE, MY CHEST BURNS. MAYBE IT'S not the run at all. Maybe as my eyes scan the distance, I realize just how little my family cares. *No one is here.*

Seeing Lindsey's parents put aside their difference to support their daughter was a bitter pill to swallow. I'm happy for her, but jealous at the same time because no one is here to support me. My goddamn brothers couldn't put their shit aside for long enough to support me in this. My father never came. Nor my mother. It's just like when I graduated from high school. The day I realized I meant shit to them. It should have been the best day of my life, but instead, my world imploded when I realized everyone was too concerned about the drama with Grant and about changing the paperwork to leave a company to Spencer. They never showed up. No one came. I was the only person with no family. That was the day I realized the only person you can rely on is yourself. Years later and nothing has changed. They're still not here for me.

You didn't ask them.

I pick up my pace, running from the incessant voice in my head reminding me this is my fault. That they're not here be-cause I never personally invited them. But they don't care. They knew and didn't come.

Faster I run.

Burning. Beating. Breathing.

My muscles quake with the pressure of my strides. My brain aches from my thoughts. I hit my stride until there's nothing left in front of me, nothing behind me. Nothing but the demons that chase me.

Finally crossing the finish line, I come to a halt and the wind smacks against my face. I look around and, in the distance, I see Lindsey. Calm falls over me. It's unearthly how just seeing her makes it all go away. Makes all the pain dissipate.

She smiles but then as fast as her smile spreads it pulls back at the exact same second I feel arms around me. Someone kisses my cheek. I turn, pulling away, and find Josie standing there. She reaches out and touches me again, first on my arm and then on my chest.

"What's wrong?"

I step back and cock my head. "What are you doing?"

"I thought you asked me to come here to be with you . . ." she trails off.

"To be with me?"

"Well, yeah."

"Josie, listen to me. Hear what I'm saying. I asked you here to support children. To raise money for the children."

"I mean, I know it's for the children, but you ask me and—"

"I asked a lot of people," I cut her off. "Josie, my girlfriend is raising money to open a boarding school for underprivileged children. *My girlfriend*," I enunciate so she gets my full message. "There's no you and me. We're over. Hell, we have been over for a long time."

"But that night—"

I raise my hands to silence her. "That night was the biggest mistake of my life. That night was a lifetime ago. Everything has changed since that night."

I turn back around, looking for Lindsey, but she's nowhere to be found. *Shit.* "I got to go."

And that's what I do. I jog off to find her. It takes me a few minutes, but eventually the crowd parts and I see her. Her shoulders are pulled back, and her head is held high. I'm no idiot, though. I can see it in her eyes. She's hurt.

She keeps busy, not acknowledging me, just pretending I'm not standing in front of her. She won't even make eye contact with me and it destroys me how much I hurt her. Eventually she'll have to look at me, so I wait. But as the crowd dissipates and she says her goodbyes, she doesn't look at me. Instead, she walks to the street to catch a cab.

With my hands outstretched, I stop her. "Where do you think you're going?"

"Home."

"Without me?"

"You seemed rather busy," she snaps back.

"Not what you think."

Her jaw tics. "Oh, it's not? So, that's not the girl you were with? The one who got you arrested?"

"Well—"

"And she's not your ex-girlfriend?"

"Girlfriend would be a stretch of the w—"

"Stop. Just stop." She pushes past me and storms off.

"What's wrong with you?" I call out.

She stops her pace and turns to look over her shoulder and glare at me. "What's wrong with me? What's wrong with you? First off, you made it sound like that girl was nothing to you."

"She is nothing."

"Then why were her h-hands," she stutters and stops herself.

Her face is red and blotchy, and I know she's holding back tears.

"I didn't welcome that."

"You didn't seem to mind. Not when she was getting *handsy* with you on the track."

"She's nothing. I don't understand. Where is this all coming from?"

"I can't compete," she mutters under her breath as I walk toward her until I'm right in front of her.

"What does that even mean? There is no competition. She's nothing and you're everything. Haven't you realized that yet? You're fucking *everything*. You're all I got. My fucking family . . ." I shake my head in an effort to control my rage. With a deep inhale followed by a longer exhale, I continue. "You're my fucking everything. I would do everything for you, but it's not enough. Nothing I do is ever enough. Now, I have you ranting and raving and talking crazy. Doubting me, for fuck's sake. Will anyone ever take me seriously?" I hiss.

"Honestly, Lindsey, I get it. I understand, but I can't deal with this right now. After everything I've been through this past month . . . Losing Linc." I pull at my hair that's damp with sweat. "I'm finally back in a good place. I took your shit yesterday, 'cause I knew you were nervous about today. But now, today . . . No. I don't need this shit. Not when my family can't even bother to fucking support me," I snap before turning to go in the opposite direction.

She reaches out and halts my movement. "Please don't walk away from me. Please talk to me," she whispers.

I turn around and look at her. Our gazes lock. "What's going on with you, Linds?"

Her upper lip nibbles on the lower one. "I just don't understand why you'd be with me when you can have someone like her. Someone not so broken."

"There's no one else for me, okay? I know you're self-conscious about your leg, but when are you going to realize I don't give two shits whether you limp or if you have a million scars running down every surface of your skin? All I care about is you. What's *inside* of you."

"But you don't know. You can't know. You can't know what it's like to have people stare, to see the looks of disgust on their faces when they see how messed up you are. What do you know about being broken, Pierce?"

"This isn't the right time," I grunt.

"Then when?"

I expel a long exhale. "Come to my place."

"Why?"

"Come to my place and I'll show you."

CHAPTER FORTY-THREE

Lindsey

WHEN WE WALK IN THE DOOR, I TURN TO HIM AND place my hand on my hip. "So, now that you got me here, why don't you tell me why you know I'm not broken?" The tone of my voice is harsh, but I'm pissed. After the track today, I'm not in the mood for this. I want to go home to my own apartment and wallow in self-pity. But no, Pierce is taking me back to his place.

"You're not broken, Lindsey." He sighs.

"And how do you know?"

"Because I know broken, and trust me, you're not. Come with me." He leads me by my arm through his apartment, up a flight of stairs and into a lofted space. I expect him to stop in his studio, but instead, he pulls me through a door I've never seen before in the corner.

The first thing I notice is he has floor-to-ceiling windows and the view is spectacular. The second thing I notice is that this is fantastic. It's like his own private gallery. I'm in awe of the space. Unlike the studio, which has large canvases on easels and paint splattered haphazardly on the floor, this room is its complete contrast. It's white and pristine, the only color coming from the painting hanging from the wall.

I move closer to look and the wind is knocked out of me.

The images on the canvas are all different. Some are buildings, some are flowers, some people, one is a room that resembles a nightclub and inside that room are two men. What catches my attention is the one man caught in the shadows, he has black eyes that are so dark they send a chill up my spine. With a deep breath I turn to the next painting; it's actually of him. But that's not what makes my chest lurch. What makes my chest wobble and pitch is the pattern I see.

"All the sketches, all those untold stories, everything I see . . . I look for broken. I search for it everywhere."

Each painting, each image, appears as if it's broken glass. Every one of his paintings are broken. Not the canvas itself, but the images he painted. The building looks like glass, hundreds of shards of glass. The flower looks like it's been smashed into pieces. The people . . . broken.

And then there's the painting of him. A tear drips down my cheek. He's beautiful in the picture but also severed into a million beautiful broken pieces of himself. His image on the canvas looks like rigid edges, tarnished pieces.

He knows broken.

He believes he's broken. He believes he's like me.

I step forward, water cascading down my cheeks. "You're not broken. You're beautiful."

"But I am."

"I don't understand. Why? I understand you lost Linc, but this is more. These paintings are not just because of Linc. Why do you see yourself as broken? Nothing is wrong with you."

"There doesn't need to be anything wrong to be broken. You can appear to be perfect, but inside . . . "

His words hang over me like a billow of smoke during a fire. They clog my lungs, making it hard to breathe. I might be physically broken, but he's mentally broken and that I can understand. For so long I've been that way, too. For so long I used my vices to hide my hurt.

To stop feeling.

That's what Pierce does. He hides behind his looks, behind his name, behind a false ego. In truth, he's broken and it's in every piece of him.

"Now you see. Now you see all of me. Can't you show me all of you?"

His question takes me off guard. I can't. I shake my head back and forth.

"What are you hiding from? What aren't you showing me?"

"I can't."

"Trust me."

I'm not sure I can. "It's not you, it's me." It's a lame copout, but it's the best I have right now.

"What does that even mean?"

"I hate to look at it. The scars . . ." I trail off.

"You shouldn't hate any part of yourself, Lindsey. Because it's part of you, and you are beautiful."

"Like your broken paintings," I say.

"Like my broken paintings."

"Why do you think you draw them?"

"I don't know. I guess I'm a little broken and I want . . ." he trails off and looks at the floor.

"And you want to find the beauty in them. Do you want to find the beauty in me?"

"There's no need. It's right there for the world to see, and I'm not talking about your face. Anybody who knows you, anybody who tries to know you, will see how beautiful you are."

I search his eyes for insincerity, but I'm met with none. So, right there in the middle of his art studio, amongst fresh paint and fractured images, I remove my pants and show him my imperfections.

"You're exquisite."

"Hardly."

He drops to his knees in front of me. He places my leg—the one that screams in pain when I walk, when I sit, when I live—in front of him. He trails his fingers down my thigh to my calf and I place my hand on his scalp for balance. Not physical balance, but emotional.

He touches me. Each jagged edge. He drops his mouth to my flesh and I quiver against the sensation. This isn't sexual. It's love. He might not see it, but as he kisses each scar, each gnarl of raised, puckered flesh, each mark that tells of a story before, of a life before, he tells me with no spoken words that he loves me.

As I let him make something beautiful of all the pieces—all of my beautiful broken pieces.

I heal.

CHAPTER FORTY-FOUR

Pierce

TODAY IS ONE OF THE BEST DAYS OF MY LIFE.

Sitting across from Lindsey for breakfast is officially how I want to start my mornings from now on. There's just something about waking up to her face, seeing Lindsey smile. As cheesy as it sounds, it makes me happy. Having her beside me makes the shit with my family not so bad. Having her see me, the real me, makes everything okay. I honestly never thought I'd feel this way, but yesterday was a game changer. I was pissed. But later, in my studio, when I bared my soul to her and she bore hers to me, things changed. Everything changed.

The idea of another girl repulses me. Even before last night I felt this way, but if there was any hint of doubt, last night solidified it. I want Lindsey, and not just for now. I want a future.

"What are you thinking about over there?" she asks as she lifts the mug to her mouth and takes a sip of her coffee.

"Just how much I like having you here."

"You getting sappy on me, Lancaster?"

I stand and make my way to where she's sitting. Looking down at her, I grin. "I'll show you sappy," I tease as I lean down and take her lips. She tastes like the cappuccino she made this morning. Like sugar and cinnamon. I lick the seam of her lips.

"Cut it out." She laughs, and I reluctantly pull away, but not before sucking her bottom lip into mine, making her moan. As I step back to my chair and sit, I smile.

"No really, though, I've been thinking . . ."

She cocks her head and waits. I don't know what I've been thinking. I don't want to be away from her, but it's way too soon to say that. We might have known each other for years, but we've only been exclusive for a little over a month. Is that enough time to know?

Yes.

I don't say any of that, though. The thought of this all falling apart, of Lindsey eventually tiring of me or realizing I'm not worth the hassle, still presses on me. So instead I give her a grin, one that makes her roll her eyes. "I think we should go back to Antibes," I blurt out.

Her eyes widen and her mouth opens, but no words come out.

"The first time we were there, I—well, let's just say I want to take you back. I want to go where it all started and give us new memories. Ones we can always cherish."

"Wow, I don't know what to say."

"Say yes. Say the word and I'll book us on the next flight I can get, bearing that Carson says we can both take off."

"Yes."

"Done. And this time, Lindsey . . . This time I'm going to make it up to you."

"Nothing to make up for. Just having you is enough for me."

"Me too. But still, I want to."

And I do. I have a lot to make up for and a lot to be grateful for. This trip will be a new beginning.

———————— •◆• ————————

After she has her coffee, we decide to head out to a diner for breakfast before heading into Polaris. When we get there, I go to the computer room to see about finding a travel agent. I've never flown commercial, so this should be interesting, but hey, with Lindsey, I don't give a shit how we fly as long as she's with me.

I'm knee deep in search engines when I hear voices outside the door.

"How much does he want now?"

I can't hear the response, but I hear the first voice say, "No way can you come up with that. Are you going to ask her?"

"No."

"You have to."

"I said no," one of the speakers says forcefully. "I just don't know what to do. It's bad, man. That shit is cut with God knows what so he can sell more of it. But I heard it's got that stuff that they are calling the lethal injection."

My jaw clenches at what he just said, Lethal injection is the street name for cocaine being cut with fentanyl.

That's what killed Linc.

I stand and head straight for the door. Pulling it open, I find Christopher and Xavier in the hall. "What's going on?" I glare at them needing to know why they are talking about this.

I need to breathe and relax or these boys will be scared and won't talk to me.

Inhale. Exhale.

"Nothing," Christopher mutters as he picks at his nail. *He's lying.*

I lift an eyebrow. "Didn't sound like nothing."

"Well, it is," Xavier says and gives Christopher a pointed look.

I don't believe them, but I'm not going to get them to talk to me. They know something. I make a mental note to ask Lindsey later today.

When later comes, I'm sitting with Lindsey sharing a turkey sandwich she bought from the corner deli. We're like an old married couple, and strangely enough, the idea makes me smile.

"I spoke to Carson about us going away to Antibes," she says.

"Great, because I spent my day looking up flights and hotels."

"He said we can take off not this weekend but the next. He's got enough staff to cover for us."

"Sounds perfect. I found a great hotel . . . what was it called again?" I try to remember the name, but it's not coming to me. When the site was up on the computer was also when the boys were outside talking. "Oh, that reminds me, something is up with Christopher and Xavier."

She places her lunch down and looks up at me, her eyes wide. "What do you mean?"

"They were arguing about money."

Lindsey's face pales, and I'm instantly on edge.

"Do you know something?"

She swallows and shakes her head, but the movement is rigid and it makes my stomach clench. She's hiding something. One thing I've learned from my past is how to tell when someone is withholding information. It's written all over her face.

I just wonder what it is.

And why she won't tell me.

CHAPTER FORTY-FIVE

Lindsey

T HE WEEK HAS PASSED, WHICH MEANS ONLY ONE MORE week until our trip. It's finally the weekend again. After an hour of cleaning up the Polaris Boys Club, I'm finally ready to join the boys in watching the weekly Friday night movie. As I'm about to step into the media room, two strong arms wrap around my waist and pull me back and into the storage closet directly next to the media room. The rhythmic beat of a heart vibrates against my spine.

"Where do you think you're going?" The words are a whisper in my ear, the voice husky with need.

"To watch a movie—"

"I don't think so," he rasps, his soft lips pressing against the pulse in my neck and licking a trail down the exposed skin. The hands that are splayed against my waist travel up, lifting my shirt. The cold air bites at my skin, doing nothing to calm the erratic drum of my heart.

"This isn't very professional of you, Pierce," I tease, my words coming out playfully, but there is no hiding the desire laced beneath them. There is nothing I want more than Pierce Lancaster right now, and he knows it.

"You've been fucking me with those beautiful blue eyes all night. How can I possibly resist you?" His hand lowers my shirt and moves down to dip into the waistband of my leggings. "I need to be inside you. Right here. Right now. So you better be real quiet."

The rough pads of his fingers caress me and I can't help but tilt my hips back, pressing my rear against him. Through my leggings, there's no mistaking how hard he is. Not even his jeans can conceal his desire for me. Pierce's hand pulls away and the sound of a zipper lowering echoes in the space.

"Take your pants off."

In the background, I can hear the boys laughing. The movie has started in the media room. Can they hear us? My body shivers at the thought, a soft squeak escaping my mouth.

"*Shh*. If you're real quiet, they'll never know, I promise. Not another sound, though."

I bite my lower lip to stifle my moans. Pushing my body farther back and rotating my hips to rub myself against him, I will Pierce to put me out of my misery. Once I lower my pants to my ankles, his fingers tug my panties to the side. I hear the familiar ripping sound as my eyes close, as my heart thumps against my breastbone in anticipation. Time stands still, measured through the beat of my heart, and against the sound of laughter floating through the metal door, the only barrier to being caught.

"I need you," I rasp, barely a whisper. I can feel his hard length pressing against my core, but he doesn't move. The torture is delicious, heady, all-consuming. With every second I wait my breath comes out erratically. And then, when I think I can take no more, he finally pushes into me.

His mouth latches onto the back of my neck as he pulls out and thrusts back in. My back arches up to meet each of his strokes as he takes me from behind, my arms pressing against the door for leverage. The door rattles. He retracts himself from my body, making me quiver with his absence.

"Slow," he breathes.

"Fast," I plead, but he doesn't heed my desperation. Instead, he draws it out, making each second seem like an eternity. Time stretches slowly, painfully, until he slams back in at a punishing clip. The door shakes.

"Someone will hear."

It doesn't stop him. Instead, he picks up his pace, fucking me brutally against the metal door.

This forbidden encounter, knowing that anyone can find us, that we might be caught, has me falling over the edge. I fall so fast, so hard, I fear I'll never put myself back together. But as Pierce slows his strokes, bracing his arms tightly around my waist, he pulls us closer together until there's no end and no beginning to where our bodies meet.

I feel him shudder inside me. I feel him get lost in the feeling alongside me. Our hearts beat in tandem until we regain our breaths. Pulling out, he turns me around and places a kiss on my lips. "Ready to watch that movie?" He laughs against my mouth.

I sigh in satisfaction. "I am now."

Once we clean off, I sneak out the door and make my way in to join the kids. A few seconds pass before Pierce walks in—struts in, more like it—like he owns the place. My face is beet red. I look thoroughly fucked, and he's cool and collected and looking hotter than shit.

It's so unfair.

He winks at me and I shake my head and roll my eyes, eliciting a small laugh from him. I search the seats to find a place to sit when I notice a bunch of seats are empty. *Where's Xavier?*

I leave the room and Pierce follows. When we step outside, he looks at me, puzzled. "Leaving so soon?" He smirks. "Want another round?"

"Xavier is not in the room. I want to see where he is."

"Really? He was dying to watch the movie."

"I know. That's why I want to find him. He'll be pissed if he misses the new Bond."

"Maybe he's shooting hoops."

Together hand in hand we walk to the gymnasium where a group of boys are whispering in the corner. *Never a good sign.* Pierce looks at me and shakes his head. He's thinking exactly what I'm thinking.

"Let's see what that's about."

CHAPTER FORTY-SIX

Pierce

WHEN WE FINALLY MAKE IT TO THE BOYS, I'M ON edge. There's definitely something wrong. After the other day and now this, I know it in the bottom of my heart that something's not right.

"What's going on over here, guys?" Lindsey asks.

"Nothing," Matthew says, but he won't meet her gaze. He looks down at the floor instead. His lack of eye contact has my back going ramrod straight.

"What aren't you telling me?" She tries to keep her voice level, but I can hear her fear.

When he doesn't answer, I turn to Rocky. "Come on, man. What's going on?"

He opens his mouth, but then Matt gives him a pointed look that shuts him up. I'm about to demand answers when Lindsey beats me to the punch and steps forward.

"Tell me now," she demands.

"It's nothing, really."

"Now." Lindsey looks around again. "Where's Xavier?"

At Xavier's name, his lip twitches.

Shit.

"Come to think of it, where's Christopher?"

Uncomfortable silence fills the air. Lindsey drops to her

knees. She's eye to eye with Matthew. There's no way this isn't hurting her. There's no way this isn't killing her leg. She does it anyway. Showing her strength. She reaches her hand out and takes his in hers.

"Please tell me," she implores.

"Don't be mad."

My stomach drops.

"I won't be mad. I promise," she responds.

"He got a text."

"What did the text say?"

"I don't know," he whispers, but even in the low tone, I can hear the fear in his voice.

"What aren't you telling me?" Lindsey asks.

"It was from his brother."

"Shit," she murmurs under her breath and an oppressive feeling starts to descend down on me. It feels as if the air is thick with something, making it hard to breathe.

"Where?" I ask, stepping forward.

He shrugs.

"You need to tell me. One of you knows. You need to tell me," she begs as all her prior composure evaporates into hysterics.

I step forward and put my hand on her shoulder to soothe her. She needs to calm down or she'll scare the boys.

"Please, Matthew," I say. "It's important. Did he say anything? Anything at all that would make you know where they would go?"

"He mentioned going to the bodega on Ninetieth."

I don't know what that means, but Lindsey must know something because before I know it, she's taking off across the hall. I dart after her, hands extended, stopping her mid-stride. "Where do you think you're going?"

"To find him." Her voice is strong and doesn't waver. There's no changing her mind, and I know what I have to do.

"Let's go." My voice is strong too, but deep down I feel quite the opposite, but no matter what, I can't show her. So I fight off the feeling of fear wreaking havoc inside me and let the adrenaline give me the strength to guide us out of the building and where we need to go.

CHAPTER FORTY-SEVEN

Lindsey

"HOW MANY MORE BLOCKS IS IT?" PIERCE BARKS from behind me. He's pissed. At the situation, at the boys, but mainly he's mad at me.

Looking over my shoulder, I answer, "Two." I wince. The pain in my leg is excruciating. I'm walking way too fast. My knee feels as if tiny slivers of glass are stripping away at the bone, but I don't stop. I push forward, no matter the pain.

"Are you ever going to tell me what the fuck is going on?" he hisses at me. "For God's sake, I thought we were partners. I thought we were in this together. I thought . . ."

The pain in his voice breaks me, and as much as I don't want to admit the truth, I do.

"I lied to you."

He stops in his tracks and looks back at me.

"When I told you I didn't know what was wrong with Christopher and Xavier, I lied. A month ago I lent him fifty thousand dollars to give his brother." Pierce's eyes go wide and I can see a vein in his throat throb. Not being able to face his anger, I turn and start walking again.

"Jesus, Lindsey. Don't you think you should have told someone?" he yells above the sound of our footsteps hitting the cement pavement beneath us.

"I know I should have, but I wasn't thinking."

"No, you weren't." Pierce's anger is palpable even with the distance, and I can feel a thaw descend. "How could you not have told me? I thought we were a team. I thought . . ." When I don't answer, he lets out a long, drawn-out sigh. "I guess I was wrong."

I want to object. I want to tell him he's wrong, that we are in this together, but I can't. Not now. Not when I have to continue. I have no other choice. I need to get to them. I need to find them before he does. I don't know what he wanted, but in this neighborhood, with these boys, it's never good. When we turn the corner, all the air spills from my lungs in a muffled cry, followed by a sharp intake of breath. I stumble forward and Pierce catches my arm so I don't fall.

I still might fall.

The scene in front of me makes me want to.

There's Christopher, Xavier, and two guys I don't know. There's also a gun.

All my nightmares of how this will go down play out in my brain. Every nightmare I've had since the day I walked into The Polaris Boys Club. I can't breathe. It feels like there's a cage around my body and it's closing in, and there's no exit in sight.

In my ear, I hear Pierce say, "Inhale. Everything will be okay." But it doesn't help. Fear is sitting on my shoulders, pressing into my spine, robbing my words, blinding my eyes, and dulling my senses. I'm incapacitated by it.

"Shut up," one of the boys yells as he steps closer.

I should move, I should run, but I can't, and no matter how much I will my legs to move they won't.

Broken.

I'm broken.

But then my body starts to shake uncontrollably as I notice

the gun is trained on us now.

"Don't move."

But I shake and shake.

"Breathe," Pierce whispers, his arm reaching out to calm me, and when his hand touches mine, I calm, steady my legs, and will them to move.

One step.

My legs feel so heavy, but I push on.

Two steps.

"Don't come any closer."

I don't heed his warning. I take another slow step, simultaneously lifting my hands to indicate I'm not a threat. "Listen to me. I'll get you the money. Just let Xavier and Christopher go." I take another step. "I promise. We won't even call the cops. Just leave them alone. I'll even add more money."

Pierce takes another step until he's next to Xavier. He's ready to pull him away. Seeing Pierce there calms my nerves enough for me to move in closer.

"You'll get me what I need?"

"Yes, I promise you. Just let us go. Let the boys go and I'll get you whatever you need. Let them go and we will deal with this."

He seems to consider it and I watch his chest, the air expelling from his lungs. The gun lowers and the breath I didn't know I was holding drifts out of my mouth.

"Okay." He nods to his friend before turning toward us again and glaring at Pierce to not move. I think we are finally in the clear until I hear a sound, a sharp intake of breath.

Pierce. It's coming from Pierce.

"You," Pierce mutters as his face pales. "It was you."

"What the fuck is he going on about?" the guy not holding the gun says.

"The drugs." My stomach revolts at the words coming out of

Pierce's lips. "You killed him."

It's as if everything happens in slow motion. The gun is lifted.

It's like all those movies you watch.

The sound of his finger pulling the trigger.

The sound of the barrel cocking.

The pop of the gun.

Deafening silence.

The scene plays out so slowly, every second feeling like an eternity. That's how it feels watching a bullet fire, watching it fly through the air, and watching . . .

"No!"

CHAPTER FORTY-EIGHT

Lindsey

EVERYTHING STOPS.

The world around me fades.

I don't see the commotion. I don't see the lights. All I see is Pierce.

Running up to him, I drop to the ground. "Pierce. Oh my God, Pierce." But he doesn't answer. Panic floods through me as I pull him into my arms, rocking back and forth. "Someone get help! Someone call someone! Someone find us!" I scream into the night, not sure who will hear me. Begging God to hear me.

Blood coats my hands. Thick and pulsing. Pouring through my fingers. I press down, but no matter the pressure, the current doesn't stop. It ebbs and flows, with no end in sight.

"No!"

His eyes flutter open. Then shut as his breath comes out in ragged, shallow gasps.

I watch as his chest concaves in with every strangled inhale.

I watch as the puddle beneath him grows, spreading across the pavement beneath him like a scarlet pool.

He's dying.

Pierce is dying.

"No, Goddammit, no!" Tears stream down my face. "Don't you dare leave me. Stay with me. Open your eyes. Someone, I need some help."

In the distance, I hear it. Sirens. Each second stretches on an endless loop until it descends upon me, suffocating me with the sound. My heart pounds heavily in my chest. It beats along with the sound of running footsteps gaining in the distance. Next thing I know I'm being lifted off him and pushed away as they work on him. I can't lose him.

I can't.

My whole body shakes.

"You need to step away." Arms pull me back.

Tears stream down my cheeks. "What's happening?"

No one answers me.

I stand frozen.

Watching, listening, crying.

Helpless.

"Throw in an IV and let's get fluids going wide-open," one says.

"Let's move."

The next thing I know they are moving toward the ambulance. I try to keep up. I try to go with them. But I can't. I can't keep up and I can't go with them.

They're inside the ambulance before I can protest, getting ready to leave. The paramedics are working furiously to save his life, to stabilize him before transport. As they try to keep him alive, I stand frozen on the street staring inside the rig.

"We need to intubate."

"I can't see anything. It's all blood."

"Let's just bag him and go."

"We're losing him."

The door slams shut.

"No! No! No! Nooooo," I scream. "Oh God." An involuntary sob tears through my chest. "Please don't leave me! Please.

Please, you can't go. You can't take him. He needs to wake up. He can't leave me. I can't be without him. He can't die. He can't die. I love him, I love him."

CHAPTER FORTY-NINE

Lindsey

NEXT THING I KNOW, I'M BEING ENGULFED IN ARMS. I strain against his hold, trying desperately to break through and go to Pierce. Christopher pulls me into his chest, whispering words I can't hear over my own wailing. This can't be happening. This can't be happening. I repeat this over and over again in my head.

"We'll get a cab," Xavier calls from the end of the alley as he runs to me, standing on the street watching the ambulance drive off into the distance.

"He's gone," I say on a sob.

"Then we have to go, Miss Lindsey. Mr. Pierce needs you." Christopher's voice cuts through my cry but only makes me fall back to my knees on the sidewalk, wanting to curl into a ball and stay here forever. Allowing my weakness to take hold and crush me, pouring out all of my sorrow.

"We have to go," Xavier yells and Christopher practically drags me up and toward the waiting cab.

Xavier offers directions to the driver, and Christopher tries to talk to me, but I don't comprehend the words he's saying. Sometime between kneeling in the alley and being placed in this cab, I'm frozen.

"Miss Lindsey. Miss Lindsey." Xavier is shaking my leg,

trying to get my attention. My head turns to him, lifeless. Numb. "Miss Lindsey, do you need to call Mr. Carson? He'll be looking for us."

I stare right through him.

"Hey, is she okay?" the driver says, drawing my attention to the front. It's then I see the fear in Xavier's eyes. It's not only me who endured that traumatic event. These kids saw the same thing. They might not love Pierce like I do but witnessing something like that at their age isn't normal. It isn't right.

"Call Mr. Carson," Christopher says to Xavier.

They're right. Someone needs to call him. I left and didn't tell anyone where I was going. Because I just took off, Pierce is hurt. Hell, he might be dead.

A sob breaks loose and Xavier pulls me into his chest and gives me a hug. "He's going to be all right, Miss Lindsey. He's strong."

I lift my head, taking him in. These boys don't need to see me breaking right now. They need to see me strong. I'm the adult here. I take a deep breath and push all of my emotions down. I try my best to sit up taller, and at least fake it. Rifling through my purse, I find my phone.

Me: At the hospital. Pierce was shot. I have Xavier and Christopher with me.

Me: I went after them when they weren't at the center.

Carson: WTH is going on? Which hospital?

Me: Mount Sinai

Me: They need you. They can't go home.

Carson: On my way.

CHAPTER FIFTY

Lindsey

WARM TEARS STREAM DOWN MY CHEEKS AS I BARREL through the doors into the hospital. My breathing is rapid and shallow and my vision is blurry as I approach the emergency room desk.

"W-Where is he?" I strangle out desperately. "I-I need to see him."

A woman dressed in scrubs comes over to me. She reaches her hand out to me to steady me. "Do you need help?" All my limbs start to shake. I'm like a twig being pushed around by the wind.

"Let me help you." Her hand touches my arm, but I pull away like a caged scared bird.

"Don't touch me." I push past her but lose my footing.

"It's okay. I have you." She holds me steady.

"I need to find him," I sob. "I need to find him."

Without him I'm nothing.

I'm hollow. Empty. Broken in two.

"Let me take care of you first. Where are you hurt?"

I shake my head back and forth, confused by her words. I follow her stare. My gaze drifts down. A desperate sob pours from my soul. My legs give out, making me crumple to the ground. But even as I fall, I can't take my eyes off my hands.

My hands.

My hands are painted with *his* blood.

"Not mine." My breaths come in gasps. "He's gone . . ."

"Who, dear?"

"The only boy I've ever loved."

"We'll find him. What is his name?"

"Pierce Lancaster. He can't die. We're supposed to go away." My body starts to rock. "He's supposed to take me back." *Back and forth.* "I never told him I loved him." *Back and forth.* "He can't die."

I can't breathe. I can't walk. I can't move.

All I can do is sob.

"He can't die."

Eventually the nurse tells me Pierce has been taken into emergency surgery. That's all she'll tell me as I'm not family. When my whimpering slows, I try to calm my shaking hands as I make the call.

"This is Spencer."

"Spencer, thi-this is L-Lindsey Walker. I-I'm calling because there's been an accident and Pierce was sh-shot." The other end of the line is completely quiet. "Sp-Spencer? Are you th-there?"

"I . . . wait. Who is this? What happened?" Spencer says, sounding very confused.

"Pierce was shot and has been taken to Mount Sinai."

"What the hell happened?" He's angry, and that raises my hackles.

"He was trying to help one of the kids from the Polaris Boys Club. A gang member pulled a gun on a couple of the kids, and P-Pierce . . ."

I hear Spencer's intake of breath. "Is he—"

"I honestly don't know. I don't know. We're at the hospital now." I say the last part a little colder than necessary. Spencer is a good guy, and I know he had his reasons to be angry, but I can't help but be protective of Pierce.

"Absolutely. I'm headed out right now. Thank you, Lindsey."

The line goes dead.

CHAPTER FIFTY-ONE

Lindsey

SITTING IN THE WAITING ROOM STARING AT THE PUTRID yellow wall, I ignore everything around me. I'm in a dazed trance. Tired, exhausted, hurting, but mostly I'm emotionally torn in two. A commotion at the door has me looking toward it. Spencer and Grant come rushing in.

"Lindsey. Any news? What's going on?" They're talking over each other, each looking worried.

"We haven't spoken to anyone yet. All I know is he's in surgery."

"What happened?" Grant demands.

I run through the whole sordid story, not leaving out any detail. Spencer wipes sweat from his brow while blowing out a harsh breath.

"Dammit, Pierce. Why does he always have to throw himself in the way of trouble?"

I surge to my feet before I even realize it, poking my finger in Spencer's chest.

"He was helping. It was me who went there, and he didn't want me to be by myself. He's a hero in the situation, and you'd best remember that. You and your brother are always sticking your nose down at him, but really it was you two who always threw him to the side and made him feel less than. He's always tried to get your attention. Good or bad, any attention was better than the cold shoulder."

Spencer's gaze lowers to the floor. Shaking his head, he pulls his fingers through his hair, grasping the roots. "I've neglected him," he mutters to himself, and I can see he is visibly shaking. "Oh god"—a strangled sob escapes Spencer's mouth—"he could have died. I was too hard on him. I-I just got lost in my own shit . . . You know we never meant that, right? We were thrown into the family business and never given a choice."

I suddenly feel foolish having yelled at Pierce's brothers in the middle of the hospital waiting room. All the emotion, protectiveness, and hurt exploded at once. I'm about to apologize or slink away when I'm saved by Carson coming through the door.

"What's going on?" He looks back and forth between Spencer, Grant, and me. I pull him to the side and give him the rundown, explaining what the boys have gotten themselves into.

"Jesus, Lindsey. Why didn't you come to me?"

"They asked me not to and I didn't want to ruin their trust in me. I should've told you. I know that now."

"Is this why you've been trying to set up a boarding school?"

I nod my head sadly. "Things like this shouldn't happen, Carson. They're kids."

"You and I both know how easy it is to fall into bad situations. It's not always kids from troubled pasts or bad neighborhoods. Every kid deserves someone who cares about them."

A tear slides down my cheek at Carson's words. What he's saying is so true. Nothing is more important than love.

"I'm going to get these guys out of here." He sighs. "I'll call their parents and give them the rundown. I won't tell them where they're staying, but to trust they are safe. I'll keep them with me."

"My hotel." Spencer steps forward. "You'll be safe at The Lancaster."

"I can't let you do that," Carson responds.

"You will let me. We're family, man. I need to make sure you're all safe."

Stepping forward, I place my hand on Carson's arm. "You should go to The Lancaster. It will make me feel better knowing you guys are okay."

"You should go too," Spencer says, turning toward me.

"I'm not leaving here."

"Lindsey." Carson tilts his head. "Come with me. You need to shower. You need to get out of those clothes."

"I'm not leaving. I won't leave him."

He pats my back before gathering the boys and leaving. Sitting back in the uncomfortable chair, I pick at my pants nervously, praying for Pierce to come back to me. Without him, I have nothing. I can't lose him, not now that I just found him.

Hours must pass of people coming and going. There have been crying families all around me, which doesn't help my fragile mind, but I keep the faith. Something deep down inside me is whispering he'll be okay. He's got to be. Pierce's parents are here now, and so are Olivia and Bridget. Amelia just left, and surprisingly, so were my parents. They sat with me, hugged me, and showed me support I could've only prayed for in the past. It meant so much to have them with me. I've since sent them home, so now, Olivia sits between Spencer and me. Holding both our hands, giving us both her strength. The doors to the back open up and out strides a tall man in a white doctor's coat. This is the guy I've been waiting to hear from. I jump to my feet at the same time Spencer and Grant do, bum-rushing the doctor.

"Who's the family of Pierce Lancaster?"

Both men raise their hands. "Me," they say in unison.

"What can you tell us? How is he? Is my brother going to be okay?" Spencer questions nervously.

"He's out of surgery, but there were complications. Your brother went into cardiac arrest. A thoracotomy was performed, in which a hole in his ventricle was identified. We stopped the bleeding. They were able to get him all stitched up and close the wound and he's in ICU. He's on a ventilator."

A sob escapes my throat. The news that he'll be all right, lifts the heaviness from my chest.

Spencer and Grant pull each other into man hugs, slapping each other's backs.

"Can we see him?" Grant asks.

"Not yet. You should be able to see him in thirty minutes. One of the nurses will come and get you when he's ready for visitors." With that, the doctor turns and walks away.

I can breathe again.

CHAPTER FIFTY-TWO

Lindsey

SEVERAL MORE HOURS PASS AS GRANT, SPENCER, PIERCE'S parents, and I fidget in our seats. Each of us takes turns on coffee rounds, needing to escape the dreary waiting room. It's my turn and I take my time in the cafeteria. I've already downed one cup of espresso, but the exhaustion is weighing heavily on me.

I pick up the holder full of coffee and I'm heading back. When I round the corner, Spencer is missing. Grant stands, helping me with the coffee.

"Where'd Spencer go?" I question.

"He got to go back."

I deflate at the news, jealousy overtaking me.

"The doctor said one at a time. He's not awake, but we're able to go back and talk to him. Mom and Dad are back there now taking turns and Spencer was going to relieve them."

I nod, secretly hating the fact Spencer gets to go before me.

"Your time will come, Lindsey. I'll make sure you get to see him," Grant says, noticing my sadness. "I let him go back first because I know I'm the last person who deserves it." He sits down, taking a deep breath. I follow, sitting in the chair next to him. "I'm the one who's thrown this family through such turmoil. Spencer had to jump in as the acting CEO of Lancaster, and I went after them. It's been one shit show after another, and it's all my fault."

"You can't shoulder all the blame, Grant," I say, trying to help. I feel sorry for him. He looks so desolate.

"I just didn't understand him. He had everything anyone could want. The parties. The lifestyle. The money. And yet he couldn't keep his name out of the tabloids. I thought he was doing it on purpose."

"He was," I say matter-of-factly. "He was trying to get your attention, and he didn't care how he got it. It was a cry for help."

Grant's shoulders slump. "We turned our backs on him. I'll regret it for the rest of my life, Lindsey." He shakes his head. "What can I do? Will he forgive me?"

The story Pierce told me peeks out through my memories, the story of Pierce, his brothers, and their dog.

"He loves you, Grant. You're his brother. He wants you in his life. Just make time for him. Be there for him."

He nods. "I promise I'll make time. Thanks for having his back, Lindsey. I'm glad he has you."

I smile. A throat clears and we turn our heads to find Spencer looking grim. "Is everything okay?" I ask warily.

"Yeah. I'm just exhausted. He slept the entire time. He looks horrible." Spencer rubs his red, swollen eyes. "I just don't know what to do. I've got to find those punk-ass kids who did this," he grits through his teeth.

"Why don't you go home and get some rest? I'll stick around," Grant offers.

Spencer looks up at us. "All right. I appreciate it, man. It's been a long day. Can you call me as soon as he wakes up?"

"You've got it," Grant promises. "Is anyone else allowed to go back?"

"Yeah, you're up."

I want to argue, but I really have no leg to stand on. This is their family, not mine, no matter how much I want to fight that.

Spencer leaves, but Grant doesn't make a move to go back. "Spencer had a rough day. He needed the rest. I'll be fine, but why don't you head home too. I can call you when he wakes up."

I shake my head. "I'm not leaving him." My tone leaves no room for argument.

"Then why don't you go back and sit with him? I'm sure he'd rather have you there than me," he says sadly. "I can see him in a bit."

"Are you sure?" I ask, hoping like hell he doesn't change his mind.

"Absolutely." He smiles.

I stand and walk toward the nurses' station. "I'd like to see Pierce Lancaster," I say apprehensively.

She quirks a brow. "I only have three men on my list."

Grant comes to stand behind me. "She's family. Please add her."

Grant goes about giving her my name while another nurse ushers me back. My legs are shaky and my palms are sweating. Standing in the doorway, my breath hitches at the sight of him lying helplessly in the bed with machines hooked to him. He looks lifeless and my stomach crunches tightly. He's as pale as the walls, which are a dirty cream color. It twists and turns in knots as I bring my hands to my mouth to stop a sob from breaking through. I inhale and exhale, counting to three, willing my breathing to slow. I don't want to go in there frightened or sad.

When I finally feel composed, or as composed as I'm going to be, I walk next to the bed, sit on the chair, and grab his hand in mine. The air is stagnant, the room cold, but his hands, they're warm. Thank God, they're warm. It's a morbid thought, but right now that's all that's floating through my head.

"I'm here, Pierce."

Beep.

The sound of the machine.

The sound of his beating heart.

"Please wake up."

Beep.

"Open your eyes."

Beep.

"Please wake up."

Beep.

"You need to wake up."

Beep.

"Pierce, I'm so sorry," I choke out. "It should not be you lying in this bed right now. I should've never gotten you involved. I don't know what I'd do without you." I sniffle.

Beep.

"I've known since the first day I saw you that you were bad news for me." I chuckle.

Beep.

"We were both drowning our issues in drugs and alcohol, just barely getting by. With everyone around us fooled into thinking we had everything when all we craved was love. Maybe that's why you and I never came together. We could feel the similarities and it scared us. At least it did me. I saw too much of myself in you, and I knew I'd lose my heart to you."

Beep.

"I never made a move, or never really tried because I knew you'd break me. But now . . . I would take any pain to have you with me. You are the best bad decision I ever made." A tear slides down my cheek.

Beep.

"You're breaking me now. Looking at you like this . . ." My voice breaks. "God, Pierce, you have to be okay. Please tell me you'll be okay. I found you and I cannot live without you." I bend forward and place a kiss on his palm.

Beep.

"I love you."

Beeeeeeeeeeeeep.

CHAPTER FIFTY-THREE

Lindsey

A NURSE COMES BARRELING INTO THE ROOM.
Oh my God, what's happening?
She stands beside Pierce's bed, frantically checking the machines, checking his vitals. I watch as the color drains from her face. She shakes, her hand twitching involuntarily as she presses a button.

The next thing I know more people run in.

"Doctor?" she questions and the sound of her fear makes me bite down on my lip. Blood floods my mouth.

"Start CPR," a man shouts. "Give me an ultrasound probe to check his heart."

I look up at the ceiling, not able to watch Pierce die. The light is too bright. My eyes blink rapidly behind the abrasive glare. But I can't look down. I won't. Tears flood my vision, making me completely blind to the scene in front of me, but I can still hear the shouts. I can still hear every word uttered.

Even without my sight, I know what's happening . . .

He's dying.

"I see fluid around. He's in cardiac tamponade."

A sob tears from my lungs. It's primal and desperate.

"Give me a fourteen-inch long gauge needle."

The pain is too much. I'm being shredded from the

inside out.

"Drain fifty-five cc's of blood."

Any semblance of composure is gone. Violent shaking. A thick, never-ending flow of tears.

I can't breathe. I can't.

Time stands still in that minute.

It stretches painfully slow, through inhales and exhales, silent prayers and tortured sobs. Hands hold me from behind as we wait. *Grant.* Pierce's parents are beside us.

Praying that his heart starts. That he doesn't leave this earth. That he doesn't leave me all alone.

Then I hear the sound.

Beep.

Beep.

Beep.

His heart has started.

The sound is steady.

He's alive.

The doctor approaches us.

"He had a little bit of blood re-accumulated around his heart. I was able to drain the blood." He looks at us and breathes before speaking. "He should be fine now."

He should be fine.

He should be fine.

But what if he's not?

What if he doesn't make it?

What if he dies?

I can't be around these people.

I can't be here.

Despite the pain, I push away and begin to run.

I run for the first time in a year.

I run down the hall, with no destination in sight.

My legs scream at me to stop. But I don't.
I need the pain.
I'm so numb, I need to feel.

CHAPTER FIFTY-FOUR

Lindsey

ONE DAY HAS PASSED. ONE LONG DAY. HE'S STILL IN ICU. He's still intubated. He still hasn't woken up. The doctor says he's doing better . . .

I don't believe him.

I watched him die.

Back in the hospital, I sit holding his hand, slumped over his body, silently begging for him to wake.

A light tap on my shoulder has me jarring awake. It's the nurse. "Dear, visiting hours are over. You have to return to the guest area."

I nod, standing from the chair. I bend over and place a kiss on Pierce's cheek. "I love you." When I reach the waiting room, I find Grant sleeping.

"Grant," I call until he rouses.

"Is everything okay?"

"Everything is fine. He never woke up," I say sadly. "I just wanted to let you know I'm going to get out of here for a little bit. I'll be back first thing in the morning, but if something happens, please call me. I left my number at the nurses' station."

He nods. "Try to get some sleep."

285

When I get to the taxi, I pull out my phone and send a text message off to Carson. I can't put off talking to the police any longer.

Me: Pierce is still sleeping. No change. How are the boys?

Carson: Still very shaken up. We're still at the penthouse of The Lancaster.

Me: I just called the police and they'll be there soon to take my statement.

Carson: Good, because Christopher has gotten three death threats via text since he gave his statement yesterday. He needs to talk to them again.

Me: Oh, God. On my way.

Clutching the phone in my hand, I stare out the window. The city rushes by in a haze of bright lights against the backdrop of the early morning. In the distance, I see commuters walking toward their destinations. To think these people are going about their lives right now as Pierce is struggling for his life has me shaking in the back seat of the cab. I'm happy I'll be there for Xavier today. I hate the fact I wasn't there with them yesterday. But I'll be there to support them now and also give my own account of what happened and everything that led up to it. If I have my way, Xavier's brother, along with all of his contacts, will be behind bars.

I'm walking in at the same time the police pull up. "Follow me," I say, motioning them in. I unlock the door with the key Spencer gave me to his penthouse apartment in The Lancaster and take them to the back where I know Carson and the boys will be. When we walk in, all three of the boys jump up and pull me into a hug. I hug them back, so glad they're safe. Looking over their shoulders, I smile at Carson and mouth a thank you for keeping them safe.

"I'd like to give my statement first, please," I say to the officers. They look at each other and motion for me to follow them. I recount every gory detail, starting from the day I found Xavier with bruises and cuts, all the way up until the alley and Pierce's last words. The words that got him shot. I told them I had just come from the hospital, and they said they would be heading there tomorrow with the hopes that Pierce would be awake and able to give his statement. Thankfully, Xavier was able to identify the other guy with his brother in the alley. There's a warrant out for both of them, and the boys will be under protection until they are caught.

I'm exhausted and in desperate need of my bed. The police offer to have a guard stand outside my apartment, but I decline. My place is locked up like Fort Knox. I pay for security and they wouldn't get three feet in my building. That's the luxury of being Lindsey Walker.

When I get home, I go through the motions: undress, brush my teeth, lock everything up, set the alarm for two hours later, and then allow my head to hit the pillow. With the way my body aches and my eyelids droop, you'd think sleep would come easily, but it doesn't. If I'm not tossing and turning, I'm dreaming of Pierce being shot.

Choosing a sleepless night over revisiting that nightmare over and over in vivid detail, I curl up and continue praying to God to keep Pierce alive. Praying that he allows me to have the life I've always wanted. A life with Pierce Lancaster by my side.

CHAPTER FIFTY-FIVE

Lindsey

THE FIRST THING I DO WHEN I OPEN MY EYES IS CHECK MY phone. He's yet to wake. Spencer texted me that the doctor says that's normal. His body needs time to recover. I don't think there's anything normal about it. If he's going to be fine, why doesn't he wake up?

Every second that passes, I lose the will to live because the part that's tethered to Pierce is slowly fading away, and with that, a little part of myself dies too. I don't know what I'd do without him. My head is filled with fear spinning out of control, and in the hospital, I can't stop them.

So I leave.

I need a break for a while, so I go to Polaris to meet with Carson. When I arrive, he surprises me with a folder full of information.

"After everything that happened, I can't agree with you more. We do need a boarding school. A better way to keep these kids safe . . . I know I've already offered to help, but it's not enough. We need to do more. We need this place opened now."

Nodding in agreement, I think of what we can do.

"I'm going to speak to Spencer," I finally say.

"That's a great idea and, Lindsey, whatever you need from Polaris, you've got it."

"Thank you," I say, emotions flooding me.

"I've looked into all the information I originally got from the state when I opened this place, and it looks like these correspond with what you would need." He hands me the thick folder. "This has all the information. All the telephone numbers, and all of the documents you'll need to fill out. If you'd like, I can help you with them today. The sooner we get them done and sent in, the sooner you can get the permits ready to go."

"I'm speechless. You have enough on your hands here. You don't have to help me."

"I want to, Lindsey. What you want to create will benefit all our kids. It'll be a great partner for Polaris."

"Absolutely. I want all your kids to stay at Seaglass."

"Seaglass?" He raises a brow.

"I'm going to call it Seaglass."

He nods, seeming to like it, whether he gets the meaning behind the name or not.

"Have you heard anything about the building?" Carson asks.

I had spoken to Spencer and Grant about a possible location and they were looking into what they could do to help. I also spoke to my father and pitched the original business plan. He asked for a few additional pieces to be added, but otherwise, he seemed very proud. "I'd love your help with these," I say, lifting the folder.

Carson and I work to finish the documents. Three hours later, we finally come up for air.

CHAPTER FIFTY-SIX

Pierce

B*EEP.*
Beep.
Beep.

Blackness engulfs me and I try to push through. My lids are heavy, my mouth parched.

Beep.

Beep.

Mustering all the energy in my body, I try to open my eyes.

"Pierce . . ."

My eyes blink rapidly.

"Open your eyes."

They flutter open and Spencer comes into focus. His face is distraught. "Spen . . ." My voice cracks, and it feels as if a million fragments of glass rip at my throat. At the sound of my voice, I hear a strangled sob. Turning toward the sound, my chest heaves at what I see. My father, his head in his hands, his body shaking with sobs. Standing next to him is Grant. His hand is placed on my dad's shoulder, trying to soothe him.

"Dad?"

A harder sob breaks loose. He's coming apart, breaking in front of me, reminding me of the last series of paintings I created—broken pieces of glass barely holding on, smashing to the ground in front of me.

Dad's sobs continue, and I look up to see Grant has a tear running down his cheek as well. When I look at Spencer, I see the same.

"You died," he whispers as rivulets of water streak his cheek.

Died? *I died*? I try to move my hands, try to leave the bed, but Spencer holds me down.

"You can't move."

I almost died. I almost never saw my family again. I almost never saw Lindsey again. Lindsey.

I would have left her alone in the world.

I almost left her alone without telling her how I felt.

"Lindsey . . ." My heart lurches in my chest. Please tell me she wasn't hurt. "Lindsey," I repeat, but this time the word comes out as a desperate cry.

"She's fine. She's okay. The boys are too. They weren't hurt, but who knows what would have happened if you didn't find them. You probably saved their lives. You're a hero."

"I'm no hero."

"You're not the villain either," Spencer says as he takes my hand and squeezes it.

My father stands from his chair and comes to the side of my bed. "I'm so sorry," he whispers. "I thought I lost you."

"We all did," Grant says, stepping beside them, creating a united front.

"We were wrong. We failed you. We should have been there . . ." Spencer trails off, and with all the energy I have, I lift my hand in protest.

"I deserved it."

They shake their heads in unison.

"I made bad choices." My voice is raspy. "But I've changed—"

"We know," my dad cuts in.

Dying changes you. It sounds cliché but it's true. As I stare at my family beside my bed, I'd never thought I'd feel this way.

No anger.

No hate.

As if when my heart stopped all of the bad died with it. When it started beating again, I was born anew. The past is the past and I'm ready to move on.

"Where's Mom?"

My dad points to the couch in the corner and I see my mother curled up in a ball sleeping. "I'll wake her."

"No, let her rest," I respond, my voice rough still from the previous intubation.

No one speaks for a minute and I wince in pain.

"Shit. Are you okay?" Spencer moves closer, his concern present on his features.

"Yeah."

"What can I do?"

"You can get her. I need her."

There's no need to clarify who I'm speaking about. They know.

CHAPTER FIFTY-SEVEN

Lindsey

M Y PHONE DINGS AND I LOOK DOWN AT THE SCREEN. It's Spencer.

Two words. Two words that change everything.

He's awake.

The numbness fades and I'm alive once more.

"He's awake! He's awake," I shout as I enter Carson's office. "Pierce is awake," I say again. "I've got to go. I've got to go."

"Go," he says, laughing. "Call me as soon as you can to let me know how it goes."

I smile, not looking back. I'm running out the door at breakneck speed, a speed I shouldn't be able to do, but nothing will stop me. I need to see Pierce.

I'm at the hospital, running in when Spencer sees me. A huge grin spreads across his face.

"He's awake, and he's asking for you."

My heart swells.

The nurse is waiting at the door, and she beckons me in. I take a deep breath and step through. He may still look like he's seen better days, with a week's worth of scruff and his skin paler than normal. His normally unruly hair is in need of a good cut, but he's alive, and he's awake, and he's all mine.

"Lucky."

That one word has me coming undone.

"Pierce," I choke out on an unsuppressed sob. Tears I didn't realize were there are streaming down my face.

His hand comes up, wiping them away. "*Shh*. Don't cry," he says. "I'm okay."

All the emotions flood me at once. "I watched you fall. I thought you were dead, Pierce. And then you died. I watched you die. I wished it had been me."

He closes his eyes as if in pain. "Don't say that. Never say that."

"I was so scared."

He squeezes my hand. "It's going to take more than a bullet to keep Pierce Lancaster down, babe. Plus I have you, you're my *lucky* charm." His teasing tone has me chuckling. It's so like Pierce to be cracking jokes in a time of concern. "So, I heard this rumor while I was asleep."

My brow furrows. "What?" I lean in.

"You love me."

My cheeks heat.

He heard me.

CHAPTER FIFTY-EIGHT

Pierce

"STOP," I COMMAND, PUTTING MY HAND UNDERNEATH her chin, forcing her to meet my gaze. "Don't ever be embarrassed about something like that." The way her eyelashes flutter stirs something deep within. A primal need for her overshadows all the pain associated with my injury.

"I said those things because you were asleep. I don't want to scare you off."

She's so fucking cute. If she thinks for one minute that she could do anything to scare me off, she's crazy.

"You have to know I feel the same, Lindsey. You mean everything to me."

A tear slides down her cheek and I wipe it away, hating to see the pain in her eyes. What she witnessed had to be traumatizing for her and the boys. I will hunt those punk-ass kids down and teach them a lesson about bringing a gun to a fight with kids who didn't do anything to deserve it.

"When we were in that alley, the only thing that went through my head was that you were dead. I thought I lost you. It killed a part of me, Pierce."

"I'm here, and I'm alive, Linds. There's no reason to be scared."

"But you were shot. What the hell were you thinking coming with me?"

She doesn't get it. I would do anything to keep her safe, including taking a bullet. "My only thought was that I had to protect you and those boys. I would never let you be in harm's way if I can prevent it. It was never a question. I was going with you regardless of what you could have said. I didn't even think about the consequences."

"Don't ever be stupid like that again." Her voice cracks.

"Babe, I can't promise that. Like I said, I'll do whatever to protect you. You've changed me." My hand caresses her cheek. I have to tell her I feel the same. I need her to know her feelings are returned. My brothers told me how she hardly left this place, and her dedication to me is something I'll never take for granted. I love her.

"I want the house in the suburbs. The white picket fence. The one-point-two kids, with you. Only with you."

A small sob breaks through her lips. I wish I could fucking kiss her, but these wires and this bed makes it impossible. I groan.

"Are you okay?" she asks, concern in her voice.

"This fucking bed. I want your mouth on mine."

She giggles, putting her hand over her mouth.

"I'm serious. I need you," I say, sounding like a fucking pussy, but I can't bring myself to care.

"Let me help," she says, standing and leaning over me. Our lips touch and I can't help it. I moan. The need for her intensifies. My hand reaches to the back of her head and I deepen the kiss. We're like this for a couple of minutes before she pulls away.

"Slow down, tiger. A nurse is due back in here anytime."

"Like I fucking care." They'd be lucky to find me only kissing her.

"They caught all but Xavier's brother, who apparently was the shooter," Lindsey says, clearly steering us away from any conversation that could result in me taking her here in this hospital room.

"It's only a matter of time before they find him. He won't get far."

I nod, wanting to find the son of a bitch myself. Punk-ass coward who killed Linc.

Her face brightens as if something just popped into her head. "I bought the property for the boarding school."

My smile is large. "You did?"

"Yep. Your brothers helped me."

"They love you, ya know?"

"They're good guys, Pierce. They mean well, and they love you. And I love them because of it."

"They do. I know that now. We spent some time before you got here catching up. We're going to start hanging out, doing brother stuff. Whatever that means. I'm glad to have them in my life again. I'm glad you got to know them, even if the circumstances weren't the best."

"Understatement of the year, Pierce Lancaster," she says with a frown.

I nod, agreeing full-heartedly. "So, about that house and kids," I redirect the conversation back to us, needing to know she's mine. Forever.

She grins. "Are you getting needy on me, Mr. Lancaster?"

Her flirting is not helping my raging hard-on. I didn't even realize that was possible given all the IVs and how fucking cold this room is, but she's managed it. "With you? Always."

"I like the sound of always," she admits with a blush.

"I need to get well, but I think we should solidify that always, sooner rather than later."

"Don't tease."

"I'm serious. I love you. You're mine, Lindsey. Now and always. Promise me."

She inhales then exhales and smiles a brilliant smile. "I promise. Always."

EPILOGUE

Pierce

FROM ACROSS THE ROOM, I SEE HER.

Lindsey Lancaster, my wife.

Well, she hasn't legally changed her name, but it doesn't stop it from being true. She is Lindsey Lancaster now. Thinking those words still brings a smile to my face. Just last night, surrounded by friends and family, Lindsey and I tied the knot.

Vegas style.

It wasn't our intention to elope to Vegas. Actually, we had a whole wedding planned. It was supposed to take place at the reception hall at The Lancaster Central Park, but alas, we couldn't wait, and I have no regrets.

I only hope Spencer will give us back our deposit. I can't help but chuckle since, obviously, there was no deposit. And since he was my best man at our impromptu wedding, along with Grant, I'll assume he's okay with the cancellation.

We didn't fly to Vegas to get married. We flew to Vegas because my pieces were going to be part of an exhibit. Rather, The Lancaster Las Vegas location recently added an art gallery and we are here to kick off the grand opening of it. When Spencer had asked if he could showcase one of my installations, I was floored. Pride flowed through every molecule. There was no question what I'd be showcasing.

Beautiful Broken Pieces.

On display in the gallery hall are all the pieces I've made this last year, before and after I met Lindsey. A few of my pieces are missing, including the one I made for Seaglass. That one I gave to Lindsey to display and inspire the kids. It was important to her to show the children that even though they feel broken, like a piece of glass left in the sea, over time the edges smooth out and create something beautiful, something unique. Something special. So now on the walls of both her safe haven for the kids and The Lancaster are special pieces that symbolize that.

That symbolize hope.

"I love it, Pierce. It looks so good. And the meaning behind it," Lindsey says from beside me.

"The world may think everything is broken and jagged in this series, but if they look more closely, it's a celebration of all the broken pieces," I say.

Lindsey nods in agreement. "The scars we all carry with us, but in truth, those scars remind each and every one of us that our imperfections are so much more. They need to be cherished. All your broken pieces are what makes you, you. And I love every part of you."

"I love every part of you, too," I respond.

"To new beginnings." She smiles a heart-stopping smile.

"And happily-ever-afters."

And learning to love every broken piece.

All of them.

Always.

Forever.

BY AVA HARRISON

Imperfect Truth

Through Her Eyes

trans-fer-ence

Illicit

Clandestine

Sordid

ACKNOWLEDGMENTS

I want to thank my entire family. I love you all so much.

Thank you to my husband and my kids for always loving me. You guys are my heart!

Thank you to my Mom, Dad, Liz and Ralph for always believing in me, encouraging me and loving me!

Thank you to my in-laws for being so cool and supportive!

Thank you to all of my brothers and sisters!

Special thank you to Dr. D. Without your help, I wouldn't have been able to make my readers cry!

Thank you to everyone that helped with Explicit.
Lawrence Editing
Write Girl Editing Services
Melissa Saneholtz
Becca Mysoor
Indie After Hours
Gray Ink
Marla Esposito
Champagne Formats
Sophie Broughton
Lori Jackson
Becca Zsurkán
Hayfaah Sumtally
Hang Le
Sarah Allen
Nita Banks

Thank you to Chad Johansson for the beautiful picture and thank you Blake Johansson for being the PERFECT Pierce!

Thank you Ena from Enticing and Give Me books

Thank you to my AMAZING ARC TEAM!

Thank you to my beta team! Leigh, Melissa, Livia, and Christine. Thank you for your wonderful and extremely helpful feedback.

I want to thank to ALL my friends for putting up with me while I wrote this book. Thank you!

Thank you to my smut moms!

Thank you to my Phi Girls for always being there!

To all of my author friends who listen to me bitch and let me ask for advice, thank you!

To the ladies in the Ava Harrison Support Group, I couldn't have done this without your support!

Please consider joining my Facebook reader group Ava Harrison Support Group

Thanks to all the bloggers! Thanks for your excitement and love of books!

Last but certainly not least...

Thank you to the readers!

Thank you so much for taking this journey with me.

ABOUT THE AUTHOR

Ava Harrison is a *USA Today* and Amazon bestselling author. When she's not journaling her life, you can find her window shopping, cooking dinner for her family, or curled up on her couch reading a book.

Connect with Ava

Newsletter Sign Up: http://bit.ly/2fnQQ1n

Book + Main: bookandmainbites.com/avaharrison

Facebook Author Page: http://bit.ly/2eshd1h

Facebook Reader Group: http://bit.ly/2e67NYi

Goodreads Author Page: http://bit.ly/2eNjYwX

Instagram: http://bit.ly/2f5H5RT

BookBub: https://www.bookbub.com/authors/ava-harrison

Amazon Author Page: http://amzn.to/2fnVJHFF

Made in the USA
Coppell, TX
17 February 2023

12963306R00180